OF ONE MIND

OF ONE MIND

A NOVEL

JB MAERTEN

Serious Wonder
·PRESS·

Copyright © 2024 by JB Maerten

Published by Serious Wonder Press, Sacramento

Edited and designed by Girl Friday Productions
www.girlfridayproductions.com

Cover design: David Fassett
Project management: Sara Spees Addicott
Editorial production: Abi Pollokoff
Image credits: cover © Shutterstock/Albert Beukhof

ISBN (paperback): 979-8-9898414-0-0
ISBN (ebook): 979-8-9898414-1-7

Library of Congress Control Number: 2024908391

First edition

For my mother

This is why.

CHAPTER 1

Rene raised her glass in response to the toast being offered in her honor, a lump rising in her throat.

"To our beloved Dr. Elder," the head nurse said. "I don't think I can put into words just how much you mean to me—to us all. You inspire us daily with your unwavering commitment to our patients. You'll be greatly missed." Lorena tilted her glass toward Rene.

The conference room was packed with colleagues in white coats and scrubs. Those who'd arrived early for the Thursday afternoon gathering had snagged the half-dozen seats around the table that served as the hub for lunches and case conferences. It was covered with a bright plastic tablecloth upon which rested a big sheet cake and a punch bowl. Later arrivals leaned against the wall or stood in front of the counter, blocking access to the all-important coffee machine. Stragglers stood shoulder to shoulder in the doorway, craning to hear. Rene was wedged into the back corner facing everyone.

The unspoken questions were evident on their faces. No doubt they'd heard the rumors about her conflict with Dr. Stauss after three-year-old Marcella's tragic death. But the conflict with Stauss wasn't the primary reason for her resignation.

Rene took a sip of the cold punch to ease the lump in her throat and began. "I was a young child when my grandfather was diagnosed with Alzheimer's." Her voice quavered, but she didn't care. "I tried my best to make sense of his words as they devolved into nonsense. I remember sitting on his lap, pretending to have a delightful conversation—even as he spoke gibberish." She needed them to understand. "I was powerless to reach him."

She steadied as she made eye contact with her friends and colleagues around the room. "That struggle to communicate with my grandfather became the motivation for my career in neurosurgery and my time here at the hospital. And now that personal history has become the impetus for why I'm leaving you. For many months, I've been laying the groundwork to launch my own research facility. Everything is now in place, and I'll start the preliminary experiments tomorrow." She paused. "I must find a way to reach people whose verbal skills are stifled by disease or injury. I must give them back their voices."

Many of her colleagues nodded, and several dabbed their eyes.

"I'll miss you all dearly." She raised her glass higher in salute. "But I leave you all . . . for Gramps."

Silence hung in the air for a few moments. Then came a round of warm applause and scattered comments.

"Bravo!"

"Go for it!"

"Hear! Hear!"

A scurry of activity followed as the swing shift scrambled to grab slices of cake before tending to their duties and as the day shift headed home. The absence of Dr. Stauss was conspicuous, but Rene was grateful for it. She'd worried he might show up and create a scene.

She worked her way to the door, acknowledging each person and accepting hugs from the nurses, aides, a physical therapist, the unit clerk, and even the floor's housekeeper, who'd come for a quick goodbye. A neurosurgeon could only do so much; treating people with issues like brain tumors and spinal cord injuries took a dedicated team. She surged with gratitude for having been a part of this talented group.

Finally, only Rene and the head nurse remained. Lorena was tearful, and Rene's eyes welled up in response. "You're setting off on an uncharted course," the nurse said. "Good luck to you."

"I'm so appreciative of your loyalty." Rene had counted on Lorena during the investigation into Marcella's death and Rene's role in the subsequent investigation of Dr. Stauss's flawed decisions. Rene still had nightmares about the child and the parents' grief.

"I just offered you an ear to talk it through. You're the one who had the courage to shine a light on what Dr. Stauss did."

The hug from the no-nonsense nurse lasted longer than Rene would have expected, before she patted Rene's back and stepped away. "Grab some of that cake to take home, why don't you," Lorena offered. "There's lots left over."

"I will, thanks. Tonight I'm just looking forward to a hot bath and going to bed early so I'm ready to kick off my experiments first thing in the morning," she said. "But I'll take a couple of pieces to have after dinner tomorrow. Rob is fixing me a special meal to celebrate."

Lorena nodded. "Sounds fun . . . I gotta run now; we've got two new admits coming up from the ER."

"Thanks again. For everything."

Rene shook the crumbs out of a container from her lunch bag and filled it with a generous portion of cake. Then she succumbed to temptation and sampled a slice of the chocolate dessert, taking a last look around the room where she'd spent so many hours debriefing cases with colleagues. She'd miss this space, the camaraderie, the urgency of saving lives.

After gathering her things, she took a last walk down the hospital hall to make sure she'd said farewell to all the patients on her caseload. It was after three, and her last shift as a hospital employee had just ended. She was free. Well, almost. Technically, she was using up her vacation balance next week, and she had to come back on Tuesday for an exit interview with her supervisor, Dr. Stauss.

On impulse, she stopped at the door of one of the most challenging cases on the neurosurgery floor. The young man was on Dr. Stauss's caseload, but she'd checked on him a few times when she occasionally covered for the senior physician.

She knocked and heard a welcoming voice respond. She'd not met any of Kyle Nichols's family on previous visits, but this time a tired-looking middle-aged man with an interested smile rose to greet her. A somewhat younger woman remained seated next to the boy's bed.

"Hello, I'm Dr. Elder," Rene said, looking back and forth between the two adults. "I've checked in on your son several times before, but we haven't met."

"Dr. Elder, good to meet you. I'm Owen Nichols, Kyle's uncle," the man said, shaking Rene's extended hand. "This is Kyle's mother, Kristen."

The woman nodded to Rene and continued massaging the boy's hand.

"I was just reading him the news about last night's Mariners game," Mr. Nichols continued.

"I understand he's quite the baseball fan," Rene said. The family had decorated the room with posters of ballplayers and other paraphernalia, which almost succeeded in making the room appropriate for a teenaged boy.

Almost. The tubes and lines attached to the boy's frame and the constant sound of the ventilator quickly dispelled that illusion.

"More than a fan. He's a star player, a big-league prospect," Nichols said with a smile that faded slightly as he looked down at the emaciated form lying motionless before them.

Rene tried to sound supportive. "How exciting." Dr. Stauss had worked a miracle to save the boy's life, but nevertheless, his rare condition would prove devastating.

"I just stopped in to say goodbye, Kyle," she said, turning to the inert young man in the bed. "Today is my last day. I'm moving on to pursue independent research. I wish you and your family all the best."

"Thanks very much, Doctor." The mother answered in place of her mute son. "We're deeply grateful to everyone for saving his life and for all the care he's received. I'm so glad we got to meet you before you left."

Stauss had spoken of the mother during case conferences, remarking on her strength and dedication. He hadn't mentioned this uncle, but the man's love was evident in the way he watched the boy, attentive and kind.

"Of course, Ms. Nichols. Kyle's a very resilient young man. His own body did the hardest work to pull him through," Rene said.

"Tomorrow we have an appointment with Dr. Stauss to get an update on Kyle's prognosis." Mr. Nichols added this with anxiety creeping into his voice.

Rene nodded, well aware of the planned meeting. Concealing her sorrow, she conjured a smile. "Good luck, young man."

Rene sat quietly in her car, resting in the cool shadows of the underground parking garage. The sight of Kyle Nichols weighed on her; the plight of the young man put an exclamation point on her decision to leave the safety of her employment to pursue her mission to give voice to those whose brains denied them words. Unfortunately, it would be some time before her research progressed far enough to help someone like Kyle.

His condition was quite different from Gramps's, but the pain it would bring to the boy and his family was deeply familiar. She stared out the windshield at the concrete wall in front of her car, thinking of that day she'd snuggled up to her grandfather on the couch.

She had loved listening to Gramps's soft voice as they read her picture books together. His long bony finger marked each word to help her follow along. She was proud of how she could sound out words, even if she didn't recognize them right off.

The main character in the story was a dog named Missy.

"'Missy was asleep in her—'" Gramps read.

His finger moved under the next word, but he didn't say it.

He must be offering her a chance to fill in the word and show how smart she was. Rene smiled up at him, ready with the right answer. But he didn't smile in return. He stared blankly at the page, his eyes empty, as if he were somewhere else. Then he caught her looking at him. His eyes went wild, afraid.

He didn't know the word.

Something inside her choked. "Doghouse," she said softly.

Gramps closed the book. "It's a stupid story," he said. Getting up, he left her alone on the couch.

CHAPTER 2

Rene was up early the next morning, gulping down breakfast and taking her Labrador retriever, Humboldt, for an abbreviated walk.

Before heading out, she allowed herself a few minutes of quiet as she moved through her rose garden, carefully selecting blossoms for a bouquet to grace her new office. Then she straightened up the house to make it presentable. Rob would be coming to prepare a celebratory dinner while she was still at the lab. Rene planned to be home by six, giving her enough time to shower and change before they ate.

The first day of experiments followed by a romantic dinner. What a perfect day!

She drove the twenty miles to her new research facility, a modest suite of rooms at the far end of a large, nondescript office complex south of her home in Lake Oswego, Oregon.

Rene smiled as she approached the building. Establishing

her own research facility had been a longtime dream. She'd spent endless hours hounding contractors to get the Carl Elder Foundation offices ready so she could get right to work after her last day at the hospital. Since the IRB—Institutional Review Board—had approved her multiphase research proposal, her dream was becoming a reality.

She keyed in the entry code, swung the door open, and strode down the hall, savoring the lingering smell of fresh paint. Everything had been built to her specifications, including the three testing rooms, where volunteers would participate in her experiments. She'd deliberately chosen a palette of soft blues in contrast to the beige sameness of the medical establishment she'd left behind.

Stopping in the break room, she arranged her roses in a vase to show off the range of yellow and orange blossoms, then moved them to the desk in her new office.

After shedding her jacket and satchel, she went into room 1 and surveyed the arrangement of the latest in noninvasive brain scanners. Used alone or in combination, these devices would allow her to conduct a wide variety of experiments involving neural modulation, imaging, and monitoring.

Just for fun, she sat in one of the two recliners and leaned back, imagining herself a participant in her own experiments. She wiggled into the seat, laying her head back, stretching her legs out, and plopping her arms on the armrests. "Perfect," she said as her body relaxed into the chair.

Thoughts of her family filled her with gratitude for making this moment possible. Gramps had left her a generous trust fund. Her wealthy parents had added to the principal and invested it wisely on her behalf. Even after paying for both her MD and PhD degrees, a substantial amount had remained, which she'd invested to fund her new research.

Her reverie was replaced by urgency. She needed to set up before her two research assistants, Aisha and Carter, arrived. The rest of the morning passed in a blur as she did test runs of the medical devices in rooms 1 and 2 and then fired up the computers in the data center.

Her assistants arrived promptly at one o'clock and followed Rene into the data center. The large room housed several computer stations and the server on which sophisticated statistical programs would compile and analyze the information that flowed through dozens of hidden cables from the testing rooms.

"I know I explained your role in these experiments in the orientation materials I sent you over the last few weeks," Rene said, "but let's go over the protocols again just to be sure we're on the same page." She handed each of them a packet and a checklist.

"This is so exciting," Aisha said. The tall, athletic-looking PhD candidate was specializing in neurobiology. Carter, a casually dressed student working on his master's in physiology, remained quiet as he reviewed the details.

"Once we get started, adjust the ultrasound frequency they get through their headsets at these designated time points"—she pointed to the list—"while the participants do their assigned tasks. The devices emit inaudible, low-intensity sound waves, which penetrate to different depths of the brain depending on the frequency. The software then generates a 3D map from the waves that bounce back, highlighting the cerebral regions most actively engaged during the task.

"Before we begin the test," Rene said, "review the subject's answers to the screening questions and let me know if they answered yes to any. If not, have them sign the consent forms, and give them a copy. Then put on their headsets, the skin galvanic devices, and the pulse monitors. Today we'll be gathering data from those devices to establish benchmarks for more sophisticated experiments in the future."

Aisha and Carter nodded in unison.

"We'll be taping the sessions, but be sure to make notes of any of the subjects' reactions." Rene referred to the list of subjects scheduled for tests that day. "Carter, you'll assist Brenda in room 2. Have her work on the geometry problems. Next week, have her do algebra."

"Got it," Carter replied.

"Aisha, have Steven listen to the audio version of *The Old Man and the Sea*. Next time, have him read the print version for our comparison."

"I understand," Aisha said, just as the doorbell sounded.

"I'll get it," Carter offered. "If it's Brenda, I'll get her ready."

Rene turned on the video feed from the testing rooms and projected them onto the big screens hanging over the computer stations. Soon they saw Carter lead Brenda into room 2.

Rene turned and found Aisha studying the framed poster that occupied a prominent place on the wall, a souvenir from the recent Science of Consciousness conference in Tucson.

"Did you attend this conference?" Aisha nodded toward the poster.

"I sure did." Grinning, Rene swiveled to face her student.

"It was fantastic. There were a couple hundred scientists from all around the world. Even some Nobel Prize winners. I was incredibly energized. No idea was too radical for them." Unlike working with Dr. Stauss, who'd tried to squash her creativity as soon as she had developed a line of reasoning different from his own. "In fact, my protocols grew out of concepts I developed after that conference."

Aisha sat down in one of the ergonomic chairs, eyes wide, brow furrowed. "I understand the procedures for the experiments today, but I'm embarrassed to say I still don't grasp all the implications of your approach."

The woman's enthusiasm tickled Rene. She'd interviewed a dozen grad students for these part-time assistant positions. Aisha's obvious fascination with research mirrored her own, making her the first choice for the position.

"You won't find my ideas in journal articles, not for a while, anyway." Rene paused, trying to come up with a quick summary. "Most neuroscientists work from the premise that our ability to form ideas and communicate them is created by electrical and chemical interactions at the molecular level among the neurons in the brain. My more advanced experiments will explore the hypothesis that it's actually at the quantum level, where atoms and smaller particles within brain cells interact, that consciousness, and thus communication, originates. Traditional neuroscientists consider my theories revolutionary. Some even call them heresy." Like Dr. Stauss.

Aisha's eyebrows went up. "'Heresy'? That's a strong word."

"Don't get me started. Rejecting new ideas in favor of accepted ways still happens, even among scientists."

The doorbell rang again.

"That must be Steven," Aisha said as she rose. "This is going to be fun."

As Aisha headed to answer the front door, Rene took a seat before the big screens, where the views from the two testing rooms were already on display. She was starting a series of basic experiments, mapping the brain activity of volunteers. The results would form the foundation for more sophisticated trials in the future. But before she could conduct more advanced experiments, she needed to finalize arrangements with the hospital for installation of their medical data analysis program, a proprietary software that would rapidly analyze the complex datasets she would be generating. By using the hospital's MDAP software, she could avoid the costly and time-consuming effort of contracting with a software developer to create her own analytical program.

Rene kept her attention on the screens and turned on the audio. Carter had finished arranging Brenda's headset and chatted with her as he waited for Rene to give the go-ahead to start the experiment. Even though the two experiments were unrelated, Rene had decided it would be easier to monitor them if they ran simultaneously.

Rene watched as Aisha reviewed the screening questions, obtained the subject's consent, and then moved through her checklist. When the research assistant finished getting Steven prepped, Rene opened the intercom to both rooms. "Everybody ready?"

Carter gave a thumbs-up. Aisha smiled and nodded.

"Then let's get started." It was still early afternoon, so she'd have plenty of time to finish up the experiments and get home in time to shower and dress for dinner with Rob.

Carter gave Brenda the geometry materials. She opened the booklet of math problems, picked up a pencil, and began to scribble. Rene then checked on Aisha's experiment; it, too, was well underway.

Watching the interns begin her experiments gave Rene a burst of satisfaction. At last she could start tackling the mysteries of the mind in hopes of relieving the suffering of people like Gramps and Kyle Nichols.

She'd always been in awe of the brain and its complexity. Oh, that mysterious human ability to think, to wonder, to even think about thinking! For all the brilliant scientists working on it, no one had yet come close to explaining how that blob of tissue resting between their ears created emotions, self-awareness, and the ability to communicate.

The researcher who solved these riddles would be the Albert Einstein of neuroscience.

Rene returned her attention to the screen, where Carter and Brenda were engaged in animated conversation. That was not part of the procedure. She flipped on the audio to listen in.

"I don't understand," Carter was saying.

"Uh, yeah, well," Brenda said, "I was working on problem three, and suddenly I felt really weird. I can't quite put it into words. It was like I was in another room, kind of like this one, but not—and somebody, a man with a deep voice, was talking in my head—"

This was odd; Brenda sounded genuinely distressed.

"I've turned off the equipment," Carter said. "Do you feel anything unusual now?"

"No, I'm OK now," she responded.

"Well, there isn't any way that this device could cause that effect. I followed all the protocols, and I didn't see or hear anything unusual." Rene cringed at Carter's judgmental tone.

"I can't explain it; I just felt really weird." Brenda sounded defensive.

Rene headed down the hall. These were her first experiments and already there was a glitch. *Damn.*

Entering room 2, she said, "Brenda, I'm Dr. Elder, a physician and the director of this foundation. I was listening in from our data center, and I want to check on you. I understand you had an odd experience. How are you feeling now?"

"I'm OK," she said. "But I really felt off-kilter for a while."

The young woman was flushed and fidgeting in her recliner but otherwise displayed no signs of distress. The monitor showed that Brenda's heart rate was a bit elevated, but not high enough to be worrisome. Still, it was important to be thorough.

Rene looked through the form Brenda had completed when she first arrived. "Are you taking any medications?"

Brenda frowned. "No. I marked that on the form."

"I need to double-check. Anything to drink before you came in?"

The young woman sat up straight. "I most certainly did not. And I don't do drugs at all in case that's what you're thinking."

"Sorry, I didn't mean to offend you. I just have to be sure." There weren't any obvious red flags in her answers. "Well, if you're feeling better, are you willing to try again?"

"Sure, I guess so. It was just—I don't know how to describe it—everything was really weird for a few moments there."

"How about if I stay with you, OK?"

The young woman seemed relieved and nodded. Carter gave Brenda a new geometry booklet and moved to a vacant chair next to the computer.

Rene set the ultrasound to the designated level. The volunteer studied the papers and began writing. Her vitals stayed steady, but as Rene adjusted the frequency, Brenda suddenly flinched, dropped her pencil, and pushed the booklet off the desk. Seconds later, her heart rate spiked and her skin-response readings peaked.

Brenda abruptly pulled off the headset and tossed it onto the table, ashen-faced and wild-eyed. "This is just too weird—I don't know what you are doing to me, but I'm not going any further."

"Wait, wait! Don't run out!" Rene was taken aback by the implication that she was inflicting something harmful upon her subject. "Please, just tell me what happened."

Brenda pulled off the pulse oximeter and galvanic skin-response sensors. Rene winced as they hit the floor. "It happened again—only more intense—like I was in two places at once."

Rene hadn't expected a subject to respond so dramatically. What could be affecting her? Was she faking?

"I had a flash of someone in a blue shirt." She brushed her hand across her face, blinking rapidly, then fumbled to grab her sweater from the back of the recliner, knocking her purse off the table in the process. "There was that man's voice again, really clear this time." Her words came out in bursts through trembling lips. "Saying something about—fishing—of all things."

"I didn't hear anything," Carter interjected.

"No, no, you don't get it." Brenda scowled at Carter, then turned toward Rene. "It wasn't something in this room. There was a super loud voice *in my head*—I couldn't concentrate, and I couldn't block it out. It was really, really freaky." She retrieved her purse and struggled to put on her sweater. "I don't know what kind of crazy-ass experiment you're doing, but I'm outta here."

Brenda dashed out of the room. Carter and Rene followed into the hallway as the exit door slammed shut behind her.

Rene wondered if the woman might have some mental health issues not caught by the screening questions. One of the symptoms of schizophrenia was the belief that one's own thoughts were coming from somewhere outside of themselves. Rene wished she could have done a basic assessment, but the woman was already long gone.

At that moment Aisha and Steven exited room 1, smiling and laughing. Aisha shook his hand before he left, then walked over to join Rene and Carter. At least one experiment seemed to have gone well.

"Well, that was different," Aisha commented.

"How so?" Rene shot a cautionary look at Carter, signaling him to remain silent.

"Steven said he enjoyed the experience," Aisha reported, "but I was surprised by his comments. He asked how we created what he called 'the interference.' He assumed that all the stuff about listening to *The Old Man and the Sea* was just a ruse and that we're actually studying his reactions to the interference."

"'Interference'? Did he explain what he meant?" Rene asked.

"He said a couple of minutes into the experiment he had a weird double vision, like he was in another room, like for a few seconds he was looking down at some papers. Then the image went away."

Rene's mind tingled—the sensation she got when on the verge of something new. "Anything else?"

"Yeah. He said it happened a second time. He was reclining and had his eyes closed, but he said it was as if his eyes were open and he was seated at a desk looking at some papers. He described seeing some lines or drawings that he couldn't make out. Then the image changed, and he saw a man wearing a red hat."

Rene glanced reflexively at Carter's crimson ball cap—and then at Aisha's royal-blue blouse—"someone in a blue shirt." Her pulse quickened.

What the hell?

"He said it was a very vivid image, but it disappeared almost immediately," Aisha continued. "He assumed we were intentionally creating some kind of interference because it was hard for him to concentrate on the audio. He also said that at one point he felt an odd burst of anxiety, like an emotion coming from someone else."

This was just too weird. One random study volunteer like Brenda might have mental health issues, but both? Rene struggled to find another explanation. "Carter, is there any way Brenda could have seen Aisha?"

Carter's brow furrowed. "I can't see how. I took her right into room 2."

"I'm confused. What's going on?" Aisha asked.

Carter raised his eyebrows.

"Brenda had a negative reaction and got so upset she wasn't willing to finish." Rene took a deep breath. "She mentioned seeing someone in a blue shirt and hearing a man with a deep voice. He was talking about fishing."

There was a pause for a couple of seconds and then Aisha's eyes got big. "You're kidding me." She looked back and forth from Carter to Rene. "No way."

"Yes way," Carter chimed in. "I heard her myself."

"And you're wearing a cap like Steven described—Brenda was working on papers with drawings—geometry, maybe?" Aisha gasped. "Dr. Elder?"

Rene scrambled for an explanation. "Perhaps . . . those two know each other and tried to pull a prank on us." She flashed again to Stauss and his hostility toward her. Could he have somehow sent these two to disrupt her research?

"But how could they have known about my blue blouse and Carter's red cap?" Aisha said, sounding unconvinced.

"Maybe they each took a photo of us and texted each other when we didn't notice?" Carter said.

Rene raised her hand to ward off more questions; this speculation was getting them nowhere. "I want you both to recalibrate the ultrasound machines to ensure there weren't any malfunctions. I need to find out if the equipment is damaged or if someone is trying to prank us—"

"Um, sorry," Carter interrupted, "but I'm kinda late to meet my girlfriend—"

Aisha jumped in. "I'll take care of checking his equipment, if that's OK?"

"Of course." Rene nodded.

"Thanks," Carter said and headed toward the exit.

She turned to Aisha. "Let me know when you're done. I'm going to review the recordings."

Rene rushed to her desk in the data center, alarmed and

intrigued at the same time. This wasn't how she'd expected her first experiments to go. She brought up Brenda's heart rate and skin-response graphs and aligned the timelines.

She located the point when Carter had turned off the transcranial ultrasound in response to Brenda's verbal reaction and identified two points where the woman's heart rate had increased markedly. The skin-response readings showed corresponding spikes. She verified that the first surges occurred just before Brenda's initial verbal reaction, and the second when Rene had adjusted the ultrasound frequency.

Aisha's knock came at the perfect time.

"I was just about to come find you. Do you want to review the results with me?" Rene asked.

"Are you kidding? You couldn't drag me out of here for a million dollars!" When Aisha had interviewed for the research assistant position, she'd impressed Rene with her grasp of neurobiology. Rene was glad she could review these anomalous results with her.

Rene described the spikes she'd seen in Brenda's readings, then brought Steven's data up on the second monitor so they could review the timing of their reactions side by side. His readings also revealed two distinct peaks, although he hadn't verbalized anything in the moment. As with Brenda, his second spike was slightly greater than the first.

"Now, here's a key question," Rene said. "Did their reactions occur at or about the same time?" The further apart the incidents, the less likely they were related.

She deftly scrolled to the recording of the first incident. On the left screen, Brenda's tracing showed the first increase in heart rate at 17:23:18. On the right screen, Steven's heart rate began to rise at 17:23:23. "Only a five-second difference." Rene's skin tingled. Could there actually be a connection between their experiences? "Let's check the second time."

Rene again scrolled through the graphs, her fingers trembling a little on the keys. Brenda spiked at 17:27:42, Steven at 17:27:44.

"Only two seconds . . . ," she said, awestruck.

She stared at the screen, searching for errors. Was she looking for mistakes simply because if there were none, the implications would be so extraordinary? She locked eyes with Aisha.

"Holy shit. Could they both have experienced the same thing?" Aisha sounded incredulous.

Rene forced down her growing excitement. "We have to be methodical, Aisha. While they may each have seen or heard something unusual at about the same time, that doesn't mean they experienced the same thing."

"Yes, you're right, of course."

"OK, here's another clue: I was adjusting the frequency of the ultrasound when Brenda reacted the second time." Rene pulled up the timeline of the ultrasound. "Look where the frequency was set each time her heart rate increased—here . . . and here. Now let's see what was going on with Steven. At the time of the first incident, his frequency setting was just a bit higher than Brenda's. Now let's check the second episode, when Brenda's heart rate increased, and she reacted so strongly."

"Look!" Aisha said. "There is a four-second period, just before Brenda broke off the second test, when both ultrasounds were adjusted to the same frequency."

Rene's voice dropped to a whisper. "It's almost as if their minds somehow . . . blended."

Impossible.

Aisha continued to scan the data. Rene sat back, stunned that the readings were so closely synchronized. Her mind spun with possibilities as they sat together in silence, staring at the computer screens.

"Dr. Elder, what could possibly be causing this?"

"It's too soon to know for sure. But when ultrasound waves pulse into the brain, they cause the tissues to vibrate. Maybe those vibrations trigger an effect on the cells, deep within the neurons."

"Are you saying that if the neurons of two people . . . vibrate . . . at the same frequency . . . they can perceive in unison?" Aisha's eyes got wide. "I can't believe I just said that."

Rene rubbed the tight muscles in her neck. She was determined to maintain her objectivity despite her excitement. She couldn't so much as hint at such a major discovery without a lot more evidence. "Let's summarize what we actually know," she said. "We can state that on two occasions, when their ultrasounds were tuned to the same or nearly the same frequencies, both subjects experienced verifiable physiological changes."

Aisha nodded slowly. "And spontaneously reported that at those specific times they could briefly . . . 'read each other's mind,' for lack of a better term."

Rene fell silent. Aisha's conclusion fit all the facts but sounded completely outlandish. "I think we should say that the subjects had some 'unexplained perceptions,'" Rene said. "'Reading minds' is hardly a scientific term, and it suggests a lot more than what we can confirm at this point."

"But ultrasounds have been used for years. Wouldn't someone have noticed an effect like this before?" Aisha asked.

"Use of ultrasounds to scan the brain is still a developing technology," she said. "Even so, the odds of anyone accidentally creating these exact conditions are remote. What we observed today had nothing to do with my planned experimental design; we were recording their reactions as part of two independent tests. It was pure coincidence that they were simultaneously subjected to the identical ultrasound frequency. And then it was only their spontaneous comments that got our attention."

"Right." Aisha agreed. "But I feel like I'm in the middle of an episode of *Black Mirror*."

Rene checked the time. *Oh, no, no, no, no!* It was after seven: she couldn't be late for Rob's dinner.

She gathered her papers and stuffed them into her satchel. "We've done all we can for today. Don't share this incident with anyone until we can get a better handle on what might be going on, OK? There's still a possibility that this is some kind of hoax or equipment malfunction."

Rene rushed to copy the information to her jump drive and carefully placed it in her bag. "Can you straighten up the testing rooms, and then set the alarm when you leave?" she asked. "The code is the first six digits of pi."

Aisha looked puzzled.

"Ah," Rene said, quickly jotting *314159* on a sticky note and handing it to her assistant.

"Of course," Aisha answered with a wry smile.

"Thanks. I'm running awfully late." Rene hurried through the front door and jogged toward her car.

CHAPTER 3

Owen sat beside his nephew's hospital bed, sick with worry. The visit from Dr. Elder the day before had been a brief break from their daily vigil, but he was tightly strung as he and Kristen waited for Dr. Stauss to arrive and give them his nephew's prognosis.

It had been almost two months since the car Kyle was driving skidded on wet pavement after he swerved to avoid hitting a deer and then rolled three times. Severe head injuries led to emergency surgeries. After weeks in the hospital, Kyle's body was no longer that of a strong young athlete. His once muscular legs were scrawny, his sinewy arms shrunken, his wrists and hands tightly held in braces to prevent contractures.

Walking over to the window to settle himself, Owen stared out over the trees and lost himself in memories of the graceful boy's last game.

—

Bottom of the ninth, a runner on first base, one out, Kyle at bat, his team—the Mustangs—behind by just one run.

As the ball left the pitcher's hand, the runner sprinted from first. Kyle executed a beautiful bunt that slowly rolled toward the third-base side of the mound, forcing the pitcher to scramble toward it and allowing the runner to reach second base safely. The pitcher's throw to first was off target, so Kyle was also safe.

Owen exchanged grins with his sister, Kristen, Kyle's mother, sitting to his right. He was pleased to see the pro scout sitting behind home plate, nodding and taking notes. Owen's best friend, Yoshi, and Yoshi's adult son, Matt, sat to Owen's left. Matt pumped his fist. "Way to go, Kyle!"

Kyle represented the winning run as he bounced on his toes a few feet from first base, eyes alert. The boy's uncle clapped, willing the next batter to get a clean hit and send Kyle and the other runner sprinting around the bases.

But the opposing pitcher amped up his game. The first two pitches were screaming fastballs, and the hitter swung late both times. The next off-speed pitch tricked the surprised batter into swinging way too early.

The next batter was the last chance for the Mustangs, but he hit a weak grounder that the pitcher easily fielded, and the game dribbled to a sad loss.

Owen growled with frustration as the other fans let out a collective groan.

Most of the players looked dejected after losing their last game of the season. But Kyle seemed upbeat, hugging teammates and opponents alike. Smiling, he stopped to speak at length to the winning pitcher, clapping him on the back.

"It's just like Kyle to congratulate a competitor on a well-played game," Owen said.

"That's my boy," Kristen said. "He loves baseball no matter what, win or lose."

Owen and his sister walked down to field level, where they chatted with Yoshi and Matt as the stands emptied. They turned away to avoid staring as the scout went over and spoke to Kyle for several minutes, but Owen snuck a glance as the scout shook Kyle's hand and left him with a big smile.

Kyle came up behind Kristen and embraced her with a big hug.

"I told you everything would work out, Mom," he teased as she turned to face him. "I just got some expert advice from that scout. He thinks I've got a real shot at the bigs. Man, I'm stoked!"

Owen's hopes leaped. Kyle had a chance to go pro! He exchanged high fives with his nephew.

Kyle's eyes sparkled with enthusiasm, his energy contagious.

Kristen laughed. "It's glorious news, hon. I want to hear all about it over dinner, so go get showered. I'm ravenous."

"Can I have the car later, to meet up with the guys over at Eric's? I can't wait to tell them."

"OK, sure. But it's a school night, so be back by eleven, right?"

"I know, Mom, I know. But the season's over; I'm not in training anymore, remember?"

"Yeah, right." She smiled. "Be back by eleven."

CHAPTER 4

Owen turned back from the window and watched Kristen gently stretch her son's legs as the physical therapist had instructed her. He took a seat and sighed. "Jeez, is that doctor ever going to get here?"

"We just have to be patient," Kristen replied quietly. "Look, I get that you think Dr. Stauss has a lame bedside manner, but he saved Kyle's life. As far as I'm concerned, he walks on water."

As Kyle's uncle, Owen had no legal authority over Kyle's care. That left the lonely burden of any medical decisions resting squarely on his sister's shoulders. So, although he found it challenging to engage with Stauss, he wouldn't vent his unease. "Sorry, I'm just really anxious."

"Me too," she said softly, glancing up from her ministrations. Kristen was only thirty-six, but her shoulders seemed locked in a permanent stoop as she continued stretching her son's limbs.

A few moments later, Dr. Stauss strode in carrying a tablet.

Owen automatically rose as the physician immediately took

command. "Good morning, Ms. Nichols, Mr. . . . uh . . ." Dr. Stauss shook Kristen's hand but stumbled over Owen's name.

"Nichols. Owen Nichols."

"My brother," Kristen reminded Stauss.

"Ah, yes, I think we've met."

Owen shook the doctor's hand, swallowing his annoyance: they'd met several times before.

"I was in earlier today and gave Kyle a thorough exam," Stauss said, briefly looking at the boy. "Let's step outside and I'll give you an update."

"We'll be back soon, hon," Kristen said to Kyle. Owen squeezed his nephew's arm before he turned to leave. They were careful to include the boy in every conversation. To act as if he wasn't aware of what was happening was too awful to consider.

Dr. Stauss led them to a small waiting room. They'd come to know well the worn vinyl floor and clusters of brightly colored but hard plastic chairs that stood out against the scuffed beige walls. They'd often huddled in that room for hours, waiting as tests were run or surgeries were performed. They'd endured the stares and shows of sympathy as other visitors overheard sobering updates from Kyle's numerous doctors. Fortunately, they had the room to themselves this time.

Owen broke out in a sweat as he and Kristen sat down across from the physician. She gave her brother a wan smile, the tightly etched lines on her face reflecting his own deep anxiety. He'd longed for this moment, when at last there might be some answers. That moment had arrived, and his gut hurt.

The balding doctor with tiny eyes wasted no time on pleasantries. "As you know, Kyle sustained significant brain trauma in the accident."

Kristen reached for Owen's hand and grabbed on tight. He squeezed back and waited, his entire attention focused on the physician sitting before them.

Stauss leaned forward, as if speaking directly to Kristen, but kept his focus on the tablet resting in his lap. "After extensive tests, we've confirmed the diagnosis of a rare condition called locked-in syndrome, or LIS. It exhibits as an extreme, complete paralysis."

The doctor's words knocked the breath out of Owen. He sat back hard in his chair.

Total paralysis. His nephew's opportunities for a full life were obliterated.

"So he's a . . . quadriplegic?" Kristen's voice trembled.

"Yes," Stauss said slowly, "but I'm afraid his injuries have implications far beyond that. When I say complete paralysis, I'm including those muscles he needs in order to speak."

Owen struggled for air as his chest tightened. Kristen put words to his confusion. "You mean Kyle won't be able to talk when he wakes from the coma?"

"No, he won't." Stauss tapped on the device and stared at the screen. "But actually, our recent tests show he's already emerged from the coma and is again experiencing the world normally." Stauss spoke softly as he studied his device. "In fact, he's regained normal brain activity, including his sleep-wake cycles. His cognitive abilities remain intact. He's conscious, as conscious as you or me."

Owen rubbed his hands across his face, trying to regain focus. His mind whirled as he tried to make sense of a diagnosis he hadn't even known existed.

Kristen's face drained of color as she spoke through ragged

breaths. "Sorry, I need you to go over all this again. Slower, please . . ."

The doctor took off his glasses and wiped them on a cloth he extracted from a case in his pocket. "Locked-in syndrome is aptly named," Stauss continued. "From the perspective of the patient, they're truly locked in. They can't move their limbs to physically escape their situation. In addition, their thoughts and emotions are confined inside their own mind because there's no way to express themselves to others."

Owen's breaths got shallow. It was as if he'd gone deaf: the doctor was speaking, but he couldn't comprehend the words.

The doctor continued. "In less severe cases, patients can blink or move their eyes, and caregivers can set up a code for communication. Some can use a special computer that displays the alphabet. The patient focuses on one letter at a time. The computer tracks their eyes and types out messages." Stauss went on. "But Kyle can't move his eyes or blink, so neither of those methods will work for him."

Kristen's fingernails dug deep into Owen's hand. Tears streaked her face, and her shoulders sagged. He could barely make out her words. "And the paralysis is—permanent?"

"Yes. I'm so sorry."

The air was warm and stale. Owen got woozy as the room started closing in on him. He shook his head. "No. This just can't be possible." Pressure built in his chest, and he stood, striding around the small room to the sealed window, frustrated in his search for fresh air. Looking out, he imagined Kyle confined inside a sealed metal compartment, pounding and pounding on the walls, yelling, screaming to get out, to no avail.

Owen turned and stared down at the physician. "What the

hell? You're supposed to be one of the best neurosurgeons in the country."

Kristen glared at him, shook her head. "Owen."

Surprised by his own sudden rage, he struggled to gather himself. He was there to support his sister, not get in the way.

Dr. Stauss kept his eyes averted. "Kyle's youth and good health pulled him through the trauma, but there are some types of injuries that are just too severe for us to repair."

Owen slowly returned to his seat and slumped down. There were a million questions he should ask, but his rational mind was shocked into submission. He put his arm around his sister's shoulders, pulling her close.

Kristen briefly laid her head on his shoulder, then sat up straighter. "There must be a thread of hope somewhere," she said, dabbing her eyes with a tissue.

"Well, there is, although I caution, it's a slim one."

A slim hope was better than none. Owen forced his mind to clear.

"There are a few experimental research studies for patients with Kyle's level of neurologic functioning." Stauss met her gaze and spoke with more energy. "The research is attempting to establish computer-brain interfaces—using electrodes implanted in the brain, for example—to achieve limited communication. There's a chance that Kyle might qualify for one of those studies."

A flicker of optimism broke through his gloom, and Owen leaned forward, focusing on Stauss's next words.

"These studies are on the cutting edge of neurological research," the doctor continued. "There have been some very hopeful results." He sounded encouraging.

Kristen closed her eyes, looking shell-shocked. Owen clung

to the physician's optimism like a drowning man reaching for a life preserver. "What are the next steps, Doctor?" he asked.

Dr. Stauss met his eyes for the first time. "Well, I'd like to contact these researchers and see if Kyle is eligible for their studies." The physician sounded matter-of-fact, even enthusiastic.

Owen's hopes jumped. All his life, he'd enjoyed computers and all manner of electronic equipment. They were the focus of his academic degrees and his career. "Yes. Absolutely. We'll enroll Kyle in any study that might help him. Surely, with all the advances in technology, there'll be something that can work for him."

"Whoa, Owen, slow down," Kristen said. "Putting electrodes into his brain? That sounds like medieval torture." She shook her head. "I'm not a fan of experimental treatments."

Surprised, Owen gave her a puzzled look.

"Kimi," she said. "Remember?"

He kicked himself for not making the connection. Her best friend had died a torturous death after participating in several ineffective drug trials. Owen reluctantly barricaded his enthusiasm; he wasn't the decision-maker here.

"How about if I just make some inquiries?" Dr. Stauss asked, focusing on Kristen once again. "You don't have to decide right now. Take a few days to process the diagnosis and come to terms with the options."

"Yes, all right," Kristen said. "I was completely unprepared for this. I need some time to absorb it all."

"I understand, Ms. Nichols," Stauss said as he stood. "If you have questions, please reach out to me. In the meantime, let's meet back in Kyle's room in a half hour so I can share this information with him." With that, he strode out of the room.

Kristen's hands were trembling. "My god, Owen. How in the world will Kyle react?"

"He must have figured out some of it," he said, trying to steady his own shaky voice. "He already knows he can't move or talk."

"But he doesn't know that it's *permanent*."

Owen took Kristen into his arms, unable to say the obvious: Kyle would never be able to tell them how he felt.

Deeply shaken by the discussion with Dr. Stauss, they went to the cafeteria to calm themselves before going back to Kyle. Owen was rattled to the core by the shocking prognosis the doctor had just given them. Still, he tried to put aside his own grief to support Kristen.

He'd spent time in this same cafeteria years before, while Kristen was in labor with Kyle. The baby's father had never been in the picture, so when Kyle was born, Kristen had asked Owen to be an active part of her son's life, to be a male role model and another adult on whom her son could always depend.

Enraptured by the newborn, Owen had accepted Kristen's offer to play a key role in Kyle's life, grateful for how the experience might profoundly enhance his own life. He'd agreed that Kristen would keep the role of decision-maker, define the rules of behavior and the consequences for breaches, select schools and activities, and make medical decisions.

Sitting in that same cafeteria so many years later, the memory of the unbound happiness of that first day stabbed him in the gut.

Their untouched coffees had cooled before Kristen met his eyes. "I need you there when Dr. Stauss explains this to him. If I get stuck or can't go on, I need you to fill in the blanks, OK?"

He nodded, even as he dreaded Kyle being told about the devastating prognosis. "Whatever you need."

"Just one thing. Please don't mention anything about the research trials Dr. Stauss is investigating. I'm leery of them, and I don't want to get his hopes up about something that might not come through."

Owen bit the inside of his cheek. His hopes were already riding on the possibility of Kyle enrolling in one of the studies. But this wasn't the time to discuss her reservations.

Kristen sighed. "It's time," she finally said.

As they approached Kyle's room for what seemed like the millionth time, noxious smells assaulted Owen once again: the odors of forced cleanliness and disinfectants mixed with undertones of hope and life, cut with harbingers of dread and death.

He tried to gather his strength for what would be an excruciating talk. How could he support an eighteen-year-old who was about to be told the entire life he'd planned was essentially over?

Though they'd seen him earlier that afternoon, seeing Kyle lying motionless in bed was even more shocking after hearing the horrible prognosis. His thin frame was laid out almost corpse-like, although the aides turned him every few hours and rearranged pillows under his limbs to prevent bedsores. The ventilator kept up a steady, life-sustaining support, while catheters and feeding tubes disappeared discreetly under the covers.

Owen held Kristen's eyes across the motionless body of the boy they loved. Would Kyle be able to hear Dr. Stauss's explanation? Would he sense his mother's presence? Would he understand her words? What would he be feeling, thinking? What would be his questions, his worries, his deepest fears?

Owen was terrified they would never know.

CHAPTER 5

Humboldt jumped ecstatically when Rene entered the house, almost knocking her over. "I'm home!" she called, worried her late arrival had ruined Rob's special dinner.

She sighed in relief when he emerged from the kitchen with a big smile and handed her a glass of wine. "I thought you just might get caught up at your fancy new office, so I planned a meal that I could finish up whenever you arrived."

"You know me so well." She smiled and took a sip. "This is lovely. Thank you so much." She leaned into him for a quick kiss.

"How did it go?" he asked.

"It was an amazing day," she said, following him into the kitchen and picking up the container of cake she'd left on the counter. "From my goodbye party."

"That'll be the perfect dessert. Hang out with me while I get everything together. I want to hear all about it as soon as we sit down."

Rene kicked off her shoes and perched on the stool at the

peninsula, sipping her wine and enjoying the scene of Rob making his way around her kitchen.

In the two years since she'd met Rob, her fondness for him had grown into genuine love. They'd started talking about Rob moving in with her, and just the other night, they'd shared their hopes of marriage and having children. She contentedly watched her boyfriend prepare their meal, excited at the prospect of merging their households and lives.

Over a candlelit dinner of luscious poached salmon, wild rice, and steamed asparagus with hollandaise sauce, Rob listened attentively as Rene brought him up to speed on the bittersweet goodbye party and the bizarre experimental results of the afternoon.

Later, they lit candles in the living room and cuddled side by side on the couch, languidly consuming the rich cake with a fresh bottle of wine.

"What a wonderful treat, Rob," she said. "If this is any indication of what it's going to be like if you move in, then pack your bags!" She gave him a gentle kiss.

He laughed. "I love to cook, so yeah, it could really be like this. Although if we have kids, intimate dinners might be rare."

She smiled. "Good point. I don't remember my parents having any romantic meals with me present. It's kind of a contradiction."

"Indeed." They exchanged quiet smiles as Humboldt let out a muffled woof and started running in his sleep.

It had been such a good couple of days: a touching goodbye party, the exhilarating afternoon experiments, a fabulous romantic dinner. Why not top it off with a new level of commitment with a man she was loving more by the minute?

"So what do you think? Do you want to move in? See how far we can take this?"

"Best offer I've had all day." He grinned.

She leaned in for a kiss, but Rob unexpectedly put his index finger against her lips. "There's one more thing I need to talk about first."

Rene pulled back, looking at him with a mixture of disappointment and curiosity. "You sound so serious all of a sudden."

He paused for a sip of chardonnay. "How about if we talk about it in the morning? I'm enjoying just being here with you and Humboldt." He smiled. "I've probably had too much wine to dive into a big discussion."

"OK, now I've gone from being curious to worried," she said, half smiling, half frowning in mock consternation. "How about just telling me the topic so I don't spend the entire night trying to figure out what this big discussion is about?"

He remained silent, tapping his fingers on the side of the glass as he stared into the contents.

"Come on. What is it?" she said, trying to ignore the twinge of anxiety growing in her belly.

"It's about religion. We haven't talked about that yet," he said in a serious voice. "Really, let's pick this up tomorrow."

"I don't understand," she said, struck by his serious tone.

"It's about us raising our kids in a religious tradition," he said.

"Ah." She sat back. An uncomfortable prickle rippled through her, and she gripped her glass more tightly. "That's important to you?"

"Yeah, it is," he said solemnly.

"Really?" She was off-balance. She'd known him for months. Where was this coming from so suddenly?

"I know, I know, this probably feels like it's coming out of the blue."

"You think?" She didn't try to hide her surprise.

"Last week, after we talked about me moving in, maybe getting married . . . I started thinking more deeply about the kind of life I want to create for my kids," he said, sounding serious. "I've realized how important it is for my family to have the same level of active involvement in a church that I had growing up."

"We've spent dozens of Sunday mornings together. You never once mentioned—"

"Obviously, I'm not active in a congregation right now," he said, avoiding her eyes. "I'm embarrassed to say I haven't even attended church since I moved to Portland two years ago."

"Well then, where is this coming from?"

"Growing up," he said, his eyes suddenly bright, "I went to Lutheran services with my parents every week. We were very active. I participated in a lot of youth activities that gave me a strong spiritual foundation. It's my responsibility to provide that same bedrock for my kids." He paused and stared into his wine again. "Even if I haven't been going to services recently."

Was the jangling feeling in her gut from exhaustion or because Rob had just opened a Pandora's box? Developing a religious practice was absolutely not on her bucket list. Still, she loved this man and was determined to keep an open mind.

"I don't need you to become Lutheran if that's what you're worried about," he said, sounding diplomatic.

Rene moved slowly and methodically to refill their glasses. She set the bottle on the coffee table before looking up to meet his eyes. "Good," she said softly. "Because that's definitely not going to happen."

Rob rubbed a hand across his face and sighed. "Have you ever attended a church?" he asked.

"Just once, with Gramps. I didn't get much out of it." There was a lot more to it than that, but she wasn't prepared to give a long explanation at the moment.

"Well, we could decide together which church to attend," he said. "Each denomination has a slightly different focus, and each congregation has its own unique vibe. It could be fun to explore together and find a church that feels like the right place to educate our kids."

Rene sat back and ran her hands through her hair. Her earlier joy had been replaced by wariness. "I don't think you should presume a religious life for me," she finally said, keeping her voice calm as she met his eyes. "If you want to attend church, that's up to you. But I have to be clear: I won't be going to church—any church."

Now it was his turn to look surprised. "It's important that we attend church together to show the kids we're united in our beliefs." He leaned forward, earnest. "As parents, we can't be wishy-washy about moral values."

She took a swallow of wine to buy a few moments before responding. "I agree; we can't be vague or contradict each other on core values. Love thy neighbor and ethical behavior are principles I think we can unify around, without having to commit to any religion."

"Yes, those values are key, but the foundations go even deeper," he said, his voice becoming strident. "Our kids have to grow up understanding that it was Jesus who brought those values to Earth, that our actions now affect the promise of heaven. They need to learn the power of prayer."

Rene's skin prickled as if the room were suddenly too warm. A bitter taste rose in her throat as she fought to ignore images of Gramps asking her to pray with him. "We can teach them right from wrong without relying on the fantasy of heaven or the fear of an invisible superauthority hovering above them," she said. Then she plunged on, fearing she was taking a fateful step over the edge of a cliff but unable to stop herself. "I reject the idea of an all-powerful being who intervenes in our lives."

Rob's eyes got big. "I know you don't go to church. But you don't even believe in God?"

Rene's stomach dropped. She needed to explain, to make him understand. "I think humans created the idea of God—"

"God created us, not the other way around!"

Rene cringed at Rob's tone. How had this lovely evening gone off the rails so fast? She forced herself to meet his emotions in a rational way. "I believe people created the notion of God," she repeated, "to help make sense of a world that feels mysterious and scary." She locked eyes with him, her next words of the utmost importance. "That's why I became a scientist: to explain things that were previously incomprehensible."

"The existence of God is a mystery you and science will never explain," he said with finality.

The blatant challenge to her identity flooded her with outrage. "As far as I'm concerned, the belief in a supreme being is pure folklore."

Rob's body went rigid, his face tight. "How come you never told me you were a stone-cold atheist?" He glared at her.

"How come you didn't tell me you were so deeply religious?" She stared back, matching his defiant posture. An ominous tension was growing in her gut; his demands could be a deal-breaker.

After a long minute, she broke the stalemate. "I think we should stop here," she said quietly.

He nodded.

"It's a weighty topic, especially after such a long day." She managed a wan smile. "It was a fabulous dinner. I can't thank you enough." Leaning forward, she kissed him lightly on the lips. "I'll take care of cleaning up, but I'm just exhausted right now."

Rob took her signal and stood, found his jacket in the closet, and moved to the door. Humboldt accompanied Rene to see him out. Rob took a moment to pat him on the head. "Good dog," he said sadly before he turned to her. "We'll talk soon."

"Of course," she said without enthusiasm.

"Sleep well." They exchanged another perfunctory kiss, and he turned and left.

She stared out the window, watching his car disappear, her body jangling. Their lovely evening had unexpectedly fallen into a deep chasm.

Rene stalked into the kitchen and surveyed the mess Rob had left, then began to load the dishwasher. The screech of the fork as she scraped the plates set her teeth on edge; she feared the tension might trigger a migraine.

How dare he spring this religious requirement on her at the last moment. Had he intentionally kept his faith hidden until she was too in love to back out?

Or was he so oblivious to the fact that she was a dedicated scientist that he hadn't understood that traditional religion didn't speak to her? Either way, he'd made a serious misstep.

She gathered up the pots and pans, letting them clang loudly as she stacked them in the sink, the smallest inside the next largest, and so on, until she had built a tower four high.

Maybe it was just as he'd said: that he'd let his faith lapse until he'd seriously thought about raising children. But what did that say about the depth of his beliefs? That was part of what was bugging her. He didn't seem like someone who cherished a religious life.

Rene squirted soap into the highest pot in the stack and put the water on full blast, watching the foam build and work its way to the top, then overflow and begin to fill the one below it.

Her parents weren't religious, though Gramps had been quite devout. When she was about six, she'd been curious about why going to church was so important and asked to go with him.

She'd followed Gramps's eyes as she walked beside him into the chapel. The warm light of the clear Sunday morning cast splotches of color across their clothes as they walked beneath the stained-glass windows. The squares of red, yellow, and blue on the floor reminded her of a hopscotch game. Gramps gazed up at the windows and smiled.

Her energetic grandfather slowed his pace as they walked toward their seats—he said he liked to sit in the third row from the front. She glanced up at him, hearing a soft sigh as they sat. His face relaxed and he nodded gently as he met her eyes. He put his arm around her, pulling her in close while keeping his eyes on the minister. She smelled his suit jacket, always a bit musty from hanging in the closet all week.

She wanted to feel what he felt, so she sat up straight to pay attention. But the Bible verses were hard to understand. The preacher was a mean old man in a silly robe who talked about people going to hell. The worst part was when the adults went up to the front and the minister said they were eating and drinking the body and blood of Christ. *Ew.*

She tried to focus on the flowers on the altar and the colors of the stained glass, but that wasn't enough. She began to feel queasy.

"Why does going to church make you feel so good?" she asked Gramps in the car on the way back to his house. She was still trying to find a way to tap into the joy he clearly felt.

"As soon as I walk into that chapel, I'm filled with a sense of awe at being in the Lord's house," Gramps said, keeping his eyes on the road. "Awe is that special feeling you get when you see something so totally wonderful, you can't even believe how amazing it is. Like when we go to the rose garden."

"Oh," she said. Now she understood what he felt. The Portland Rose Garden was her favorite place in the entire world, filled with so many colors and smells that she couldn't get enough of it.

But knowing the word for what he sensed in church didn't help. Maybe there was something wrong with her; she'd had a lot of reactions to being at Gramps's church. But she definitely hadn't felt awe.

The waterfall of bubbles filled the bottommost pot and over-flowed into the sink. She turned off the water and tried to en-vision a future Sunday morning with Rob and their children sitting together in a church pew, praying to God, and listening to a sermon filled with promises of eternal life. She could see them clearly in her mind's eye.

Sadly, she just couldn't see herself.

She wiped down the counter and started the dishwasher. She'd finish up the pots later. Fortunately, no migraine had taken hold.

She plated the last of the chocolate cake and refilled her glass of wine. After snagging a couple of doggy treats from the cookie jar, she headed upstairs.

Humboldt followed her to her bedroom, where she exchanged her work clothes for her most comfy sweats. Moving to the small bedroom she claimed for her home office, Rene rewarded her pooch with a treat.

She windmilled her arms to release the remaining tension from her fight with Rob, then allowed herself a moment to savor that first bite of cake. Next she fired up her computer, eager to tackle the mysteries lurking on the jump drive in her satchel.

She scrolled carefully through the ultrasound images of the subjects' brains. How in the world could Brenda describe Aisha's blue blouse and hear a deep voice talking about fishing, while Steven saw Carter's red cap and the geometry problems?

She zoomed in on the brain maps generated by the ultrasound for a more detailed look, scouring the images for anything that seemed unusual.

She sucked in a quick breath. There it was.

Both subjects had showed a surge in activity in a totally unexpected region in their brains—the right temporoparietal junction in the brain—an area unrelated to either of their tasks. The burst of energy started just before the simultaneous increase in their heart rates.

Her jaw dropped. The specific area that had lit up in both Steven's and Brenda's scans was activated by tasks that required understanding the mental states of other people. It was sometimes referred to as "the empathy region."

Rene closed her eyes, trying to imagine what it would be like to have her mind invaded with the sights seen and sounds heard by someone else. How might her brain react? One response would surely be to try to understand the mental state of the person whose perceptions she was receiving. Indeed, she remembered that Steven had reported some "anxiety at a distance." *Like it belonged to somebody else!*

She sat back in astonishment. Something very unexpected had happened, something consistent with her theories, but something she hadn't predicted. She could come up with no explanation other than that some kind of awareness sharing had occurred.

How could she prove this to the doubters?

Bursting with adrenaline and fueled by chocolate, she spent several more hours immersed in the brain maps, searching for other potential connections.

It was nearing dawn when Humboldt whimpered, urgently requesting a visit outdoors to take care of his business. Rene pulled herself away from her computer and led her furry friend downstairs to the sunroom door.

Refreshed by the cool night air, her racing thoughts slowed. She took the short path through her beloved rose garden, basking in the faint aroma of her charges. The darkness muted the colors of the flowers' bright blossoms. The normally dark crimson of the Black Magic did in fact look black, the John F. Kennedy a muted white gray.

The flowers were her symbol of all the human brain meant to her. The tightly packed buds revealed spectacular spirals of color and scent that were so like the delicate folds of the brain, which hid some of the most magical mysteries of the universe.

Her best friend made his rounds of the perimeter, looking for just the right spot. She was grateful when he found it around the hedge, away from her cherished flowers.

One of her many trips to the Portland Rose Garden with Gramps came to mind. She must have been about four years old. As she'd surveyed the acres of flowers bearing more subtle shades than she'd ever found in her box of crayons, she'd abruptly become *aware*—aware of *herself*. Suddenly she could not only see things, but could also *think* about seeing things, even think about thinking. She was different in some mysteriously fresh way, not sure what had changed, but she understood that something important had just happened to her.

After a while, she led Humboldt back into the house and returned to her bedroom, preparing to grab a quick nap before beginning her day.

She struggled to get comfortable in bed. What would it be like to have someone else's perceptions flooding into her mind? Being in two places at once? Hearing someone else's voice inside her head? Seeing things even with her eyes closed? Hearing two sets of sounds might be like sitting in a noisy restaurant, but if she had her eyes open at the same time, would it be like double vision? How would she separate her own experience from the other's?

She needed to recreate the experiment and experience it herself. She'd call Aisha first thing and see if she could join her at the lab. And though she didn't know what she would unearth, she intuitively understood that the cutting edge of her research had just gotten razor-sharp.

CHAPTER 6

After her near-sleepless night, Rene headed for the foundation early the next the morning. Putting aside her fight with Rob to focus on the surprising results of the experiments, she called Aisha at seven thirty. The younger woman sounded startled and sleepy but jumped at the chance to follow up on the previous day's findings. Rene promised to bring bagels and cream cheese for breakfast if Aisha would meet Rene at the lab as soon as she could.

While Rene waited for Aisha to arrive, she went to her office and logged on to her computer. Two new emails from the previous day greeted her: Carter reported that after he'd left for the day, he'd been contacted by an employer with a job offer, so he was resigning from his position. Rene nodded to herself. Aisha's enthusiasm more than made up for the loss of Carter.

The second message came from Dr. Ainsworth, director of the Columbia River Institute for Neurological Research, inviting Rene to discuss "an opportunity" she might be interested in.

She'd heard rumors that CRINR's board of directors would be making moves to give the institute a higher profile, so any offer from Ainsworth was certainly worth the time to check out. She sent her acceptance and added the meeting to her calendar for a week from Monday.

Still at the computer, she printed out two sets of consent forms, one for Aisha and one for herself. Rene was about to take the unorthodox step of being a subject of her own research, and she'd follow basic procedures as best she could.

After making the rounds of the data center and the testing rooms to verify they were set up, she was brewing a pot of tea when Aisha arrived. "Perfect timing," Rene said, smiling as they sat down at the small table to share their breakfast.

"I can't stop thinking about those two participants," Aisha said. She paused, a bagel partway to her mouth. "It seemed like they shared their perceptions more clearly when the ultrasound frequencies were nearly the same."

"I agree. I hypothesize that synchronizing the frequency is key. That may be the sweet spot where the sharing becomes most complete."

"Do you think that if the frequencies align in that sweet spot, two people could share not only their perceptions but also their thoughts?" Aisha asked. "Could people actually have a conversation without talking?"

"That's exactly what I hope to test today," Rene said, flashing a mischievous grin. Aisha reminded her of a younger version of herself—smart and eager to plunge into the research. She just might turn out to be the full-time assistant Rene would need long-term.

Between hastily taken bites of bagel, Rene described the

information she'd gleaned after studying the volunteers' brain maps overnight.

Aisha's eyes got big. "What do you think's going on?"

"At this point, one person's perceptions are somehow being observed or witnessed by the other. I'm tentatively naming this phenomenon the Witness," she said, smiling.

"I like that name," Aisha said. "It captures that sense of sharing perceptions but doesn't sound as cheesy as 'mind reading.'"

"Exactly. If you're ready, let's go try this Witness technique and find out for ourselves," Rene said, draining the last of her drink.

Aisha put down her half-eaten bagel and stood. "I can't wait!"

Rene walked to room 1, Aisha to room 2. They communicated over the intercom as they secured the transcranial ultrasound headsets on their foreheads.

Rene's hands shook with excitement. If she and Aisha could transmit even simple impressions to each other, that would be the breakthrough of her career, the tool she'd dreamed of, allowing people with brain dysfunctions to communicate—but no, she couldn't dream about that right now. She needed to conduct this trial as objectively as possible.

Rene connected her headset to her TCU controller, and Aisha confirmed she was ready. "OK, let's turn on our TCUs and adjust them to the frequencies on the checklist," Rene said.

As their devices began generating silent sound waves, Rene suddenly started seeing double and felt the spin of vertigo. The new images were extremely confusing, yet so exhilarating that she forgot to breathe. She gripped the armrests to steady herself and closed her eyes. Then she realized she hadn't been seeing double in the traditional sense; rather, she was receiving visual input from Aisha's eyes *in addition to* what she herself was seeing directly. With her eyes closed, she saw only Aisha's hand adjusting the controller in the other room. She was mind reading!

Her voice trembled a little as she gave her instructions to Aisha. "OK, you said you have a photo on your phone to share with me. Concentrate on that picture. I'll keep my eyes closed, and we'll see what happens."

Rene wasn't sure what to expect. Would Aisha's photo appear in her mind as if her own eyes were open? She tried to stay open to whatever might come.

She felt an odd sensation, almost as if her brain were . . . tingling. What was happening? Suddenly, she saw Aisha's hand holding the phone, which displayed a photo of an elderly man standing next to a white car, some kind of classic. A wave of nostalgia and heartache washed through her from out of nowhere.

"Aisha, are you looking at a picture of a man and a white car?" Rene's heart was thumping so hard she was afraid she wouldn't be able to hear the response.

"Yes, yes, yes! Oh my god!" Aisha answered.

Rene pressed on. "Is this photo important to you? I'm sensing sadness."

"It's my uncle and his prized '65 Impala," Aisha answered shakily. "He recently had a stroke and can't drive anymore."

Rene received another burst of foreign grief, flooding her with compassion for her colleague.

"Thanks, Dr. Elder." Aisha's soft response came over the intercom. It took a few seconds for Rene to realize that Aisha had received Rene's comforting response before she'd said anything aloud.

"Can I try now?" Aisha asked, sounding excited.

Rene laughed. She was settling into the experience, eager to see what more they could learn. "OK. Keep your eyes closed while I look at my photo." She'd selected a favorite, one of Humboldt. She concentrated on her pooch, remembering Humboldt's joyous romp through the forest during a hike with Rob in the California Sierras.

"I'm seeing a big dog—is that yours?" Aisha said.

Rene knew that Aisha had recognized the dog even before her assistant verbalized it over the intercom. "Yes! That's Humboldt!"

"I knew you would say yes even before you said it," Aisha said.

"Me too! I get your meaning and emotions directly through the Witness; the spoken words are just a sterile echo." She was jubilant. "Let's stop talking."

Aisha's agreement came an instant later. Their shared amazement ping-ponged between them at the speed of thought.

Rene returned to the photo of a younger Humboldt in the mountains, remembering him chasing a ground squirrel and Rob calling him back—and Rob—she couldn't help it, the thought of him brought up memories of their fight, flooding her with angst. In an instant, she unintentionally transmitted all this to Aisha, whose surprise reverberated back to her just as quickly.

Rene recoiled after unwittingly revealing such intimate memories. Her deep vulnerability, humiliation, and bursts of regret flashed to her colleague, whose own distressed reaction was immediately returned. Rene pulled off her headset abruptly, breaking their connection before her uncontrolled thoughts could make matters worse.

After a few moments, Aisha came into Rene's room. "You OK?"

"Um, this is really awkward," Rene said, unable to make eye contact. "I guess that's obvious. Maybe this isn't a very good time for me to be trying the Witness. I've got a lot going on at home and—"

"Say no more. I get it. I mean, this kind of sharing seems to work, but there might be some downsides to instantly knowing what someone else is experiencing." Aisha offered a small smile. "Anyway, I'll take off now. Just let me know when—or if—you want to pick this up again."

Aisha seemed as eager to escape the uncomfortable moment as Rene.

"Sure. Will do." Rene pretended to adjust something on the controller and didn't look up. "I'll be in touch."

Rene heard the exit door click shut and closed her eyes. For a brief instant, she'd been *known* by someone else as intimately as she knew herself. Despite her discomfort, the intimacy of that direct *communion* with Aisha left her tantalized. Two people fully exposed, each a witness to the full vibrancy of the other's moment-by-moment thoughts and feelings? Her body hummed with the resonance of their connection.

This just might be it, Gramps.

CHAPTER 7

Owen paced as he and Kristen waited in the well-appointed reception area of Dr. Stauss's clinical office to hear the results of the physician's outreach to researchers. Owen had spent the past few days clinging to the hope that Kyle would be eligible for at least one of the experimental programs Dr. Stauss had mentioned. These last moments of tension before hearing the outcome were hard to bear as the wait stretched on forever.

Stauss's seating area offered dated copies of *Time* and *People* magazines to distract worried families. Kristen aimlessly flipped through one before tossing it down and turning to stare vacantly at the door to his office. Owen worried about the dark turn her mood had taken since Dr. Stauss had given them Kyle's prognosis. She'd obviously been losing weight ever since the accident and had told him she wasn't sleeping well.

Owen walked around the room. The walls were covered with Stauss's framed diplomas, awards, and certificates intermixed with photos of him in the company of civic leaders and a famous football player whose life he'd saved. Owen turned away, disgusted. This display didn't impress him; all that mattered was whether Kyle would have access to the latest research.

When the receptionist finally escorted them into the office, Stauss rose and motioned toward some leather chairs clustered around a small coffee table, then sat directly across from Owen and Kristen, his tablet once again resting on his knees.

Dr. Stauss leaned forward and looked intently at Kristen, again barely acknowledging Owen. The physician began with his typical brusqueness. "I wish I had better news for you, Ms. Nichols."

Owen's blood turned cold. Kristen clenched the armrests of her chair.

"After we spoke," the doctor continued, "I contacted several researchers who are enrolling people with severe brain injuries for research into ways to communicate," he said, then frowned. "But in each case, the answer was the same—there are aspects of Kyle's head trauma that preclude his participation in these studies." The physician shook his head. "I'm sorry if I got your hopes up."

Owen's frustration peaked. "So this is the worst-case scenario, then? It leaves Kyle with no ability to communicate whatsoever? With no hope for further recovery? And no technology to help him? Really? Is that the best you can do?" He looked to Kristen to back up his outrage.

Instead, he found her looking at him with pleading eyes. "Owen, I didn't want Kyle to be some experimenter's guinea pig, anyway. He's already being tortured enough."

Owen blinked and sat back. Surely technology offered them the best chance to help Kyle. He turned back to the physician. "You just can't tell us there's no hope."

"I know this news is terribly disappointing," Stauss said, sitting back in his chair. "It's difficult to accept in this age where technology seems to have a fix to every problem—but yes, that's the situation at this point."

Owen felt as if he'd run into a brick wall. He'd always held a deep passion for computers and advanced electronic equipment. But when it mattered most, technology wasn't there for him. Nevertheless, he also had held a deep-seated confidence in innovation. "Damn it, I'm convinced there'll be some breakthrough in the future. We'll find it."

"Owen, let it go, OK? I don't want anyone to muck around with Kyle's brain." Kristen's face crumpled. "He's suffering enough."

Owen bit the inside of his cheek. This wasn't the time or place to disagree with her.

"With those research options off the table, you're now faced with some important decisions." Dr. Stauss broke eye contact and began fiddling with his tablet as he unexpectedly switched gears. "It's been two months since Kyle's injury, and his vital signs have stabilized. However, I'm sure you realize that he'll always need considerable ongoing care. He'll be fed through a tube going into his stomach and kept on a ventilator to assist his breathing. He'll need someone to bathe him and—"

Kristen moaned, tearful, shaking her head at each element of Kyle's prison sentence. Owen put his elbows on his knees, head in his hands. His insides were being strewn over hot coals.

"He'll need constant turning to avoid bedsores and someone

to do range-of-motion exercises to prevent muscle contractures." The man's voice was quiet but firm as he continued to look down at his device. "He'll live, likely for decades, in total paralysis and isolation, never able to initiate or respond to any human communication."

Owen's jaw muscles clenched in time with the harsh recital of Kyle's condition. He glared at the doctor. Couldn't this jerk find a gentler way to make his point?

Finally, Stauss looked up at Kristen. "I'm sorry, I know this is brutal, but I need to discuss all the potential scenarios with you, Ms. Nichols. So here goes."

Owen braced himself. *What now?*

"As his guardian, you have two options," the physician continued. "One is to arrange for a long-term care facility—"

"Can you recommend some suitable care homes, top-quality places that could handle a case like Kyle's?" Owen interrupted. Here was something tangible where he might regain a bit of control.

"I don't generally make referrals to specific facilities. But in the Portland area, Rockridge Place is the only facility with the capability to provide the extremely high level of care Kyle needs," Stauss continued. "I asked our discharge planner to check, and they have a room becoming available next Friday." Stauss paused. "It may be some time before they have another vacancy. I have to warn you, they're very expensive."

"Kristen can't decide based on cost. We're talking about Kyle's quality of life." Owen's voice came out more stridently than he'd intended.

Despite her tears, Kristen pierced Owen with a resolute gaze. "I agree. Quality of life is exactly what we need to be talking about." Her voice rose. "Owen, do you genuinely think that living for decades in a care home, lying motionless with nothing to do, having no life purpose, having a machine breathe for him, needing diapers and tube feedings, is the quality of life Kyle wants?"

"We'll work together to get him the best care." Owen spoke directly to her, surprised by her comment. "What other choice is there?"

"Doctor?" Kristen turned to the physician.

"I don't have an opinion about what you should do, Ms. Nichols," he responded, sounding more compassionate. "But it is my responsibility to review the other option that you're alluding to, as hard as it is to talk about." He paused, tapping his pen against his hand. "You could elect to stop his life support and end his life in a painless and comfortable way."

"What? End his life?" A fresh shock swept through Owen. Numb, he looked at Kristen, assuming he would see a look of revulsion at the mere thought; instead, she was nodding, tearful, as if it were a possibility worth considering. His body was stricken by a deep chill from the inside out. Surely they wouldn't disagree on something so important.

"Ending life support becomes legal," the physician said, "when a patient's suffering is severe, the prognosis is that death would be imminent without continued medical intervention, and when no hope of recovery is possible. This is the point we are at with Kyle."

The doctor's words reverberated in Owen's mind: "death would be imminent," "no hope of recovery is possible." His optimism vanished. Kristen gripped his arm tightly, as if sensing his reactions.

"It's certainly not a decision to make without a lot of consideration," Dr. Stauss continued, focusing on Kristen. "The ethics department would expect you to consider what Kyle would want—if you know. There are tricky ethical and legal issues you'll need to navigate, should you decide to go down that path." Stauss looked from Kristen to Owen. "He's eighteen, right? Does he have an advance directive?"

"No. The social worker did help me get approved to be his legal guardian, though," Kristen said, her voice shaking. Her eye twitched.

"Well, then you must decide for him. You may have had conversations with him that would indicate his wishes. If not, you must rely on your own understanding of who Kyle is, and what you believe he would want." Here he looked Owen in the eye. "And I must emphasize that your decision must be based on what the young man would want, not what you want."

Owen's mind was spinning, desperate to remember anything that might give a clue to Kyle's preferences. That would be key in supporting his sister through this dilemma.

Dr. Stauss plunged on a bit more sternly. "That said, I also urge you to consider how this decision would affect the quality of your own life. It's without a doubt the hardest choice a mother could ever have to make."

Kristen let out a barely audible cry and reached for the box of tissues on the coffee table.

For a moment, Owen was relieved that he wasn't the one who had to make this decision—then was hit by guilt at his own selfishness, knowing that Kristen bore this burden alone. He couldn't protect her from this. Then another horrible possibility struck him: What if he disagreed with Kristen's decision?

"On the one hand," Stauss continued matter-of-factly, "you have to decide if you're able to commit to the long haul, to take on the emotional and financial burdens of caring for him for the rest of your life."

"We have a big reserve from Mom and Dad's estate that you can draw on," Owen said to his sister, who kept her eyes on the doctor. "So don't make money the deciding factor." He'd carefully invested the principal of their parents' estate over the last twenty years, and it had accumulated considerable earnings and interest.

Stauss looked down. "Nevertheless, Ms. Nichols, I strongly recommend that you consult a financial advisor if you are considering placing Kyle in a care home. You must have a realistic financial plan for how to pay for his care if you were to die before him, which is a possibility."

Kristen gave a small nod, somehow taking in the practicalities.

"I've known patients with locked-in syndrome to survive for decades," Stauss said. "Furthermore, if your financial resources were to run out, Kyle could end up in a facility where care may not be up to the standard you would want for him."

Kristen bobbed her head mechanically, her fingers crumpling the tissue into a smaller and smaller ball.

"On the other hand," Dr. Stauss said, as he stared at his tablet again, "are you prepared for the emotional consequences of ending the life of someone you brought into this world? That decision would also change your life forever—"

"That's exactly what I'm worried about. I can't imagine what life would be like without him," Owen said.

Kristen's head dropped. "I need some time to work through this, Doctor."

Owen couldn't agree more. "This has to be about what's right for Kyle."

Unbidden memories surfaced. Only days after their parents' deaths, Kristen and Owen had sat in front of the social worker from Child Protective Services. His sister's eyes looked swollen from crying, but her attitude oozed with a sixteen-year-old's defiance. At twenty-six, two years after his previous girlfriend had miscarried their child and then dumped him, Owen lived alone, a bachelor enjoying the single life. Suddenly he was faced with a life-altering decision: let Kristen go into foster care or take responsibility for her himself. Without hesitation, he'd agreed to become Kristen's guardian. He'd guided her through several years of grief-fueled rebellion until her unexpected pregnancy forced her into adulthood. Now it was Kristen's turn to make a momentous decision of her own, an even harder one.

"I do understand the need for careful reflection." Stauss adjusted the tablet on his lap. "But because Kyle is stable and there's nothing more we can do for him here, he'll be discharged soon. Insurance coverage for hospitalization will also stop for this stay. The hospital is full, and other acute patients need to be admitted."

What the hell? Owen broke into a sweat. They were being backed into a corner.

"But if Kyle went to the facility you mentioned, Rockridge Place, then I could make the other . . . decision at some point in the future, right?" Kristen said.

"Unfortunately, no, not if he lives at Rockridge," Stauss

said. "The medical director there, Dr. Guramurthy, is adamant that he won't agree to end life support for patients residing at his facility. His board of directors is in total agreement with his philosophy."

"How can he refuse if I were to authorize it?" Kristen asked.

"In Oregon, health care providers are under no duty to participate in withdrawal or withholding of health care. I've debated this issue with Dr. Guramurthy several times. He strongly believes in safeguarding patients from situations where families commit to long-term care, then later change their minds for selfish reasons; for example, deciding 'now it's just too hard,' or 'now it's just too expensive,' or 'now we're just too tired.'"

"But surely there are allowances for things to change," Kristen said.

"You could revisit the decision to end life support if Kyle's condition worsens and we readmit him to the hospital." Stauss nodded. "But if you move him to Rockridge, for all practical purposes, you're committed to that course of action until such a time as his condition deteriorates. I have to caution you, though," Stauss continued more slowly, "Kyle is young and otherwise healthy, and though I can't predict this with certainty, it's possible there wouldn't be any significant change to his condition for quite some time. For planning purposes, his care at Rockridge could well be a path that you would stay on for years, perhaps decades to come."

"Isn't there any other facility that has more flexibility?" Kristen asked.

"In my opinion, Rockridge Place is far and away the best placement for Kyle, not just in this area, but anywhere in the Northwest," Stauss said. "They have a very low staff-to-patient ratio and well-trained providers across all the disciplines, especially respiratory and physical therapies. Dr. Guramurthy is sometimes even ahead of me with his knowledge of the latest research." Stauss paused for a moment. "And just in case you're wondering, I don't have any type of financial ties to Rockridge or a personal relationship with Dr. Guramurthy."

"This isn't something to decide quickly, Doctor," Owen said. He needed time to talk with Kristen, to plead the case for Kyle's life, if necessary.

"Today is Tuesday. The bed will become available at Rockridge Place Friday of next week." Stauss's tone wasn't unkind, but it was firm. "You'll need to decide by then."

"Ten days," Kristen said, her words so soft Owen had to strain to hear.

The window offered a view of the darkening late-afternoon sky as the physician's admonition sank in. Every beat of Owen's heart was a tick on the clock marking down the time until the deadline for Kristen's decision.

Kristen swayed as she stood. "I'll get back to you, Doctor." Owen extended his arm for her as they walked out. She held on tight with a trembling hand. How in the world could his sister ever make such a choice?

They walked into the quiet of the reception room. The members of another family awaiting the doctor averted their eyes; Kristen's pain was all too obvious. Maybe those folks would get positive news from the brilliant neurosurgeon. He and Kristen sure hadn't.

CHAPTER 8

Rene consciously relaxed her grip on the steering wheel as her car approached the hospital parking lot. She needed to be calm and centered for this one last responsibility, a face-to-face meeting with Dr. Stauss.

Using her access card for the last time to open the gate into the lot was like entering a time warp. Nothing in the garage had changed, but the last few days of work at her lab and the argument with Rob had transformed her, as if an eon had passed since her goodbye party.

She found a parking spot in the doctors' section and sat in the car for a few moments, recalling how important this institution had been to her, remembering the patients she'd cared for—those she'd helped and those she'd lost, and those caught somewhere in between.

But that was from a different lifetime.

Pulling out of her reverie, Rene steeled herself for the upcoming appointment. She retrieved her hospital-issued laptop from the back seat before exiting the car, walked briskly to the elevator, and punched the button for the eleventh floor, where the administrators and medical directors had their offices.

Her antipathy increased with each floor the elevator ascended. The life-and-death work of the institution was carried on in the emergency room, operating suites, wards, and intensive care units; not in the offices of the big egos who dwelled on the upper floors. She was long past being intimidated by the luxurious suites or their illustrious occupants, but her intense scorn for the doctor she was about to meet still turned her stomach sour.

The door opened on the eleventh floor to a half-dozen people waiting to enter. Gritting her teeth, Rene dodged the crowd. Stauss had one of the four corner suites on the floor. She entered his generously sized reception area and greeted his assistant, Janine, at the desk guarding the door to his office.

"Sorry, Dr. Elder, Dr. Stauss isn't quite ready for you yet," the woman said, looking embarrassed.

Rene was on time for her appointment but wasn't surprised that Stauss would keep her waiting. An obvious power play.

"If you want to give me your laptop and access key, I can turn them in to HR for you," Janine said.

"You're so thoughtful." Rene smiled. "It'll save me a trip downstairs."

"I'm sorry to see you leave us," Janine added, sounding genuinely regretful as she took custody of the items.

Rene had always liked this woman, even when things with Stauss went off the rails. "Thanks, Janine. I'm really going to miss you and the folks on the neuro floor," she responded, omitting Stauss's name.

"Today's Tuesday. Wasn't last Thursday your final day?"

Janine printed out a receipt for the devices and handed it to Rene. "For your records."

"Thanks," she said, folding the paper and putting it in her satchel. "I had my exit interview with HR last week. Dr. Stauss requested this final meeting, and this was the soonest he could work me in."

"Ah." Janine nodded as she took an incoming call.

Rene sat and considered the man she was waiting to meet. Dr. Stauss was nearing retirement. He'd worked his way up from a young intern to the chief of Neurosurgery in record time and had held that honor for nearly three decades. Along the way, he'd pioneered techniques that permanently implanted electrodes in his subjects to track their brain functioning. Many considered his research techniques as best practice; Rene had rebelled against those methods months before and was instead focused on noninvasive devices such as transcranial ultrasound.

She'd deeply respected Stauss's reputation for innovation when she applied for the position in his department, but she'd become repulsed by the unrelenting ambition that she believed had led to the death of Marcella Lopez.

Four months earlier, Stauss had performed a craniotomy to treat the child's severe intracranial pressure. Rene observed the surgery, and in her assessment, the child would probably survive. But Stauss made a grave miscalculation by needlessly extending the surgery. The girl's status plummeted, and she died.

After a sleepless night, and too intimidated by her arrogant supervisor to confront him, Rene had reported the incident to the hospital's medical director and risk manager, triggering an internal investigation. To her knowledge, the results had yet to be finalized.

Rene boiled with contempt as she surveyed the expensive furniture, the fine art, and the fabulous view from the top floor of the medical complex. The man she'd once revered had indeed saved many lives and made countless contributions to the profession. But a child had died unnecessarily at his hands. She'd never forgive him.

Janine finally nodded for her to go in. A calm resolution descended upon her: she was only here to complete the required formality of meeting with her supervisor one last time.

"Rene."

"Dr. Stauss."

Stauss made up for his small stature with a deep voice that commanded attention. Two chairs were placed in front of his oversized desk, but he didn't invite her to sit.

"Thanks for coming in, Rene," he said.

Rene's gaze was steely, her voice cool. "I'm just here for the final meeting you requested." It was hard to believe at this point, but they had successfully collaborated during those first few months after he'd hired her.

Stauss adopted an artificially pleasant tone. "I'm glad you came in. I'll keep it short. I just wanted to tell you in person that I've canceled your request for hospital privileges."

"You have to be kidding. What? Why?"

"You've made it abundantly clear that you've left patient care behind for research. Your foundation doesn't have a track record demonstrating quality of care for patients treated in their clinical trials, and I want evidence of that first." Stauss smirked, his bushy eyebrows practically bristling.

The news was a slap at her professional reputation. She had had an excellent patient care record while employed at the hospital. He knew that.

More crucially, being denied privileges meant she wouldn't have access to the hospital's MDAP software that she had been counting on to analyze her research data. But there was no way she was going to grovel in front of Stauss or beg him to change his mind. She'd just have to contract with an independent software developer and design her own damn program.

Rene glared at her former supervisor. "Thank you for telling me," she said, making no effort to hide her sarcasm. "It means so much hearing it from you, face to face."

"Yes, the personal touch is always best, isn't it?" he said smugly, lounging back in his leather chair. "So my little research protégé is off to try her wings."

She held his stare, vowing not to engage. How could this man be so compassionate when speaking with patients and yet so vile behind the scenes?

"Aren't you the lucky one to have a wealthy family who can support your hobby?" he continued. "Some of us have had to work for our opportunities."

Rene bit back a smart-ass response. Then her thoughts spun to the potential of her own research. Suddenly the sting of the insults from Stauss evaporated. Her scowl morphed into a smile. "Is there anything else you'd like to say, Doctor?" she asked.

Stauss stared at her for a few moments, then turned to his computer screen. "You're done here," he said.

Rene walked out without a second glance.

CHAPTER 9

Owen and Kristen walked into her home like automatons, stopping at the hall closet to hang their jackets, uncertain what to do next. Owen didn't want to be alone. He followed Kristen into the kitchen.

"I'll heat some soup." Kristen opened the cupboard and reached for a can.

"I'm not hungry." Food was the last thing on his mind.

"We should try to eat."

He paused at a family photo hanging on the kitchen wall. He had the same photo hanging in his own condo. It was a shot of their parents at the airport, happily waving goodbye before boarding a plane for Mexico. They'd never returned from that trip: they'd gone deep-sea fishing and lost their lives in a boating accident.

He recognized this twilight zone of shock and uncertainty as he and Kristen drifted around the kitchen in silence. He recognized the feelings from the day he learned his parents had been

killed, from the day Carol had miscarried. He wasn't any better
at coping now than before. Perhaps worse.

In the background, a can opener cranked, the soup sloshed
into a bowl, the microwave hummed. He opened the silverware
drawer to get spoons.

Owen railed against their new reality. Outraged at the in-
justice of Kyle's disability, he threw a spoon across the room
and into the sink. Kristen turned in alarm, then nodded. She
turned back to the cutting board, slicing bread ever so slowly
and methodically.

Owen and his sister sat down at opposite ends of the table in
the breakfast nook, slumping over the cooling bowls of soup, trying to eat. Kyle's empty chair faced out toward the window. The
boy had long claimed this prime seat so he could see if friends
were gathering outside for a pickup game. If no one appeared
by the end of the meal, he and Owen would head out back for a
game of catch.

A string of memories came to mind as he aimlessly stirred
his soup. "Remember," Owen said, his voice cracking, "when
Kyle was just a little tyke, maybe five or so, we'd go outside to
play with his plastic bat and Wiffle ball, and he'd always insist
that we sing 'Take Me out to the Ballgame' before we could start
playing?"

He glanced at Kristen. The anguished look on her face
stopped him from further reminiscing.

"It's like some evil force kidnapped Kyle and confined him
inside a steel vault," Kristen said. "We know he's inside, begging
us to release him, and we walked away."

Owen visualized the vault, heard the pounding as they

turned and abandoned him. He was awash with guilt that had no basis: they were helpless to release him. He took a spoonful of the steaming soup, hoping the heat would soothe the tightness in his throat. It didn't.

"I've never felt so powerless," he said. "Even when Kyle was in surgery and we were just pacing in the waiting room, not knowing if he would live or die. At least then we knew someone was helping him. I'm so terrified now, knowing there's nothing anyone can do."

"I think coping with this is harder than if he'd died . . ." Kristen spoke softly.

Owen shivered. If the boy had died, his funeral would already be over. They'd be deep into their grieving, but they'd be moving on. So they were "locked in" too, in a certain sense. The rest of their lives would be dominated by LIS, just like Kyle's.

"Kyle's lost everything—he's so profoundly alone," she continued.

"We'll be there for him every day," Owen said. "And Matt, Yoshi, all his friends from the team." He was trying to be supportive, but the words rang hollow even to him.

Kristen brushed them off with a shake of her head.

"No, it's not the same, of course," he amended. "I'm not trying to say that. It's a huge adjustment."

"An insurmountable adjustment, maybe." Kristen stirred her soup aimlessly.

Insurmountable? With Kyle, nothing seemed insurmountable. Owen let his spoon drop into the bowl with a clang. "What are you saying?"

"I'm terrified to admit it, but—"

"But what?"

"I—I wonder if Kyle would have chosen to die in the accident if he knew he would have to face this for the rest of his life."

"Good God, I can't even imagine him reacting that way."

"Really?" Kristen's voice quavered. "The accident catapulted him into another reality, a reality that he wouldn't want any part of."

"If anyone can adapt to this kind of change, it's Kyle. He's the epitome of an eternal optimist. We have to honor that part of him," Owen said, dredging up his resolve. "We have to support him until the technology develops. There are a lot of universities researching artificial intelligence and brain-computer interfaces. People who are paralyzed are operating artificial limbs. Some researchers are proposing nanotechnology to repair brain circuits."

"Well, if you feel that strongly about it, I'm putting you on the case. Go ahead and dig into the research, and when someone's got it all figured out and they truly know what they're doing, then we can talk." She paused. "But you know what happened with Kimi, right?"

"Of course." He stifled a groan. "That was awful." Her best friend's last months had been excruciating.

Kristen shook her head and focused on her soup. "I've been thinking about Nana and Mom," she said as she stirred her soup thoughtfully.

"How so?"

His younger sister considered him curiously. "You know what she did, right?"

Owen shrugged. "I know Mom took really good care of Nana, right up until the end, so she could die at home."

"Oh, Owen," Kristen said regretfully. "I bet Mom never told you."

"What?" He didn't have patience for guessing games.

"Owen, Nana was suffering terribly. She asked, no, she begged Mom to help her die, to get away from the pain. So Mom squirreled away Nana's medicine, a few pills at a time, and then gave her a fatal dose."

"What? No. Come on, how would you know that? You were what, nine at the time?"

"For God's sake, Owen, don't be so condescending. I was ten, but that's beside the point. The day she passed, Nana told me she was ready to die and not to be surprised if she was gone in the morning."

"Maybe she sensed it was coming and just tried to warn you."

"Damn it, Owen, I asked Mom about it several years later. She swore me to secrecy, but she told me all the details." Kristen gave him a steely look. "Owen, Nana asked Mom to help her die."

Owen sat slack-jawed. "I was in touch with Nana all the time I was away at college. She never said anything to me about wanting to die."

"Dad was the only other person who knew. He was there when she passed."

"Dad was in on it too? Neither of them told me."

"Think about it. At that time, helping someone with a terminal illness to die was still considered murder. Murder. Mom could have gone to jail. Literally. So don't be upset that they kept it a total secret, even from you. They had to."

He hated the direction this conversation was going. Kristen

was implying that Mom's and Nana's actions gave his sister permission to apply the same logic in Kyle's situation.

Kristen's gaze came back into the room. "I learned from Nana to come to terms with death. Death can bring great peace. If you hold on too tightly, life itself can become unbearable."

"But—" Owen sputtered.

"In fact, I would have helped Kimi if she'd wanted it."

"Seriously? You'd have . . . ?"

"At one point I asked her about a death with dignity. There's a process now to do it legally," Kristen said, her voice shaking. "But she couldn't handle the thought of taking her own life. I wish she'd been willing, though. It would have saved her a lot of suffering."

"I can't imagine wanting that for myself," he said.

Kristen's face reddened. "You have no idea what it's like to make this decision. I gave him *life*. I'd give my own life for him if I could. I can't believe I'm considering ending his."

She was moving too fast for him. He felt nauseous. He came around the table, bent over, and put his arm around her. "Don't decide right now. You need to sit with this for a while, work your way through it." He squeezed her shoulders. "I'm here for you, no matter what."

Kristen gradually calmed and managed to eat most of her soup. Owen stayed long enough to do the dishes, then headed home, deeply distressed. Her insights into Nana's and Kimi's wishes intensified his own anxiety. Kristen's goal seemed to be ending Kyle's suffering rather than improving his quality of life through future medical advancements.

He'd support her no matter what—that's what he'd said. Kristen had become his priority when he'd become her guardian.

He'd reaffirmed that commitment when she turned up pregnant. But he'd also pledged to be a surrogate father for Kyle. What if supporting Kristen and defending Kyle led him in opposite directions?

He drove his Prius into the one-car garage, glancing sadly at his surfboard hanging on the wall. He hadn't hit the waves since Kyle's accident and longed to see it dripping with seawater, not cobwebs.

The garage opened into a tiny entry next to a small room he'd converted into his home office. He took the stairs up past the second-floor living area with its large TV, where he, Kyle, and Matt had often watched sports together.

On the top floor, he avoided the spare bedroom Kyle had used when he stayed over. He entered his own bedroom and found his cat, Qwerty, just waking from a nap on the back of the recliner under the window. His feline buddy jumped on the bed, playfully tangling herself in the clothes as Owen undressed and tossed shirt and pants on the comforter. The cat's antics found a small crack in Owen's stupor, and he tussled with her in the mess of his discards.

Qwerty soon abandoned him and headed for her food bowl in the kitchen. Owen opened the bottom dresser drawer and pulled out a box of treasures he'd gathered through the years.

Several years before Kyle's birth, a woman he'd been dating for only a few weeks had surprised him with a pregnancy. Enamored with the idea of having a child, he'd proposed to Carol just so he could be an active father. Then she lost the baby, and he'd been heartbroken. But when she broke up with him soon thereafter, he was secretly glad, realizing he'd been spared a loveless marriage.

He retrieved an envelope at the very front of the box and removed the sonogram of his son. He'd called him Paul, though he and Carol had never discussed names. Owen had kept the photo all these years, having passionately loved that child from the moment he'd learned of his conception.

As he had many times before, he ran his finger softly over Paul's image, as if he could feel the child through the aged paper.

What if Kristen ended Kyle's life support? How could he possibly bear the loss of his nephew, the boy he loved as his own?

He gently replaced the photo and closed the drawer. Once in the shower, he leaned his forehead against the cold tile and let the warm water pound his aching back.

A bit refreshed, his appetite returned; he made himself a ham-and-cheese sandwich, to go along with a cold beer, and took them down to his ground-floor office.

He fired up his computer, determined to see what he could find about research projects for Kyle. Dr. Elder had said something about starting her own research project, so he typed her name into the search engine.

Several links to her name came up, some of them more than two years old. There was her dissertation from the California Institute of Technology in neuroscience as well as several publications she'd coauthored with Dr. Stauss.

The newest entry, posted a couple of weeks earlier, was a press release about the opening of the Carl Elder Foundation offices. He followed a link to the website and found a picture of Dr. Elder next to a statement of the foundation's mission: *To develop noninvasive techniques to assist persons who have lost their ability to verbally communicate due to illness or injury.*

He read the line several times to make sure, then sat back in surprise. The statement sounded exactly like what Kyle needed. The foundation's address was near Portland, south of Lake Oswego. Why had Dr. Stauss failed to mention this to them?

He needed to talk with Kristen.

CHAPTER 10

When Rene woke, her thoughts immediately jumped to the argument with Rob and the voicemail he'd left, saying he'd come by her house this evening. Rene had been in limbo for five long days since they'd fought over the role of religion in their future. Prior to his message, neither had reached out to bridge the sudden gap that had opened between them. Her gut told her the mutual silence did not bode well.

"We need to resolve the issue from Friday night," he'd said in the recording. "I don't want this to drag on any longer than it already has."

Her heart had dropped at his tone; it was in such contrast to his typical warm banter. And though his statement didn't include an ultimatum, it was implicit in his words and the noticeable edge in his voice.

Why had he assumed that she believed in God? Did he think she'd dutifully attend religious services, all the while only pretending to believe and hoping the kids didn't sense the truth? He'd drawn a line in the sand. Would he be willing to retract it?

She got out of bed, stopped in the bathroom, then padded downstairs. Making her morning cup of tea was her form of meditation. She filled the electric kettle with filtered water. While she waited for it to boil, she packed the infuser with her favorite black tea. She always insisted that her beverage be steeped in a glass teapot, which she filled from the kettle. As she lowered the infuser into the roiling water, the dried leaves immediately began to unfurl.

She had a genuine love for Rob. They'd had many happy times together: their trip to Ashland to attend the theater in the quaint Oregon town; their vacation to Montreal had been like a visit to France itself; sumptuous dinners, breathtaking hiking, and kayaking adventures. It had all been such a refreshing balance from her grueling schedule under Dr. Stauss.

But had all the excitement led her to miss the essence of the man? Had she mistaken their shared enjoyment for shared values? Why hadn't they talked about religion sooner?

She watched the second law of thermodynamics force the tannins from the leaves, dispersing the rich burnt-umber color into the clear water.

Her thoughts spun. Would she still consider marriage if he did back off from his demands, or had her trust been too badly damaged to recover? Was it worth explaining why his presumption was so offensive?

The liquid surrounding the strainer gradually became richly darkened, while tendrils of fainter shades tentatively reached out to the limits of the container. The eddies of color were mesmerizing, a counterpoint to the steam swirling from the surface.

Should she try to explain her path to atheism?

She'd been eight years old, standing next to Gramps's bed. She looked into his blue-gray eyes, the eyes she'd inherited from him.

"Pray for me," he said, his weak voice barely a whisper. Rene folded her hands dutifully, bowed her head. And she prayed. She prayed with every ounce of her being. She didn't really know how to pray or what to feel, but she tried hard. She imagined God and prayed for Gramps to get better, to read with her again, to once again speak in sentences that made sense. She prayed until she was prayed out and then tried some more. When she finally looked up, he'd fallen asleep. "I'll figure this out, Gramps. I promise," she said.

The nurse was waiting when she tiptoed out of the room. "How're you doing?" she asked, her kind brown eyes meeting Rene's.

"I prayed like he asked, but I don't think it's going to make any difference."

"It made a difference to him."

"Maybe, but I prayed for him to get better, and he keeps getting worse. Am I doing something wrong?"

The older woman's voice softened. "No, hon, you're not doing anything wrong. We have to trust that God knows what's best."

The nurse's words hit a painful chord of doubt that had been growing in her for some time. If God wasn't going to heal Gramps, then what was God good for? Why bother praying if all you got was the opposite of what you needed?

Her thoughts seemed illegal, and she worried that she might be punished somehow. But nothing bad happened to her.

Gramps died soon thereafter. Her prayers hadn't made a bit of difference. Gramps's faith had failed him, and in so doing, had betrayed her as well.

The light pouring through the glass of her teapot alerted her to that perfect moment of equilibrium when the entire contents had become a rich, glowing red brown. It was time to pour her cup of tea. She took the steaming glass mug to the kitchen table and sat, looking out at her yard.

The first sip was the perfect temperature to warm her through, and she relaxed with satisfaction. She savored the rich flavor that engaged her senses as she searched for answers deep within herself.

Her foundation was built on ethical values and an awe for life in all its fullness, an elegance revealed by the rigors of science. She knew her purpose and had confidence in her truest self, without the need for any god or godlike concept.

It was abundantly clear that she couldn't participate in religious worship that held no meaning for her. She couldn't abide indoctrinating her children in a belief system she found utterly false.

Beyond all that, Rob's requirement that she abide by his religious vision and participate according to his rules was an unforgivable breach of all that she held sacred about a healthy marriage.

She stared out the window, noticing the clouds moving away. There was hope for a sunny afternoon. Rene slowly finished her tea, deeply sad but thoroughly resolved.

CHAPTER 11

Owen finished loading the dishwasher and carried a bowl of pretzels out to the dining room. Yoshi was soon to arrive for their monthly game of chess. This was one of the few evenings Owen had set aside for himself since Kyle's accident. He was sorely in need of a diversion and just preparing for this long-standing tradition with his best friend was giving him comfort.

He pulled out his grandmother's chess set from the cabinet and placed the pieces in their proper places.

The chess set took him back to the many games he'd played with Nana at her kitchen table. Her kitchen had broken all the stereotypes. It wasn't a space where she'd spent endless hours cheerfully cooking for an eager family. It never smelled of roasting turkey or freshly baked chocolate chip cookies. The counter space was meager and sometimes cluttered with groceries or unwashed dishes. She wasn't unclean, she was just busy with other things.

It was at that kitchen table where Nana had taught him to

play chess. "Always hold your head high if you've done your best," she'd say when he was downcast at a loss. She was as delighted as Owen when he finally beat her on his own.

The most important element of the kitchen was Nana's textile art hanging on the wall next to the table. Her true passion was weaving, and she had created large tapestries on an enormous loom in the converted garage.

The kitchen piece centered on striking patterns suggesting a sunrise over dusky gray hills. Owen had spent many hours staring at that tapestry as he waited for Nana to make her chess moves. At times he would get lost trying to trace the colored threads and reconstruct how so many separate strands could be woven into such a powerful image. The complexity of the design made the intricacies of a chess game seem insignificant.

"It's like life," Nana said to him one afternoon when he had asked what the design meant. "Complicated. Confusing. But the way everything is interconnected can create something beautiful."

He'd protested that he'd never be able to make something so lovely.

"Just do your best, Owen," she'd said, repeating her mantra. "Your best will always be enough."

The vintage chess set and the tapestry were the only belongings that he'd wanted from Nana when she died. That tapestry now hung over his own dining room table, which was where he and Kyle played Strat-O-Matic Baseball each winter and where he and Yoshi would play chess on her board that night.

He stared at those threads once again, trying to sort out the news that his grandmother had been ready to die, had enlisted her daughter—his own mother—and that she had, in fact, taken steps to end Nana's life. He shook the memory from his head; he didn't want to deal with his reactions yet.

He'd just finished setting up when Yoshi arrived. Owen ushered his friend to the main level and offered him a beer.

Yoshi accepted the drink and took his seat at the waiting chessboard. "I love this set," he said fondly, smiling at the hand-carved marble and quartz pieces. Yoshi, too, had learned chess from Owen's Nana.

Over the years, Owen, Kristen, Kyle, Yoshi, Matt, and, of course, Kimi had formed their own nontraditional family. Owen's and Yoshi's parents—all deceased—had been neighbors. Owen and Yoshi became best friends in kindergarten, and the families had remained close.

The two men made their first moves, pretzels crunching as they settled into the comfortable rhythm of chess and conversation.

"How are rehearsals going?" Owen asked. Yoshi taught music at the university and played clarinet in the local symphony.

"Pretty slow right now. We're learning some new pieces for the next concert. First rehearsals are always pretty rough." Yoshi moved a pawn and reached for a pretzel. "I have an important solo in one of the pieces, so I've got a lot of work to do on my own."

"A solo? Cool. Be sure to get us tickets, OK?"

"Of course."

Several minutes passed as Owen considered his next move. He'd minored in math and loved strategy and statistics, and he easily remembered patterns that stumped others.

"I haven't talked with Matt lately," Owen said, countering Yoshi's move with his rook. "What's up with his job search?"

Matt had recently completed his master's degree in biology and moved back home to live with his father until he landed a professional position. He was working as a barista in the meantime.

"He's working his contacts, putting out lots of feelers. No serious bites yet." Yoshi studied the board.

"Hmmm."

"Any idea what Kristen's thinking about Kyle?" Yoshi asked.

Owen moved a pawn before answering. "As far as I know, she's still considering the options laid out by Dr. Stauss."

Yoshi crunched on a pretzel as he considered his next move. "Has she asked for your opinion? Seems like she usually checks in with you before making any big decisions."

"No, but she knows where I'm coming from. I guess we'll all find out her decision at Friday's family conference."

Each of the six of them, including Matt, Kyle, and Kimi—before she died—had from time to time called everyone together for a group discussion when faced with an important choice. Over the years, they'd discussed Kristen's decision to take a low-paying job as an attorney for a nonprofit, Matt's choices for college, and Kimi's wishes for a memorial service when she passed. Such was the level of trust among them.

"The stress is taking a heavy toll on her," he continued after Yoshi moved. "She said she isn't sleeping well."

"And you?" His friend inquired with raised eyebrows.

"I'm not sleeping either." Owen met Yoshi's eyes. "I'm worried about her, and when I'm not worried about her, I'm worried about Kyle. And then I throw in some extra worry about not keeping up with my work, just to keep myself worried all the time."

Yoshi smiled ruefully. "Yeah, I've lost plenty of sleep as well.

Last night Matt and I ran into each other in the kitchen at two a.m. We started reminiscing. Do you remember the time you and I took Kyle and Matt to that Mariners' game? Kyle was what, six? During the seventh-inning stretch, he stood up on his seat to sing 'Take Me out to the Ballgame,' and he turned around and made like a conductor so everyone around us would sing too? He was so enthusiastic everyone laughed."

"That's one of my favorite memories."

Yoshi chuckled, then captured Owen's knight.

The room was quiet while Owen considered the board. He settled on capturing one of Yoshi's pawns. He rubbed his fingers over the smooth, cool marble as he removed it from play, thinking that Nana's hands had caressed this same piece. If only she were here to advise him.

"When I visited Kyle today," Yoshi said, "I thought about how Matt and I were up in the middle of the night worrying about him. Then I wondered what was going on in Kyle's mind. If we're so worried, what must it be like for him?"

"That's exactly what I'm desperate to understand," Owen said as he selected a pretzel.

Yoshi looked up from studying the game. "At retreats I attended, the sensei emphasized meditation as a way to understand the workings of the mind. I relied on my practice when Kimi was dying," he said. A sad look passed over his face and then disappeared. "I got to thinking that meditation might help both you and Kyle. You could meditate together, you know, listening to podcasts to guide you, using headphones. There are lots of secular teachers. You don't have to buy into any philosophy or religion."

Qwerty hopped onto one of the dining room chairs and seated herself, staring at the board as if considering strategy.

Yoshi studied the board again, then finally made a move.

Owen took a sip of beer. Yoshi had been through a lot with Kimi, and if meditation had helped, maybe there was something to what he was saying. But Owen had a more urgent question. "How did you come to terms with Kimi's death, Yoshi? Or have you?"

Yoshi's eyes glistened. "There's not a day, not an hour that goes by that I don't miss her terribly." His voice was husky. "But I guess, instead of being sad for what I lost, I try to be grateful for what we had."

"I like that way of looking at it," Owen said. "I'll always be thankful for the time I've had with Kyle. I spent so many evenings with him, playing Strat-O-Matic Baseball, coaching Kyle on how to weigh the percentages. He took the game seriously, memorizing statistics and learning strategy. He was planning to be a coach after he finished his career as a player."

"You sound like he's already gone," Yoshi said. "He is still in there, right?"

"Yeah, yeah, of course 'he's still in there,' as you say, but I can't reach him. We've lost that forever." Owen let out a deep sigh and moved his rook.

Yoshi's eyes were sad. "I wouldn't feel this intense pain if I hadn't loved Kimi so much. So the pain reminds me of our love. In some ways I've even come to cherish the pain."

"'Cherish the pain'? Seriously?" Owen searched his friend's eyes. "I can't imagine that. I still hurt for the baby that Carol and I lost. It's been nearly twenty years, and sometimes it's like it happened yesterday. I don't think I can handle it if Kyle dies."

Yoshi spoke to him kindly. "Meditation lets me step aside from my grief and just observe the sadness coming and going. At first it seemed like nothing could possibly ease the pain, but I've gotten better at it over the years. Meditation helps me find peace of mind when I'm most lonely."

Owen stared at his bottle of beer, grief circulating in his gut.

As silence settled once again, Qwerty slowly stretched a paw toward one of the captured pawns at the side of the board and gently batted at it. The solid piece didn't move. Owen reached over and pulled the cat onto his lap to foil the interference, but the feline immediately jumped down and scampered into the kitchen.

Yoshi took his time, then moved his knight.

Owen tried to discern his opponent's strategy but couldn't concentrate. He could usually figure out the patterns of the game without effort, but this time, his analytic powers failed him.

Yoshi changed the direction of the conversation. "I had an idea while I was visiting Kyle, maybe an unorthodox way of looking at things. You might find it kind of radical—"

"Please. I could use some ideas." Owen looked over at his friend hopefully.

"Maybe even offensive—"

"Just go for it, Yoshi." He took a swig of beer and waited.

"All right, then hear me out. There are these Buddhist teachers, masters—expert meditators if you will. They go on extended retreats, sometimes for months, even years, to calm their minds and get in touch with their inner nature. They get away from everything. They take a vow of silence. They have no agendas, no goals, and no deadlines to meet. They spend all their time contemplating, meditating. All without talking. And they end up with this deep, deep understanding of what it means to be human," Yoshi said thoughtfully. "They exude this amazing, calm presence. They can experience almost anything and not be disturbed."

"Not offended yet," Owen said, taking another sip.

"Well, here it comes. Imagine that Kyle is on a retreat."

Owen sat back, startled.

"He's away from everything," Yoshi continued, "not talking with anyone. No agendas, no goals. He has all the time in the world to meditate, to contemplate. Well, when you look at it that way, maybe having LIS might be an opportunity a person wouldn't have any other way to explore what goes on inside their mind, with no outside distractions."

Yoshi's insight took Owen aback. "An 'opportunity'?" He snorted. "That really is a bizarre way to look at it."

"I know, it must sound kind of, I don't know, weird."

"You think?" Owen stared at him. But this was his best friend talking. He tried to keep an open mind.

"But maybe for Kyle he could be like a Buddhist master who spends the day meditating, taking a vow of silence. There's an entire universe to explore in our own heads, and I think we might only experience it when we're still, totally quiet."

"It's one thing to choose to be still but another thing altogether to be forced into it and not able to get out of it," Owen protested. "I know you're trying to find the silver lining in a black cloud, but come on."

"Look, I know Kyle didn't choose this," Yoshi said, holding Owen's gaze. "But he does have a choice about how he responds."

"Well, that's true enough," Owen said slowly. He'd completely lost track of the game and made a random move that he immediately regretted.

Yoshi pounced, closing in on Owen's king.

Owen had bumbled his last move, and the game had slipped away. "Damn, I can't think straight. I'm just going to concede."

"We'll call it a draw," his best friend responded, marking the score sheet where they kept a running tally of their competitions going back years.

"Look, maybe 'opportunity' isn't quite the right word." Yoshi resumed making his point. "But Kyle is such a resilient kid, he might take this situation as a challenge."

"'A challenge'?" It had never occurred to Owen to look at it in that way. He grabbed onto this thread of hope for dear life. "Kyle did love to be tested," he said, nodding to himself. "What always stood out was his optimism and determination in the face of obstacles."

"Absolutely," Yoshi said. "We've seen that in him since he was a little kid."

"I remember his last game, right before the accident," Owen said. He stared up at the tapestry. "Right down to the last out in the bottom of the ninth, Kyle believed that the Mustangs could pull out a victory."

"Yeah, and when they lost, he never got discouraged," Yoshi added. "He even congratulated the opposing pitcher."

Owen's hope gained some traction. "You know what?" He looked up at Yoshi. "I do trust Kyle's positive spirit. It *defines* him. Maybe he does have the inner strength to survive a situation as desperate as this one." Owen closed Nana's chess set, filled with a new solace and clarity.

"He's a special kid, that's for sure," Yoshi said.

Owen put the chess set in the cabinet, then sat at the table with his friend. "I like your idea of meditating with Kyle. It might be good for both of us," he said. "You know, all along I've been trying to come up with ways to support Kyle, and this just might be it." He smiled at his best friend. "Thanks, Yo. For the first time in weeks, I feel a little bit optimistic."

CHAPTER 12

Rene answered the door, dreading this meeting. She scolded Humboldt, whose exuberance threatened to knock over Rob as he came in bearing flowers.

"I want to apologize for the way things ended the other night," Rob said first thing, then handed her the bouquet.

"Wow. Well, thanks," she said. Her mood lightened a little.

"I had too much wine for a discussion that important," he went on.

"Yeah. Me too. Come on in. I baked some cookies. I'll start some coffee."

"Better let me make it," he said, smiling. The fine points of brewing coffee were his domain; she took the lead when it came to making tea.

She returned his smile, and they walked into her kitchen. "The cookies smell great," Rob said as he moved to the Breville Barista Express, an artisanal coffee machine they'd bought for her counter.

"Just out of the oven." Rene sat at the peninsula just as she had the other night before their entire relationship had gone off the rails. She savored this moment. It was all so familiar, so right.

When the coffee was poured and the cookies selected, he sat across from her on the other side of the peninsula.

"I do want to apologize," he said. "And not just for the other evening. Over these last few days I've had to come to terms with things." He looked down into his coffee.

She reached across the counter and took his hand. "So tell me. We need to get everything out in the open." Where had his quest taken him? He'd brought flowers, apologized. Was it possible he'd back off from his demands after all? And what would she say if he did?

"I so love you," he started, leaning forward intently. "I think you'd be a wonderful mother. But my commitment to raising my kids in a faith tradition and attending church as a family is even stronger today than it was last week."

Her hopes evaporated.

"I haven't been actively religious in years. There was no way for you to know that my faith is so central to me. I wasn't clear within myself, and so of course I wasn't clear with you." His eyes were filled with regret.

"And you're suddenly clear now?" she said, unable to suppress the sarcasm in her voice.

"Yes. I went to church last Sunday. I hadn't gone for a really long time—as you said—but being there reinvigorated my commitment." He held her eyes.

"How did it make you feel, to be there in church?" It was an important question, the key to understanding the depth of his faith. It was the same question she'd asked Gramps years before.

"It confirmed that having an active church life is the right thing to do," he said. "It just makes so much sense to immerse my family in the traditions I grew up with, that my parents and grandparents lived."

"But how did it make you *feel*?"

"I don't understand." His brow furrowed. "I felt sensible, I guess. Like a responsible future parent if that answers your question."

Rob's response lacked that heartfelt spirituality she'd experienced in Gramps. His answer made it clear she was making the right decision.

He raised his eyebrows and offered a questioning gaze. "Is there any chance at all that you might find a way to fit into that picture?"

The lump in her throat constricted her voice. "I've been doing a lot of thinking too," she said quietly, keeping her anger restrained. "And I'm equally clear that participating in an organized religion isn't something I can agree to. It's just not who I am, and I certainly would never pretend about something that important."

"I was afraid you were going to say that." His eyes were sad. "I was truly shocked that you don't believe in God. You never gave any indication that you were an atheist." His voice had an edge. "I'm kinda pissed about that."

"Well, let's talk about being pissed." Rene's hackles rose. "I don't go to church, read the Bible, or pray. My behavior is consistent with that of an atheist. You, on the other hand, rarely go to church, and never read the Bible or pray. That isn't consistent with someone who requires that of their spouse."

"Are you calling me a hypocrite?" His eyes were narrow, voice taut.

"I'm not calling you anything." She glared at him. "But I'm the one who was misled." She stood up and turned to look down at him, spitting out the words, rapid-fire. "How dare you. How dare you spring something so important on me at this point in our relationship."

"I didn't—"

"Don't make excuses." She jabbed her finger toward him. "I was ready to live together. I've never lived with anyone before, but I was ready to commit to you. To have kids. And now, from out of nowhere, you start making demands about going to church?"

"I just assumed—"

"Don't give me that bullshit. Anyone who's paying attention would see that I'm not religious. Do you see me? The *real* me? Or am I just a baby factory to you?"

"No, I never—"

"What other demands do you have hidden away? Huh? Am I supposed to vote the way you do? Dress the way you like? Wear my hair to please you? Do you even have a clue why I can no longer trust you?"

He sat there, silent. His eyes were blazing, lips tightly pursed.

She paced around the room, glaring back at him. Finally, she leaned against the counter on the other side of the kitchen. They stared at each other until Rob finally broke eye contact, sighing.

"Maybe I deserved that," he said, his tone becoming softer, sad. "Look, I respect that you have to abide by your own truth.

I won't try to convince or convert you," he said. "But I'm going to say this one thing because I care about you: someday you'll be forced to reckon with a power that's greater than yours, a power that transcends science, a power that can transform you."

How condescending could this man get? Rene just shook her head and sealed her lips. Any retort she might make was pushed aside by the heartache welling up.

"We got so close," he said, his eyes downcast.

She said nothing. She'd been open and vulnerable to this man, and he'd betrayed her trust. There was no going back. There was no going forward either.

Humboldt came over and nuzzled Rob's hand.

"He'll miss you," she said, through the tight lump in her throat.

Rob ruffled the dog's ears, then met her eyes. "Me too." Then he stood and they walked slowly to the door, Humboldt by Rene's side. "I'll be in touch about a time to pick up my things," he said softly.

He reached out for a hug. She leaned forward, keeping her body stiff. Then he turned and left for the last time.

Humboldt sat quietly as she knelt and buried her face in his fur.

CHAPTER 13

Owen arrived early to help Yoshi and Matt with dinner preparations for the family meeting Kristen had called.

The Imai and Nichols clans had several meeting traditions, including a very specific menu. Years ago, when Yoshi and Kimi called the first such gathering to announce their pregnancy with Matt, Mrs. Imai, Yoshi's mother, had been too frail to cook for everyone. So she'd coached her son, Yoshi, on her family recipe for sukiyaki, a one-pot dish Westerners like the Nicholses tended to appreciate. They received rave reviews for their collaboration.

For dessert that evening, Kimi had insisted on chocolate cake with fudge frosting in addition to the more traditional pan-fried mochi, a rice cake stuffed with sweetened bean paste. The elder Mrs. Imai had disapproved of the culinary merger, but Kimi had only laughed, delighted by the rich combination.

As he carried dishes out to the dining room, sadness tightened Owen's chest. He was setting places for just four: himself, Kristen, Yoshi, and Matt. The last family conference had included Kyle and Kimi. It had been the occasion of Kimi's devastating revelation that she'd ended clinical trials and was going into hospice. She'd died less than two weeks later.

Owen moved slowly past the two chairs that would remain empty. He'd always assumed the next family conference would be a joyous occasion where Kyle would announce that he'd signed with a minor league team, or that he'd accepted an athletic scholarship to play at a university. Instead, Kristen would share her decision about Kyle's fate: long-term care or end-of-life support.

He gently placed each piece of silverware on the tablecloth, filled with reverence for the momentous family transitions marked by these dinners.

Kristen arrived soon after, dressed in a tailored gray pantsuit she often wore for courtroom appearances. Owen greeted her with a big hug, troubled to see her drawn, tired expression.

"It was a rough session in court today. The stress about Kyle heaped on top of work at the law firm is taking a major toll on me," she said grimly. "Hey, Yo, that sukiyaki smells fabulous," she called out toward the kitchen. She waved to Matt, who was bringing food out to the table. "I'm starving."

"Good timing, everything's ready to eat," Yoshi answered, scurrying around to serve the hot meal. "Go ahead and sit down."

"Ah, I'm starting to feel human again." Kristen kicked off her shoes and took a sip of warm sake.

"There's chocolate cake for dessert, with coffee. And mochi, of course." Yoshi smiled at Kristen as he served the meal.

"You're the best, Yo." She returned her old friend's smile. "I can still see your mom wincing at the sight of us eating chocolate cake after sukiyaki."

"Kimi always said it was one benefit of cultural assimilation," he acknowledged with a smile.

Owen sampled the steaming broth, cooling the impact with a bite of steamed rice. The mild flavors and cooked vegetables soothed him. He craved the buzz of the sake but stuck with his sparkling water.

As was tradition, they held off the discussion about Kyle until after dinner; still, everyone understood the stakes were high, and their usually spirited conversations were muted.

As they ate, Yoshi shared the latest on the upcoming performance by the orchestra. He'd been tapped to play the dramatic opening clarinet solo in "Rhapsody in Blue," and he briefly updated them about the rehearsals.

Matt, the newbie barista, tried to provide some light relief, sharing silly anecdotes about the characters that frequented the coffeehouse where he worked.

Owen smiled, but his laugh was forced. He left most of Yoshi's meal untouched.

After dinner, they settled in the living room. "As Kyle would say, it's time for the chocolate cake," Kristen said as Yoshi emerged from the kitchen with a tray of small plates.

"And mochi," Matt added. Only Yoshi and Matt enjoyed the mochi; neither Kristen nor Owen had ever developed a taste for it. A silence descended on them as they waited for Kristen to call the meeting to order.

Owen hoped he'd agree with his sister's decision. He was walking a thin line—he desperately wanted Kyle to move into long-term care. The alternative, death, was unthinkable. But supporting Kristen was his priority: she and Kyle were his only living relatives. He vowed he wouldn't let this rip them apart.

"I've realized there's no perfect answer." Kristen finally started as she faced the three men. Matt sat with his elbows on his knees, looking down. Yoshi's face was knotted with tension. Owen forced himself to remain still and maintain eye contact with Kristen. He had to stand by her no matter what.

"I can argue both sides," she said. "Sometimes I'm convinced that the most loving thing would be to let Kyle go, but then I think he's still fighting and wants to keep trying. I have no way of knowing." She stopped, gave a heavy sigh, then repeated herself. "I have absolutely no way of knowing."

Owen put his arm around her and pulled her close.

Yoshi came around to sit on her other side and took her hand.

Matt fetched her a box of tissues and Kristen dabbed at her eyes. "Thanks, guys. I so wish Kimi were here. This is the hardest decision I've ever had to make."

Kristen eventually picked up her thoughts, sounding calmer. "I did get a chance to tour Rockridge Place this afternoon, and it's lovely." She gave Owen a small smile. "The staff is experienced, and I was thoroughly impressed by Dr. Guramurthy, the medical director. The possibility of Kyle living there gave me a lot of comfort."

Owen let go a small sigh.

"Right after I left Rockridge, I went to spend some time with Kyle. I thought being with him would give me some guidance." The three men were completely focused on her.

"While I sat there, I noticed the smell, not for the first time.

I guess it's from the disinfectants, the sheets and gowns, the medications, the bodily fluids, I don't know, maybe the isolation. It's more of a stink. It's an awful odor that follows me home and lingers on my skin." She crinkled her nose, gave herself a little shake.

"You know, as soon as I get home from the hospital every day," she continued, "I immediately take a shower, open all my windows, wash my clothes. I didn't think much about it until today, but I do all that just to get the odor out of my mind, to keep my house from getting infected with that stink."

Owen nodded, though he didn't really understand where this was going. He'd expected her to present them with rational arguments for her decision, pros and cons, like the attorney she was at work.

"It's weird, I know I have this huge decision to make, but that's all I could think about today. The stink."

She looked off through the window over Yoshi's shoulder, into the darkening evening. Owen's foot began to jiggle, and he forced it to stop. Would Kristen ever get to the point?

"It suddenly occurred to me that Kyle has lost so much," she said, "but not his sense of smell. It smells clean at Rockridge. His room would have big windows, looking out on a lovely courtyard. There are flowering bushes under all the windows, filled with birds and insects." She looked calm, her voice quiet.

"I can't make him well, but there are some things I can do for him. I can get him out of the stink. I can bring him freshly washed pajamas. I can bring in fragrant flowers. Most importantly, I can open the windows and give him fresh air." She made eye contact with each of them, stopping with Owen. Eyes locked with her brother's, she said, "Kyle's going to Rockridge."

Owen squeezed his sister's shoulders again, drawing her close. "Thank goodness," he said.

"I won't be able to do this alone," she said. "I'm going to need all of you."

"I'll be by your side every step of the way," Owen said. "I'll manage the estate so you can afford the best care for Kyle. And I'll work to find ways to improve his quality of life."

She held his eyes as if evaluating the testimony of a witness on the stand.

Matt came over and knelt in front of Kristen. "He's my best friend. I'll come and listen to games with him all the time. And I'll help Owen with his research."

Her eyes teared at the young man's offer. "Kyle couldn't have a better friend, Matt. You've been there for him all along."

Yoshi's voice was husky as he addressed her. "You were there for Kimi. Through all her pain. I'll never be able to repay you for all you did for her." Yoshi's eyes filled and she took his hand. "But that aside, I am Kyle's godfather. I'll be there for whatever you need."

"Thank you, all of you. This is the best decision I can make at this moment." She was clear-eyed, resolved.

Owen gave her a hug, releasing tension that had been building inside him for weeks. At least Kyle had a chance. He silently vowed he would make sure Kristen never, ever regretted this decision.

"I'm exhausted," Kristen said, rising from the couch. "I'm calling it a night. Yoshi, thanks for hosting."

"Of course," he answered. "But wait just a second, I'll box up some of that cake for you to take home."

Kristen smiled. "Perfect. Chocolate is definitely my drug of choice right now."

Owen saw his chance. "Hey, Kristen, do you remember that Dr. Elder who stopped by Kyle's room to say goodbye to him, about a week ago?"

"Uh, yeah. Why?"

"It turns out she's doing research that might be relevant to Kyle. I want to follow up with her, but I want to make sure you're OK with it first."

"Give it a rest, would you, Owen?" She sighed. "Frankly, I don't have time to fool around with untested techniques."

"I get it, Kristen. But what if I just checked it out a bit further? You don't have to do anything. What could it hurt?"

"All right, all right. I don't have enough energy to argue with you. If you want to go down a rabbit hole with Dr. Elder, that's fine with me."

Yoshi came back into the room and handed Kristen a plastic container.

"Thanks, Yo," Kristen said. "Owen, if you go see this Dr. Elder, why don't you take Yoshi and Matt along? They can relate to my concerns about experimental treatments. But don't get me involved until—or should I say 'if'—her techniques are proven to work and are safe to try with Kyle. Understood?"

"Got it," he said. "Proven and safe. Absolutely."

It was after ten when Owen finally pulled into his garage. The family meeting had been hopeful and left him energized. Not only had Kristen settled on Rockridge Place for Kyle, but she'd given him the green light to contact Dr. Elder.

Owen went into his home office and sat at the computer without even taking off his coat. Bringing up the website for the Carl Elder Foundation, he found the contact information and began crafting an email reminding Dr. Elder of her visit to Kyle's room. He outlined the way the foundation's mission statement resonated with his nephew's need to communicate.

He ended with a request to drop by her offices and talk further. After giving a definitive push of the Send button, he forwarded a copy to Kristen and asked her to confirm that she'd OK'd Owen, Yoshi, and Matt to meet with Dr. Elder about Kyle's situation.

Satisfied that he'd done all he could, he bounded upstairs, hoping for a rowdy game of "fishing pole" with Qwerty.

CHAPTER 14

Rene padded downstairs in her bathrobe and slippers to let Humboldt out the back door for his morning business before putting water in the electric kettle and then going to the front door to get the newspaper. Her thoughts were already consumed with designs for the next Witness experiments.

It was unusual to find the paper on her doormat; usually it was just thrown in the general direction of her driveway. Oddly, there was an envelope tucked under the paper: *Rene* was all it said on the front, but she instantly recognized Rob's handwriting.

She shuffled back into the kitchen and sat at the table, glancing at the vacant spot on the counter where the espresso machine had lived until Rob retrieved it, along with all his other belongings, while she was at work Friday.

She remembered the debate they'd had at the kitchen supply store, analyzing the pros and cons of different high-end machines as if the decision was a matter of supreme importance.

She was more than willing to let him have the stupid machine. She wasn't interested in arguing with him over *stuff*.

She considered the envelope in her hand. He'd brought her newspaper up to the door and left a note in the dark of the early morning; it was a coward's way out, a way to avoid talking with her face to face. She pulled out a single sheet with a few lines written in his nearly illegible handwriting.

> *Rene—I've gotten the last of my things. I need*
> *to make a clean break, so I'm moving back*
> *home to Cincinnati. I've realized that if I want*
> *my family to have an active church life, then*
> *I should get involved in a congregation first.*
> *I hope to meet my future partner there. I've*
> *reconnected with some old church friends as*
> *a start. Maybe someday I'll contact you, but*
> *for now, like I said, I need to make a clean*
> *break.—Rob*

Rene let the note fall to the table with a snort and got up to fix her breakfast. At least the man was following through on his abruptly rediscovered religious path.

She scrambled a couple of eggs, toasted some bread, and slathered the slices with homemade pomegranate jelly, a gift from Lorena.

She'd met Rob a few years after she'd snagged the coveted position under renowned neurosurgeon Dr. Stauss. For these last two years, she'd woven her profession and love life into a lovely tapestry with these two men as the weft and warp. Her head and heart, mind and body, had all been stimulated and fulfilled.

But ultimately, the design proved flawed, and the fabric disintegrated. Stauss revealed himself to be an unethical tyrant, Rob a different kind of autocrat.

Rob's decision to move across the country was unexpected, but it really didn't matter. She hadn't considered trying to forge a friendship out of the remains of their romance; the memory of his surprise demands and their different value systems would always be a barrier.

She tore up Rob's note and tossed the pieces into the recycling bin. *Good riddance.*

She devoured her eggs and toast, savoring the sweet tartness of the pomegranate jelly as she stared out the window at her prized roses.

She was ready, even eager, to start over and create her own existence independent of her mentor and her lover. Her future love life was yet to be revealed, but she had her specially designed lab to enjoy. She couldn't wait to get back to the foundation offices and tackle the myriad questions posed by her Witness discoveries.

But first, the mysterious meeting with Dr. Ainsworth was just a few hours away. Her thoughts buzzed with questions about the potential opportunities mentioned in his invitation.

The hospital's underground parking lot was both familiar and strange as Rene drove in for her meeting with Dr. Ainsworth. Familiar because she'd parked there hundreds of times before, at all hours of the day and night. Strange because she had to drive past the section designated "Doctors Only" and park with all the other visitors and patients.

Heading into the separate building that housed CRINR's headquarters, she waited with a half-dozen others to take the elevator; without her white coat, no one took the slightest notice of her.

This reminder of her change in status triggered her simmering anger at Dr. Stauss for blocking her request for hospital privileges last Tuesday. She still fumed over his ridicule. Hopefully, she wouldn't run into him while on campus.

CRINR was a spin-off of the hospital, existing as a separate legal entity but retaining formal organizational links with the hospital. As director, Dr. Ainsworth was the official liaison between the two organizations, reporting directly to Dr. MacKenzie, the hospital CEO, and meriting one of the corner offices in CRINR's administrative floor.

Arriving at the top floor, she turned toward Dr. Ainsworth's suite. The receptionist nodded in the direction of the director's open door, where she could see Ainsworth and Stauss were seated at the conference table, chatting amicably.

Stauss—could she not be rid of that man? Rene forced herself to smile and keep moving forward; apparently Stauss was going to be included in this meeting whether she liked it or not.

Dr. Ainsworth adopted a formal demeanor when she approached. "Dr. Elder. Welcome. Have a seat." He motioned toward a chair across the table from her former supervisor.

"Thanks for inviting me," she said to Ainsworth, shaking his extended hand.

"You know Dr. Stauss, of course."

"Doctor," she said, trying to sound as if encountering Stauss was the most natural thing in the world.

Stauss offered only the smallest of nods in her general direction.

She hadn't been in Ainsworth's conference room before. The room was tastefully appointed in a light Danish-modern look, quite the contrast to Stauss's heavy dark furniture. Apparently, the top administrators had a lot of discretion and money to devote to their preferred decor.

Rene composed her face and turned her eyes on Ainsworth.

Although Dr. Stauss was more senior by any measure—age, reputation or influence—Director Ainsworth carried himself with the assurance of someone clearly in charge of this meeting. As Ainsworth seated himself, Rene steeled herself for interacting with these two alpha males in their white coats.

"Thank you both for joining me today," Dr. Ainsworth began.

Rene offered a small smile in Ainsworth's direction, hoping to convey a sense of self-assurance despite the fact she had no idea what was coming.

"I'll get right to the point. The board of directors of CRINR has recently expanded its mission," Ainsworth said. "They're taking CRINR into the big time, moving out of the ranks of the small-time institutions, and establishing us as an international leader in neurological research." Ainsworth paused, looking pleased with himself as he glanced back and forth at them with a grin. "I assume you have both heard of the Kavli Prize?"

Rene nodded. "Of course." The international Kavli Prize garnered the winning researcher a million dollars and conferred considerable honor upon their sponsoring organization. Several Kavli Prize laureates had gone on to win the Nobel Prize. Her pulse quickened.

"The institute's going to submit a nomination for the prize?" Stauss asked. "It's about time."

Ainsworth flashed a smile. "I thought you might be pleased," he said, sitting back. "The two of you are the most accomplished and innovative researchers in the neuroscience department," he continued, "so you are both up for consideration to be the institute's nominee. But the board was divided about which of you to select, resulting in a stalemate."

Rene shot a quick glance at Stauss, who was staring grimly at the director. She wasn't sure what to make of Ainsworth's mention of a stalemate but took some comfort from the fact that Stauss didn't look at all happy about it.

"The board's comments covered a wide range of perspectives." Ainsworth's tone became more serious as he turned to the man across the table from her. "Your work, Dr. Stauss, is based on your contention that inserting electrodes directly into the brain remains the best if not the only way to develop communication tools for patients with brain dysfunctions. Several board members were concerned that your approach is obsolete, perhaps even dangerously so." He gave Stauss a long look.

Stauss registered his opinion. "Humph."

"That is in contrast to your approach, Dr. Elder." Rene leaned forward as he addressed her. "Some found your use of noninvasive modalities to be revolutionary; other board members found it too controversial to qualify for the nomination for such a prestigious award."

Stauss smirked at her from across the table. No doubt he enjoyed hearing someone else challenge her assumptions. She smiled to herself, thinking of the potential significance of her recent findings.

"Ultimately, the board decided it was important to send a message by nurturing an up-and-coming talent and avoiding the perception that any one researcher automatically had a lock on the nomination."

Ah. So her involvement was more about the perception of her than her actual contribution. And even if she were the institute's nominee, she knew it would be unlikely for the prestigious award to go to a newbie researcher like herself. She started to sour on this supposed opportunity.

"In order to break the stalemate," Ainsworth went on, "the board is offering each of you the opportunity to submit a detailed case study of a single patient who shows significant improvement in their ability to communicate as a direct result of your techniques. The deadline is eight months from now. The board will review your case studies and select one of your projects as our nominee for the Kavli Prize."

"What?" Stauss said. "Come on, Ainsworth, surely the board isn't putting my research on the same level with Elder's?" Stauss's face was bright red. "I've been working on this project for years, with regular support from the CRINR." He brought his fist down on the table with a thump.

Rene clamped her jaw shut and kept her face neutral.

"It's that damn investigation into the Marcella Lopez situation, isn't it?" Stauss continued, leaning across the table toward Rene. "This is your fault, Elder," he said, pointing his finger at her. "Your allegations are sabotaging my research."

"I don't have any influence with the board, Doctor," Rene shot back, her voice steely. "You're their longtime favorite. Don't blame this on me."

"Enough," Ainsworth commanded, holding his hand out to

stop any further bickering. He glared at them in turn and held his silence until Stauss settled back in his chair. "To be clear: CRINR is legally affiliated with the hospital, but functions as a separate organization. Hospital personnel matters are confidential. Therefore, the CRINR board members know nothing of the suspension that the data safety monitoring board has currently imposed on your research, Dr. Stauss. The DSMB confirmed to me that the suspension will remain in place until the risk manager's investigation is complete."

"Then there's an issue I need you to resolve," Stauss interjected as a hint of urgency crept into his voice. "I have a full schedule of patients with whom I consult. People travel from all over the country seeking my advice. I've intended all along to recruit some of them for my research. With the Kavli nomination on the line, I need to schedule them soon, so I can identify the patient best suited for my case study."

The director didn't hesitate. "Absolutely not," he said in a cold, rigid tone. "For the moment, the DSMB has suspended all aspects of your research. You aren't to even hint about your work to any patients or families. You may not so much as whisper that you may have a treatment waiting in the wings until and unless the hold on your research is lifted."

"Are you kidding? Any delay in my research gives Elder a huge head start, Charles. We're in head-to-head competition for the Kavli nomination, after all. This favoritism toward her isn't right."

"Look at it this way, Dr. Stauss: as you yourself just said, CRINR has been supporting your research for years. You have dozens of completed experiments. Are you telling me you don't already have a single patient who can serve as your case study?"

"Well, I do, of course, but—"

Ainsworth cut him off. "Dr. Elder is just now getting her project underway for the first time, so you already have a clear advantage."

The muscles in Stauss's jaw tightened but he remained silent. Rene silently cheered Ainsworth's rebuttal. Maybe Stauss's long political reach into the hospital and the Columbia River Institute for Neurological Research might not protect him after all.

Ainsworth paused. "Am I understood?"

Dr. Stauss shook his head. "But—"

"No 'buts,' Doctor. I have the full backing of the hospital's lawyers. Understood?"

The two male doctors locked eyes for a long moment. Stauss dropped his eyes first, then responded in a low undertone, "Understood."

Rene kept her face expressionless to hide her satisfaction at watching her former boss get brought down a notch.

"Dr. Elder, your research has the Institutional Review Board's approval to work with human subjects, and so you have a green light to recruit for your case study or use past patients."

Rene nodded her acknowledgment.

"Any other questions?" Ainsworth looked from Rene to Stauss and back.

"Yes, actually," Rene said. If Stauss could be bold, so could she. "If CRINR really wants this competition to appear fair, then the hospital should issue me a license for the MDAP software. I'm in discussions to design my own program, but it won't be ready in time for me to analyze the data I'll generate for the case study."

"You still have access to MDAP, Dr. Elder," Ainsworth said,

"even though you're no longer employed by the hospital. It's one of the perks of having privileges here."

"Actually, I'm not eligible for any of those perks." Rene turned a glare on Stauss and allowed a tinge of her bitterness to seep into her voice. "My former medical director rejected my application for those privileges just the other day."

"Bill?" Ainsworth said, looking over at Stauss. "What the hell?"

"I didn't think she'd ever need them," the defiant physician said as Ainsworth stared him down.

"You need to fix this, Bill." The director's voice was grim.

It looked like Stauss was about to snap back at Ainsworth, but instead he clenched his jaw shut.

"Bill? Authorize Elder's privileges as a community physician as soon as this meeting is over. And expedite the paperwork." Ainsworth pushed. "Got it?"

Stauss broke eye contact with the director. "Yes."

"To avoid any delay in your research, Dr. Elder, I'll direct Mai Cheng from the institute's IT department to install the software at your facility as soon as possible."

"I very much appreciate it," Rene said, doubly pleased at having secured the software and beaten Stauss at his own game.

Dr. Ainsworth rose and the others followed suit. "That's it for now. I'll keep both of you posted on future meetings."

Stauss pushed back his chair and strode out of the room, while Rene offered her hand to Dr. Ainsworth. "I'm very excited by this opportunity," she said. "The board won't be disappointed."

"Don't assume that because Dr. Stauss's research is temporarily on hold that CRINR will automatically decide to nominate your project," the director said in the same stern voice he'd used with Stauss. "Your work will have to stand on its own merits."

"Of course. I wouldn't have it any other way," Rene said. "Thanks again, Doctor."

Out in the hallway, Stauss was waiting for her. "Don't spend a lot of energy on this, Rene. I've got the nomination in the bag."

"Bring it on, Bill," she responded as the elevator arrived. It was the first time she'd ever called him by his first name. She liked treating him as a peer for once.

As the elevator doors closed her in, Rene had to admit that Stauss did have the edge. He'd been honing his techniques for several years and brought a considerable reputation to the table. If the Kavli nominations were due today, his existing body of work would already make a highly credible entry into the international competition. In contrast, her nascent theories were based on only the slimmest of very early data.

It was clear that she was the underdog. In fact, Ainsworth had basically said that she was only being considered to give the impression of an open process.

What went unsaid was that the board had to be very careful: the investigation of Stauss's judgment in Marcella's case could well seep into the rumor mill. CRINR had to conduct a neutral selection process that would stand up to scrutiny by the Kavli judges.

Still, the odds of being nominated were clearly against her. She briefly fantasized about going back to Ainsworth's office and withdrawing from the competition. She'd love to confront him, call out the sham process and be done with Stauss forever.

But then again, the odds against her having stumbled on a

technique that allowed people to share their thoughts were even higher than her chances against Stauss. Besides, just the access to MDAP software made it worthwhile to stay in contention.

She'd have to complete a colossal amount of work to meet the institute's lofty standards and beat out the favorite for the nomination. It was time to get to work.

CHAPTER 15

Rene laughed at herself while she waited for Aisha to prepare the two volunteers. Earlier that morning, standing at the kitchen counter in her pajamas, she'd faced Humboldt, who listened respectfully.

"I'd like to thank the Kavli Foundation for this great honor," she'd practiced. Humboldt cocked his head. "I gratefully accept this award in the memory of my grandfather, Carl Elder, my inspiration."

"Yes, thank you, thank you," she'd intoned to the applauding audience, aka the hungry pooch. Then she'd held out the treat Humboldt had been waiting for. As he licked his lips and looked at her expectantly, she'd laughed aloud before sitting down with her oatmeal.

Now seated in the foundation's data center, she took herself to task. The fantasy ego trip she'd taken earlier was a warning not to let CRINR's interest in her work go to her head. It would be all too easy to let the potential nomination take over her true motivations to help injured patients communicate.

She returned to the plans for the day. Mai Cheng and a couple of techies from CRINR had arrived promptly at seven. They'd uploaded the MDAP program onto the foundation's server and configured the computers to display the results. Then they trained Rene and Aisha so they could get the most out of the custom application.

Now it was time to begin the first experiment to be analyzed by the institute's MDAP software. This was where the real work began. Although she'd abruptly terminated her test with Aisha, she'd gotten a strong sense of the potential of the Witness. The news that she was being considered for the Kavli nomination meant that every experiment would be subject to intense scrutiny: she needed to conduct her trials carefully, both to advance her understanding of the phenomenon and to stand up to critics.

In her previous experiments, the staff had managed the TCUs from the respective test rooms. However, Rene had planned her facility so that she could also control them from the data center. She turned on three of the big screens hanging over the data center desk, two to observe the subjects, and a third to display the data. The screen to her left showed Aisha prepping Claire, the first participant.

"Once we get going," the assistant explained to the subject, "you'll see a series of common objects projected in these VR glasses. For example, you might see a bicycle or a fire engine. You'll see a different picture every ten seconds. The ultrasound device you're wearing will chart your brain activity as you observe different types of objects. All you need to do is to concentrate on each picture."

Rene silently applauded Aisha's clear and concise explanation.

"That's it?"

"Yep," the assistant said. "Just focus your attention on the object, so the readings are as clear as possible, OK? I'll let you know when we're ready to begin."

Rene smiled. The participant had readily accepted their explanation for the experiment. Aisha hadn't told Claire that there was a second subject already set up in room 2. On the second big screen, Rene turned on the video feed of Frank, who sat quietly, waiting for them to start.

Rene was pleased with her simple plan: as Claire concentrated on a single item, Frank would be shown an array of ten objects, one of which was identical to the one seen by Claire. He'd been told to select whichever one of the ten objects most stood out to him. Like Claire, Aisha had led him to believe that they were studying his brain activity as he made his selection.

In truth, they'd dubbed Claire "the sender" and Frank "the receiver." They were testing the hypothesis that if one subject, Claire, focused her attention on the object, that image would be shared with the second subject, Frank, which would in turn influence his selection. The odds of Frank choosing Claire's object by chance was one in ten; they were hoping for a significantly higher agreement rate.

Aisha joined Rene at the console. "Let's do this," Rene said, exchanging a fist bump with her assistant.

Aisha grinned and flipped the audio switch. "Ready to go, Frank?" she asked. The man in room 2 gave a thumbs-up. She switched to room 1. "Claire, we're about to start. Are you ready?"

"All set," the woman replied.

Rene signaled to Aisha to close the mike. "Let's begin. I've set this third monitor to let us view the results in real time. Here on the split screen, we'll observe each set of images. The left side of the screen will display the object that the sender is seeing. On the right we'll see the ten options shown to the receiver, highlighting the one he chooses."

Everything else in the room faded from Rene's attention as she focused on the third screen. Could this work? It seemed like something out of a science-fiction movie.

The software had been programmed to randomly select the sender's object from a large database of common items, as well as nine distractors that the receiver would view. The tenth object would match that of the sender, though its location on the receiver's screen was also random.

The first set of images popped up on the monitor. On the left was a single tennis ball. The right side showed ten objects; the tennis ball was third from the left.

Rene held her breath. A few seconds passed and nine of the ten objects disappeared, leaving only a photo of a pair of pliers. She exhaled slowly. Frank hadn't picked the correct image.

The second set appeared. A pair of glasses replaced the tennis ball. The receiver picked a blender. Rene winced. Wrong again.

Then:

- car—tricycle
- beach ball—teacup
- rose—daisy

Three more wrong answers in a row. Finally:

- cat—cat

"A match!" Aisha said. But that was followed by another fourteen misses.

Rene had come prepared to test three frequencies. "I'm going to try the second alignment to see if that makes a difference," she said after studying her notes.

Aisha nodded and let the volunteers know it was time to start again.

The second alignment also produced unremarkable results. Aisha fidgeted in her chair.

"Don't be discouraged," Rene said. "We learn as much from a failed trial as from a successful one." Rene adjusted the settings once again.

Then:

- pencil—pencil
- spool of thread—spool of thread

Two correct answers in a row. Aisha let out a hoot. Maybe they were on a roll. Then:

- purse—ring
- umbrella—gloves
- briefcase—briefcase

Three out of the five was well above chance, enough to give

Rene a surge of hope that this might actually work. Of the next fifteen tests, the subjects matched six times.

"Twelve out of twenty!" Aisha said. "That's sixty percent!"

Rene allowed herself a small smile. "This alignment looks promising, so we'll move on to phase two. For a control test, we'll do ten sets where we turn off the TCU connection and transmit no ultrasound. The volunteers won't feel any difference. After those ten, we'll switch back to using the TCU and continue alternating until we've done two hundred sets—one hundred using the TCU and one hundred without."

Frank selected no correct objects during the control set, and Rene moved on to another round with the TCU on. This time he selected five correctly. Rene sat back, sharing a quick smile with Aisha, who bounced in her seat.

Rene became more confident with each subsequent round. Though she lost count of successful selections, it seemed clear that the results were greater than chance.

When the tests were over, Aisha left to disentangle the volunteers from the electronics and thank them for their time. Meanwhile, Rene tried to hold her excitement in check as she directed the MDAP software to tally the results, and test whether there was a significant difference between the control and TCU sets.

Aisha returned and Rene projected the results onto one of the overhead screens. "How did they react?" she asked Aisha. "Did they report anything unusual or concerning?"

"Frank didn't say anything. Claire mentioned that sometimes she found it hard to concentrate on what she called the 'highlighted' object, because she also saw faint images of other items being projected."

"Ah, that makes sense," Rene said. "She was probably perceiving the images that Frank was being shown. The Witness is a two-way street, so I'm not surprised. Did either of them seem upset or distressed by the experiment?"

"Not at all. In fact, they both said they were kind of bored by it."

"Perfect. Well, let's look at the data." She prepared herself, muscles tense. "OK, after one hundred control sets—the receiver got twelve correct. Statistically, we'd have expected a match of ten out of one hundred, so that's about right."

Rene and Aisha exchanged quick nods. So far, so good.

"And now, drumroll, please—here are the results when using the TCU. Out of one hundred sets, the receiver got—seventy-eight correct!"

Rene's heart was slamming. She'd just witnessed something amazing.

"Whoa! That's just—I can't believe what I just saw." Aisha stood up and did a little jig as she clapped hands with Rene, who was grinning broadly. "This was a clean research design, Dr. Elder, and one that can be easily replicated. I can't think of any flaws that might challenge the results," her assistant said. "This is just—astounding!"

Rene smiled with satisfaction. These results were just the sort of objective, statistical data that would appeal to the institute's board as they chose their nominee. Rene just needed to find a patient for the case study. She had already identified several patients from her previous caseload who might be interested in participating. In addition, Owen Nichols was scheduled for a visit the next afternoon . . . perhaps his nephew might be a candidate for her case study.

A complex array of emotions played out across her face—triumph, relief, excitement. But her words were modest and quietly spoken. "I think we're on to something really important here, Aisha."

CHAPTER 16

It was pouring rain at just before three Wednesday afternoon when Owen stopped at Yoshi's to pick up him and Matt.

"Did you guys sign your NDAs?" he asked as they got into the car.

He'd emailed Rene Friday evening after the family meeting. She'd returned the message the next morning with an invitation to tour her facility as long as he, Yoshi, and Matt signed nondisclosure agreements. She'd emailed him the blank form, and he'd forwarded it to the other two.

"Yep."

"Got it."

"So Kristen didn't want to come along?" Yoshi asked as Owen pulled away, heading toward the complex where Dr. Elder's offices were located.

"No. She's concentrating on getting Kyle moved to Rockridge Place."

"What do you know about Dr. Elder's work?" Matt asked from the back seat.

"She's coauthored a couple of papers with Dr. Stauss. Her current focus is to develop noninvasive methods to help people with brain injuries communicate."

"Sounds perfect."

"We'll see. I googled the Carl Elder Foundation," Owen reported as he drove. "It's a new organization, independently funded by a family trust. Their website is quite professional. The members of the board of directors all seem to have solid credentials."

Matt nodded. "She's lucky to be able to set her own goals," he said. "Big Medicine provides almost all the funding for medical research, and they control the topics that get attention."

"Yeah, you can't do that kind of research out of someone's garage," Owen said as they pulled into the parking lot.

The drenching rain continued as they bolted toward the entrance that was tucked in next to an accounting firm. Modest lettering on a white door identified it as the Carl Elder Foundation. Owen found the door locked and rang the doorbell.

After a long minute, Dr. Elder opened the door and welcomed the men into the waiting room.

Relieved to be out of the downpour, Owen wiped his feet on the entry mat, shaking droplets off his jacket and pulling the hood back from his face. The room was starkly furnished with a few side chairs, a small coffee table, and a lamp. The comparison with Stauss's luxurious and self-promoting office was immediately obvious. Owen relaxed, pleased by the lack of pretension.

"Thank you so much for agreeing to see us," Owen said.

"You were in on Kyle's case, so when I read your foundation's mission statement, I just had to follow up."

"Of course. My office is at the end of the hall." Dr. Elder led the men down the corridor. Owen was eager to look around and tried to take in as many details as he could as they walked past an open door marked "Room 1."

"Let's talk first and then we can take a tour," she said. "But let me take a second to introduce my assistant, Aisha Jackson." Dr. Elder stopped at the door of a small office where Aisha was staring intently at a computer screen.

Owen stepped forward into the cramped room and shook hands with Aisha. Yoshi and Matt nodded to her from the hallway. Owen eyed the stacks of paper and the dozens of yellow sticky notes tacked around her computer screen and workspace.

"Would you get ready to run the next experiment while I meet with our guests? The subjects are scheduled to arrive in a half hour," Dr. Elder said to Aisha, who nodded.

Owen turned to move back into the hallway so Dr. Elder and Aisha could finish their conversation. His eye caught a single sticky note stuck to the doorframe next to his shoulder: *Alarm—314159*. Owen stared at it for a few seconds, then smiled to himself. He recognized the numbers as the first digits of pi.

"I'll work on the manual until they get here," Aisha said to Dr. Elder. The assistant motioned toward the thick green binder on her desk labeled "Witness Project Procedures."

"We're preparing the protocols for our next series of experiments," Dr. Elder said to the men. "Aisha is compiling all the step-by-step procedures."

Owen waved goodbye to Aisha as Dr. Elder led them to her

office, where they draped their wet rain gear over the backs of their chairs to dry. Soon they were crammed around her small conference table.

Rene settled into her chair and considered the three men who sat before her. "It's quite unusual to discuss a patient's possible participation in a research project without that person's guardian present," Rene said. "May I ask, Mr. Nichols, how you all are related to Kyle?"

"Please, call me Owen."

"Owen," she said, nodding, without reciprocating the informality.

"I think you know that I'm Kyle's uncle," Owen began. "Yoshi is Kyle's godfather. Kristen and I have known Yoshi since childhood. He's my best friend." Owen smiled at his buddy.

"Matt is my son," Yoshi said.

"I'm Kyle's best friend," Matt said. "I just finished my master's in biology, with an emphasis on research, so I'm especially interested in your experimental design."

Rene nodded. "Congratulations. That's a big accomplishment."

"Kristen, Kyle's mom, gave us the OK to learn more about your research," Owen said, "but of course she remains the decision-maker about Kyle's care. We won't be talking about him or his condition specifically. We're only here to find out what, if anything, your techniques might have to offer. We'll keep Kristen informed."

"Agreed. My discussions with you are only exploratory in nature. If I were to decide that Kyle is an appropriate candidate for my research, Ms. Nichols would have to become fully involved. If, and when, we reach that point, I'd give her a detailed explanation of the research for the informed consent necessary for me to work with Kyle."

All three men nodded, so Rene continued. "Were you able to bring the NDAs?"

"Here you go," Owen said, handing over the completed papers.

"I want to make absolutely sure that no rumors get started about my early findings. I hope you understand."

"It's wise of you to require NDAs. I work with inventors and manufacturers who rightly fear industrial sabotage is a genuine danger."

"Did you have any questions about the provisions?" Rene asked.

There was a short pause, then Matt spoke up. "Can we tell Kyle what we find out?" he asked. "He's the one who has the most at stake. And obviously, he can't give away any protected secrets."

"I don't think we should tell him," Yoshi responded firmly before Rene could gather her thoughts. "Not until we know if this has the potential to help him. As hard as it is, I don't think we ought to get his hopes up for something that might not pan out."

Owen nodded. "I agree, it's better to wait."

"Yeah, OK, OK," Matt said. "I get that."

She was struck by the sense of caring the men exhibited. They seemed interested and responsible. Still, it wasn't ideal to approach a potential research participant indirectly through a relative and family friends. Ms. Nichols was clearly reluctant to get involved, so even if Owen and company were persuaded, she still might block the study, making this and future meetings a waste of time.

But Kyle's situation was compelling. A beloved young athlete was trapped in the silent, motionless prison of locked-in syndrome. Helping someone communicate despite such a devastating disability would mean everything to her. She'd been too young to help Gramps. She'd been unable to save Marcella. But it would be worth every moment of her time to make a meaningful difference for this young man and his family.

"With that formality over, how about that tour I promised?" Seeing nods all around, Rene led them back down the hall to room 3.

"There are three identical test rooms where I conduct experiments on what I call the Witness," she said as they entered the small space. "The rooms are designed to ensure that tests going on in the other rooms can't influence one another." She paused to give them a chance to survey the room. "That instrument between the two recliners is the dual controller for transcranial ultrasounds, or D-TCU," she said, pointing to a device about the size of a shoebox with two digital readouts and a few recessed dials.

The setup clearly intrigued Owen. "What are the headsets sitting on top of it?"

"Each headset has a transducer that converts electrical current to the specific ultrasound frequency we select."

"May I?" Owen asked, gingerly picking up one of the headsets.

Rene nodded.

Yoshi stood just inside the door, watching everything with interest but not touching any of the equipment.

"The side tables hold the headphones and virtual reality goggles that control the auditory and visual input the participant receives," she explained as she showed off her well-equipped lab.

"This is fascinating," Owen said. "I'm surprised that this is all that's needed to create the—what did you call it—the Witness."

"Actually, only the headsets and the D-TCU frequency controller are needed to engage the Witness itself. The other instruments allow us to monitor the physiological responses of the participants."

"I'm aware of ultrasound equipment—is this dual controller already on the market?" Owen studied the device.

"Oh, no, I've been working on the design for some time, even before I opened this lab." She allowed herself to brag a little. "In fact, I intend to apply for a patent for the design."

"Interesting. I've consulted on a lot of patent applications in my work." Owen looked at her with admiration. "It can be a difficult and tedious process."

"Apparently so. I'm dreading the time the paperwork will take away from my research."

Yoshi piped up for the first time. "Is any of this dangerous? We have to convince Kyle's mother that it's totally safe."

"Good question." Rene smiled at the quiet man with black hair and dark eyes who stood a couple of inches shorter than her. "Probably the worst that could happen is if someone tripped over all these cables," she said. "Ultrasound technology has been used for years in medical settings, and our devices are set at frequencies known to be safe."

Yoshi smiled and nodded.

"Your facility seems quite impressive, Dr. Elder," Owen said, his eyes bright.

"There are so many hypotheses I want to test, I'm just exploding with ideas," she said, gesturing with both hands. "But we're proceeding methodically; just doing basic steps, laying a solid foundation on which to build more complex trials."

"Do you have any results you can share with us?" Owen said when the tour group stopped in the data center.

"Would you like to see the data from our most recent experiment?" Rene asked.

Owen nodded. "That would be great."

Rene described the purpose and setup of the experiment. "I'll only show you the split screen of the sender's object and the receiver's choices to preserve the anonymity of the participants," she explained. "I'll run the tape at triple-speed so I can show you all two hundred trials in just a few minutes."

Owen quickly caught on to the rhythm of the trial: the sender's object and the receiver's ten choices popped up on the screen, then nine of the choices vanished, leaving only the receiver's selection.

The tape moved too fast for Owen to keep count, although it seemed like the number of correct answers increased markedly over time.

Each correct answer brought Owen a spark of hope: as preposterous as it sounded, all indications were that the volunteers were engaged in a limited form of mind reading! He was thrilled to be on the track of research that might have a tangible impact on Kyle's quality of life.

"I tried to keep track of the number of correct answers. I think it was close to 75 percent, right?" Owen said when the tape concluded.

"You're good." Rene smiled. "The receiver matched the sender 78 percent of the time, when random chance is close to 10 percent."

"Kyle will never need to match objects like in this experiment," Owen went on, bouncing a little in his chair, "but if images can be shared, then maybe words, and even thoughts too! Your work has the potential to be the lifeline I was hoping for. If it pans out, it could improve Kyle's quality of life immeasurably."

"Seventy-eight percent concordance—that's extraordinary!" Matt's eyes were big, excited, then wary. "My degree's in biology, Dr. Elder, but I've never heard of anything like this before."

"I'm working at the intersection of neuroscience and physics," she said. "Like most sciences, these fields are quite compartmentalized, and cutting-edge ideas that cross academic boundaries haven't progressed into mainstream studies yet. That said," she continued, "these results are quite surprising to me as well. I have a lot of work to do to understand what's happening here."

The young man turned solemnly to Owen. "These results are amazing," he said, "but I think it's too soon to talk with Kristen."

"I have to agree," Owen said, looking at Rene, calming himself to assess the situation with professional caution. "I've sat through too many meetings with solo inventors and manufacturers who overpromise what their devices actually do. Sometimes one-off results like this vaporize under deeper scrutiny."

"I appreciate your thoughtful approach," she said, "and you're exactly right. Even if we replicate these results, there are lots of unanswered questions."

"This has been very helpful, Dr. Elder," Owen said as the men stood and pulled on their rain gear. "I'd like to get updates about the research, if that's OK with you."

"Definitely. I'll keep you in mind as my work progresses."

"I'm not a scientist," Yoshi said, as he smiled and shook her hand. "But even I can see that the implications of your work are staggering, not just for Kyle, or even for medicine. Either this is one of the most revolutionary scientific findings of all time, or—"

"Or I'm a complete quack." Rene finished for him, chuckling.

Yoshi nodded, his smile growing into a grin.

Rene's video left Owen thrilled with possibilities. He needed to hear his friends' reactions as he navigated the car through traffic to drop Matt off for his shift at the coffeehouse. The rain had stopped, but the roads were still wet, and he drove cautiously, aware that his mind was still back in Dr. Elder's office.

"Well, she's quite something, don't you think?" Yoshi broke in to his train of thought from the front passenger seat.

His best friend was flushed, and Owen gave him a knowing look. "Uh-huh," he said.

"Yeah, Dad, I thought you were there for the tour," Matt said to Yoshi, "but you kept your eyes glued to Dr. Elder the whole time."

"Was I that obvious? Jeez, that's embarrassing."

"I don't think you offended her—I think she liked you too," Matt said.

"You think?" Yoshi sounded a little giddy.

All three laughed.

"OK, Yo, I need you to get serious here," Owen said. "What did you think?"

"The science is way beyond me, but I found her very sincere and highly professional," Yoshi said, sounding thoughtful. "If she'd been Kimi's doctor, I'd have trusted her right off."

"Really? That's a high recommendation."

The widower's tone turned mournful. "We consulted with a lot of doctors while she was sick. I got to be a pretty astute judge of who Kimi would be willing to work with. Dr. Elder's explanations were clear, and she willingly answered questions. She was hopeful but didn't make any promises. Kimi would have appreciated that."

"Yeah, I liked her too," Owen said as they waited at a red light. "Matt, what'd you think?"

"I have some familiarity with medical research," the young man said, leaning forward from the back seat. "And everything struck me as very professional. When the technique is fully developed, I do think it might majorly improve Kyle's life. Totally."

"Really?" Owen was filled with optimism. Matt cared deeply for Kyle, and he also had a keen nose for charlatans.

"Like Dad said, everything seemed professional," he continued, his voice brimming with enthusiasm. "I mean, I came in a skeptic, and I'm leaving as a convert."

Owen imagined communicating with Kyle using Dr. Elder's equipment, filling him with hope. "Thanks, guys. I'm so glad you came along to check this out," he said, pulling to a stop in front of the coffeehouse.

"It was an honor," Matt said as he opened the car door. "I think the research we just observed may be the start of scientific history."

After the men had departed, Rene returned to her desk, envisioning again what it must be like to be a healthy young man suddenly stricken with LIS, imagining the depth of his desperation. She'd noticed the pain and worry radiating from Owen and his friends. Studying the brain in the abstract was exciting and safe, but it was inherent in experimental techniques that things didn't always go as planned. Once she identified a patient for her case study, be it Kyle Nichols or someone else, she'd inevitably be drawn into that family's roller coaster of hope and possible despair.

Abruptly, her thoughts filled with unwelcome memories of Marcella's bitter parents and her helplessness in the face of their anger after they lost their only child to Stauss's poor decision. The pressure of the responsibility roiled in her mind, as she recalled the parents berating her. Rene stuffed the memories of Marcella back into the compartment where they'd been safely locked away. She'd have to be very careful while conducting this case study. She couldn't afford to lose herself in another family's pain ever again.

CHAPTER 17

Owen brought pizza and a bottle of wine to Kristen's on a Thursday evening almost three weeks after Kyle moved to Rockridge.

Matt was visiting with Kyle, freeing Kristen and giving Owen his first opportunity to spend time alone with his sister since the family meeting.

Kristen greeted him in faded sweatpants and a rumpled T-shirt, looking as worn out as her clothes. She'd seemed much more relaxed after making the decision to move Kyle, so her appearance shocked him. He couldn't remember ever seeing her look this bedraggled. "Are you OK, Sis?"

She shrugged and let him in.

He gave a passing nod of acknowledgment toward a picture of his parents and set up the pizza on the kitchen table.

The counter was uncharacteristically messy, and unwashed dishes were stacked in the sink. A laundry basket overflowed next to the washer in the next room. Owen saw the old aluminum bat he'd bought for Kyle on the boy's tenth birthday leaning against the wall nearby. He recalled Kyle's excitement as they'd gone to the sporting goods store and Owen let him make his selection. Kyle had kept the bat near the back door so it was always handy for a little game of pepper in the large backyard.

Moving mechanically, Kristen put plastic glasses next to paper plates and then folded paper towels for napkins. A gloom descended onto his chest: Kyle's empty chair was still waiting for them.

Kristen sat down across from Owen, worry lines etched on her face. He reached for the corkscrew, concerned about the toll Kyle's move was taking on her.

"How am I?" she asked. "I'm flat-out exhausted. I've never been this tired in my entire life. So thanks for bringing this wine—though I fear one glass will put me under the table."

"I thought Kyle's transition to Rockridge was going well. Is there a problem?"

"Not exactly," she said as she took a sip of the merlot. "Remember how hopeful we were before Kyle was transferred?"

"Of course." Owen remembered the excitement that Kristen had exuded after her decision to move Kyle, how she'd decorated the boy's new room with photos and his trophy for sportsmanship the day before the transfer.

Owen and Kristen coordinated their efforts on moving day. Kristen oversaw preparations at the hospital and collected Kyle's belongings before following the ambulance to Rockridge Place, while Owen stationed himself in Kyle's room at Rockridge, ready to watch over the boy's arrival.

The quiet was broken when the door swung open and Rockridge staff wheeled in Kyle, then transferred him from the stretcher to his bed. A respiratory therapist with neck tattoos switched his airway from the portable ventilator to a solid cabinet-sized one at the head of the bed; other staff reattached IV fluids, catheters, and feeding tubes to their new poles on and near the bed. Their routine competence boosted Owen's confidence in the transfer.

Kristen came in last, smiling and carrying a box of cards and other odds and ends she'd collected in Kyle's hospital room during his lengthy stay. When she directed the attendants to orient the bed near the window, Kyle's new nurse, Larry, introduced himself and explained Kyle would need to be out of direct sunlight to avoid sunburn. He guided Kristen to Owen's side, then asked that they step out so he could check Kyle's catheter.

"Wow. What a whirlwind," Owen said as he and Kristen walked out to the lobby to wait. Although his sister was beaming with relief, his own enthusiasm was tempered: Kyle's environment had improved, but his physical condition hadn't.

"I'm so happy about having him live here, away from the hospital environment. Thank you so much for everything you've done all these weeks," Kristen said to Owen.

"Has something changed?" Owen asked as his attention shifted back to Kristen. He took a sip of wine.

"I assumed that when he moved to his new room, away from the clinical smell of the hospital, that his gaunt appearance wouldn't affect me so much," Kristen said. "But the room and grounds at Rockridge are so homey that his disability stands out even more." Her glass shook a little as she took a drink.

He hated seeing her so forlorn. She was right. It wasn't getting any easier seeing the boy lying there, wasting away. He clung to the belief that Kyle's resilience would carry the day, but her doubts brought his own lingering fears to the surface.

"He has no privacy. He can't pee or poop without someone having to clean him up. They move him like he's a rag doll, trying to prevent bedsores." Owen reached out and took her hand, heartsick to hear her talk that way. She wiped her nose on her sleeve, and he got up and found the tissues.

"Now I'm anxious about Kyle's stability after the stress of the move," Kristen said. "At least Dr. Guramurthy is watching him closely too." She took another sip of the wine. "I might like Dr. Guramurthy even better than Dr. Stauss. He seems really grounded."

"Well, that's good to hear. I've always thought Stauss had an oversized ego."

"Owen, stop. He saved Kyle's life, so what he says is gold."

"We'll have to agree to disagree on that one." Owen slid slices of pizza onto their plates. Kristen left her piece untouched.

"I was hopeful, but now I'm just feeling desperate again, thinking of his lost opportunities." Her voice shook. "Look at the stack of mail on the counter. Those are from the universities he applied to." She started to cry. "The first two were acceptances with full athletic scholarships. I couldn't open the rest." She bent over, crying harder.

He moved his chair over and put his arm around her, rubbing her back and staring out the window at the yard where he'd spent hundreds of joyful hours playing catch with Kyle. His earlier optimism drained. How could their lives have changed so horribly? "I'm so sorry," he said. She sat up, reaching for a tissue.

"Well, you asked," she said, wiping her nose. "So go on now, eat your pizza while I finish my wine."

The limp pizza had cooled on his plate; he was no longer hungry. How was she ever going to get through the next few months, years, or even decades with Kyle in long-term care, given the toll this was taking on her? He'd been optimistic after what he observed at Rene's offices. If only he could recapture that enthusiasm and transfer some of it to Kristen.

Owen gave his sister a few minutes to recover while they picked at their food. In light of his NDA, he broached the topic carefully, hoping to share a tiny bit of his optimism. "Kristen, I want you to know that I've been in touch with Dr. Elder. Remember her, from a couple of weeks ago?"

Kristen picked up her wine glass and stared into its contents.

Owen plunged on. "Yoshi came along, to make sure I asked all the right questions, and Matt, too, like you suggested."

"I really don't care right now. I told you I don't want to know anything about it unless it's proven and safe." Kristen was surprisingly firm, given how emotional she'd been just a few minutes before. "The only way I can survive is to keep a steady course and focus on what's right in front of me in this moment," she continued, draining her glass.

"I was just going to say that—"

"I'm sorry, Owen. I'm too exhausted to talk about this any further. You should finish eating and then go on home."

Owen filled with sadness. Kristen was standing at the brink, and he dared not push her. He choked down his earlier excitement along with the congealed cheese on his cold pizza.

CHAPTER 18

Rene lay tangled in her covers, wide awake in the early morning after a restless couple of hours. For the last two weeks, she and Aisha had run as many experiments as they could by day, then analyzed the resulting flood of data late into the evenings. The results were consistent: subjects repeatedly showed high agreement in the image-sharing experiment. An electric thrill zapped through her each time the MDAP program spit out a new round of results.

She lay on her side, barely able to make out the shadowy form of the dog slumbering in his kennel next to the bed. One unfortunate result of her obsession was that she often had way too much adrenaline coursing through her to sleep through the night. On top of that, Rob's absence from her bed brought a relentless heartache that made deep sleep even more elusive.

She inhaled deeply, enjoying the cool morning air. Her next experiment would test the possibility of two healthy participants having an actual conversation. If that proved possible, then she would begin working with patients who might benefit, assuming their families were interested and supportive.

Owen had called, and she'd agreed to meet with him later this morning; taking careful measure of the man was her top priority. Her assessment would guide her next steps regarding Kyle.

Her compassion went out to the three men of Team Kyle who'd observed her experiment two weeks ago. Owen comfortably mixed his roles as deeply concerned uncle and intrigued professional; Matt absorbed her research methodology and showed genuine appreciation for how her theories might help his best friend; and Yoshi—well, Yoshi was quite a thoughtful guy, and she had liked him right away. But Kristen was still an unknown yet essential wild card.

Rene sighed. There wasn't any going back to sleep. She threw on her sweats and sneakers and headed out for a long walk with Humboldt in the breaking light.

Later that morning, she and Owen took seats in the comfortable armchairs in the nook in her office at the foundation. The small table between them held a helter-skelter stack of books, many with bookmarks stuck partway through. Nearby, a well-exercised Humboldt turned circles in his bed, eventually curling up for a nap.

The long walk in the brisk morning air had allowed Rene to work off some residual energy and left her alert for her meeting.

Owen left his mug of freshly brewed coffee on the table, untouched. His tight face radiated distress.

"Kyle's situation is eating Kristen alive," Owen said, his face knotted with worry, "even though we thought it would get easier when he moved to Rockridge. It's been over two weeks, and her stress is higher than ever."

"I can't imagine how hard this must be for her," Rene said, warning herself not to take on his grief. "And for the rest of you, for that matter."

"I've been convinced from the beginning that there'd be a technology that would improve his quality of life," he said, leaning forward, eyes intense. "Your Witness technique is still our strongest hope of communicating with him."

"I get how urgently you want to make progress," she said, meeting his eyes. "But we still have to proceed carefully."

"I just have to find out what he needs, what he's feeling," Owen continued. "Every day that Kyle lies in bed without communicating is torture for him and Kristen—for all of us."

Her heart ached for him, setting off alarm bells. The conversation suddenly became as much a check on her own reactions as it was about Owen's. Though she was drawn to Kyle Nichols's dilemma, it was cases such as his that tested her. Marcella's death was still taking a toll on her; she didn't dare take on another such burden.

She brought Owen back to the harsh realities. "The kind of conversation you want to have with Kyle is immeasurably more advanced than the experiment you saw on tape," she said, her voice quiet but firm. "That kind of dialogue may not even be a possibility. It's premature to draw any conclusions."

"The potential is obvious, though," he said, brow furrowed. "If pictures can be recognized between people with that kind of accuracy, then surely words, sentences, even just ideas, can also be understood."

"Maybe. But Aisha and I tried to have a conversation using

the Witness. It was extremely disorienting, and we didn't get very far." She cringed at the memory. "You can't add to Kyle's suffering, no matter how much you want this to work," she added. She carefully watched for Owen's reaction.

"If I tried the Witness with Kyle and he freaked out, of course I would stop," he said with conviction. "But I've been involved with Kyle his entire life. It's not like I would be a stranger walking around in his head."

Rene paused. The truth was that she and Aisha did have brief success sharing their thoughts. Their attempt had been scuttled by her own humiliation at accidentally sharing her troubled love life, not because one of them had become panicked by the unusual sensations. Perhaps if she and Aisha were old friends, she could have worked through her reactions.

"I take your point," she responded carefully, "but I can tell you from experience that connecting directly with another's mind is intensely disconcerting."

He didn't react and she switched gears.

"Before I pioneer the Witness with someone as vulnerable as Kyle, we have to demonstrate that the kind of dialogue that you're hoping for is actually possible."

"What would that involve?"

"I would require that you try the Witness first, with someone other than Kyle as your partner," she said matter-of-factly. "Whether we go on to work with Kyle would depend first on your tolerance of that experience, and second, on your success at carrying on a dialogue with that person. Call it a trial run."

"Would that really be necessary? I know I sound impatient, but I've already seen a lot about how it works."

"As I said, being inside your own mind and someone else's at the same time is extraordinary, unlike anything else you've ever experienced," she said as embarrassing memories of her own reactions came tumbling back. "You need to be ready for the possibility that you might find it too bizarre to go any further, no matter how committed you are to using it to help Kyle."

"I'll tough it out, no matter what it takes," Owen said.

"I know you're determined, but it just makes common sense to prepare you first so you can guide Kyle through the experience." She needed to keep Owen's expectations realistic. "Having that experience will help you both if and when we get that far."

Owen exhaled a loud sigh. "OK, OK, you make a logical point." He nodded. "I'll agree to a trial, if that's what it takes."

"Good. You would need to find a partner, someone you're already close with, to approximate the same level of intimacy you would have with Kyle."

As Owen considered this, Rene was hit by the realization that she herself wasn't intimate enough with anyone to meet the requirement she'd just established for the Witness experience. With Rob out of her life, there was literally no one else who met that basic element of closeness.

She had a sinking feeling. Had she made the wrong choice?

"Well, Kristen is my first choice, but she wouldn't be interested at this point. Yoshi might be willing," Owen said, nodding. "He quite enjoyed our tour."

"Well, there's something else you need to consider, as disturbing as it may be," she said, giving him a steely look. "It's possible that although he's conscious, Kyle may have lost some or all of his ability to verbalize. He may not be able to think in words in the way you imagine. Brain injuries can have that effect."

Frowning, Owen narrowed his eyes.

She leaned forward with a stern expression, preparing to test his resolve by painting a stark, worst-case scenario. "You might connect with him only to encounter a chaos of disjointed sensations and feelings, or even just total blankness, like a sort of black hole." She paused for effect. "What if you go into his mind and find *nothing* there? Are you prepared for that?"

Owen's face went white, and he sat back. "I hadn't thought of that." He opened his mouth as if to speak, then sat back again, staring out the window with unfocused eyes.

Rene watched him carefully.

"That . . . that would be devastating, for sure. I'd be horrified to find out that . . . that he's already . . . gone . . . mentally," he said, his voice quavering. Then he locked eyes with her. "But we can't know that unless we try, can we? At least we'd have some clarity, as terrifying as that might be."

She returned the gaze, then sat back and considered. Owen seemed willing to face the most difficult experiences that the Witness could bring him. She read his reactions as true courage, not bravado.

She considered her next move. Working with Kyle might generate leads that would help thousands of others with severe brain dysfunction. It would be truly amazing to determine that *any* two people were able to establish a meaningful conversation in the Witness, much less if one of the two was suffering from a severe brain injury.

She decided to take the plunge. "I've laid out my concerns and requirements. If you're still interested . . ." She waited for his reaction.

Owen was even more solemn than before. He nodded. "I'm

absolutely ready to go forward," he said. There was an edge of steel in his voice that gave her additional confidence.

"Then I'm willing to proceed as well," she said.

Owen's posture visibly relaxed as he raised his mug. She brought her own cup up with a smile, and they clinked their agreement.

Rene added another condition. "If the trial goes well, you'll still need to get permission from Dr. Guramurthy at Rockridge before we attempt the Witness connection with Kyle."

"Why? You did say this ultrasound device is harmless, right?" Owen asked.

"The use of transcranial ultrasound in medical settings has been approved for many years. Nevertheless," she continued, "Kyle's a patient at Rockridge, but I'm not on the medical staff there. I can't just walk in and use a device on another doctor's patient without permission. It would be a violation of medical ethics, and it could compromise my license."

"I can see that, sure."

"And Kristen, of course. She would have to agree before we could ever work with Kyle." Rene was getting more and more curious about this absent member of Team Kyle, who held all the responsibility for deciding whether to proceed. When would she get to talk with her, and how might that affect her own willingness to pursue this research with the woman's son?

"Uh, sure. Of course."

His response sounded more tentative than she'd expected.

She narrowed her eyes. "Is that going to be a problem? Kristen's consent is nonnegotiable."

"It's just that she's totally overwhelmed with Kyle's day-to-day care," he said slowly. "She doesn't want me to discuss any research options with her until I've thoroughly checked them out first."

Another concern popped up. "Sorry to pry, but is there a father who would need to give consent? That might complicate matters."

"No, the biological father isn't involved."

"I feel awkward probing like this, but I'm not clear . . . ?" Best to find out early how this family was structured, before getting in too deep.

"It's not my story to tell," Owen went on, shifting a little in his chair. "But when Kristen was a teenager, she went wild for a time," he said. "She hooked up with a boy at a party. She never knew the boy's name or how to track him down, so she's been going it alone all along. Getting pregnant extinguished that wild streak in a hurry," he added, seemingly trying to preserve his sister's current credibility. "She's been a great mom. I fill in as a male role model. She had our parents' trust for financial support, and she even went to law school after Kyle started first grade."

"Ah." That explained Owen's involvement in his sister's life and his passion for helping his nephew.

"I think Yoshi would join me for the trial run," Owen said, obviously eager to move forward. "How soon could you set it up?"

"We'd have to do it in the evening. Our schedule is filled during the day for the next two months." She checked her calendar and found an opening four days hence. "How about this coming Tuesday evening?"

"OK. I'll have to check with Yoshi and make sure it doesn't conflict with his rehearsal schedule."

Rene gave him a quizzical look.

"He plays clarinet in the symphony," he explained. "I'll get back to you later today. And thank you so much, Dr. Elder!"

Rene showed Owen out, shaking hands with him at the door. She was alight with excitement as she watched him walk to his car. What secrets of consciousness might she unearth if she were to work with Kyle? This could be a huge step toward helping people with severe brain dysfunctions.

Back in her office, she reviewed their meeting. The prospect of this trial run ignited her inner sleuth. Rene suspected the Witness held many more secrets, and she was committed to uncovering them all.

CHAPTER 19

Owen ignored the greetings of staff and shoved open the door to Kyle's room at Rockridge Place early Tuesday morning. There was nothing particularly different to trigger his temper, he was just reacting to the ongoing crush of aggravations that Kyle's situation posed day after day.

It had been three weeks since the young man had been moved from the hospital to Rockridge Place. Team Kyle had developed a schedule of their visits to keep the boy company, and this morning was Owen's turn.

Kristen had decorated his room with sports posters and found a prominent location for Kyle's favorite action figure from his childhood, Buzz Lightyear. His new room had a good-sized window overlooking the landscaped courtyard.

On the small dresser across from the boy's bed stood a framed photo of Kyle with his mother. The thought of Kristen pulverized the already broken pieces of Owen's mood into dust.

Every day he witnessed the grief etched on her face, the dark circles under her eyes, the slouch of her shoulders.

The photos of Kyle's athletic accomplishments and the coveted sportsmanship award were there too, reminding Owen of all that had been lost. The boy's muscular body had become a limp skeleton, forever attached to tubes to keep his nutrition going and his wastes removed. It just wasn't fair.

Owen groaned, desperately tired of the constant rhythm of the ventilator that sustained Kyle's breathing; it created an aggravating pumping noise loud enough to block out the sounds of the birds outside the window.

Owen's helplessness surged in the face of Kyle's endless silence. *Get up! Move, dammit!* he nearly yelled, just barely holding himself back. He wanted to shake the boy to get him to say something, as if he were an obnoxious teenager on a power trip.

The selfishness of his own thoughts mortified him. Feeling guilty, he turned and walked to the window. He knew all the platitudes about life not being fair, but still he wanted to let out his frustration on someone, anyone. He stared out at the well-manicured yard, as the anger slowly subsided.

It was clear he needed something to calm himself. He hoped the meditation podcast he'd brought would do the trick. He untangled the aux cable, splitter, and two sets of headphones he'd brought to block out the hospital sounds that might disrupt their session.

On his way in, Owen had checked with Larry, Kyle's nurse, asking if it was OK to turn off the lights. Larry worked well with Kyle, exuding knowledge and compassion that everyone on Team Kyle recognized and appreciated.

After fussing with the wires, and securing the headphones around both their heads, Owen finally had the setup ready. "Kyle, I'm going to play a podcast of a beginning meditation instruction," he said as he pulled up the link on his phone. "I think meditation is something we can do together to help both of us deal with our new circumstances. It's Yoshi's idea. I hope you like it."

He turned off the room lights and hit Play, settling down and focusing on the teacher's instructions. Sitting up straight, feet flat on the ground, he followed his breath; gradually the sound of the ventilator faded from his awareness. Being there next to Kyle was all that mattered.

Owen took a series of deeper breaths at the teacher's direction. The instructor guided Owen to sit on a boulder by a shady, quiet stream. He suggested that he attach his worries to the leaves floating by and watch his cares gently drift away.

The voice was soothing, the words calming, and the music tranquil. As time went on, Owen gradually felt calmer. With his nephew lying nearby, he meditated in a place of quiet serenity.

Eventually the teacher's voice gradually brought him back into the room, relaxed and settled.

Opening his eyes, the dim light from under the door outlined the simple beauty of Kyle's face. A profound love for this special person overwhelmed Owen. He sat there quietly for a few more minutes, basking in gratitude for the joy his nephew brought into his life.

Suddenly a piercing alarm broke the rhythmic sounds of the ventilator, and the hair on the back of his neck lifted.

Something was wrong.

Helpless in the face of the specialized equipment, he rushed into the hall to find Larry already striding purposefully in his direction.

To quell his panic, Owen stepped aside as Larry checked the readouts and examined the boy. Owen put his hand on the boy's hot forehead while the nurse summoned Dr. Guramurthy.

"He's spiking a fever," the medical director said after listening to the boy's lungs. "I suspect a lung infection, perhaps pneumonia. Let's get him back to the hospital right away."

Dr. Guramurthy called for an ambulance while Owen, terrified, rushed to contact Kristen.

Owen was puffing, having run up the stairs to the Neuro-ICU, too worried to wait for the elevator. He rushed up to Kristen, who'd beaten him to the hospital. She was looking through the glass panel into Kyle's room, watching the nurses inside ministering to her son.

"Oh God, Owen, I'm so glad you're here."

He nodded, trying to catch his wind.

"He was only at Rockridge for three weeks, and already he's back in the hospital," Kristen said. "How could things have gone so wrong so soon?"

Owen pulled off his coat, sweating from exertion. "Dr. Guramurthy said it's a risk of being on a ventilator. His temperature spiked, and now they're going to check if he has pneumonia. But Dr. Guramurthy and Larry were great, they got an ambulance right away."

"The attending physician has started antibiotics, and they said they'll look at the cultures and then see if they need to adjust them. They hope they can get it under control within a few days." Kristen's exhaustion was on full display. "This is a disaster."

"He's had grueling days before—I'm betting he'll get through this too." Owen tried to reassure her, though he, too, was spinning with anxiety. The sudden downturn in his nephew's condition had left him badly shaken.

"I don't know, Owen," she said, shaking her head. "I'm starting to doubt my decision to move him to long-term care."

Her words were an electric shock, sparking another surge of fear and leaving him speechless.

"Maybe it was the right decision at the time," she continued. "But it's hitting me how hard this will be for him, lying motionless for years. Now he's suffering even more, and if he has pneumonia . . ." Kristen's shoulders were slumped; she appeared years older. "This must be living hell for him. He must have wished he'd died at the scene."

"Kristen—"

"I mean it, Owen. This is no way for him to live. Now that he's back in the hospital, I'm just not sure that I can continue to torture him."

Another wave of panic ripped through Owen. He'd just made plans to explore the Witness with Yoshi. He felt they were closer to connecting with Kyle. "This is definitely a setback, but let's see how it plays out, OK, before making any major decisions?" He tried to sound reassuring.

She shook her head, looking pensive, unsure. "I'm going back in to sit with him. I have to make sure they're giving his meds on time. We can only go in one person at a time, but can you stay too, please?"

"Of course, I can stay for a couple of hours. I called Matt.

He's coming when he gets off at six, so we'll take turns. Do you want me to bring you something from the cafeteria before I leave?"

She nodded and entered Kyle's room, careful not to get in the way of the nurses as she went to the head of the bed and smoothed the boy's hair away from his flushed face.

Was Kristen right? Were they putting Kyle through more pain than he'd ever choose for himself? Maybe Kyle was ready to die. . . . That was a conclusion Owen didn't want to accept. It was more urgent than ever that he and Yoshi complete that night's trial with Dr. Elder.

CHAPTER 20

Rene arrived at her office a little after noon, refreshed after a leisurely morning, a relaxing breakfast, and a long walk with Humboldt in the brisk fresh air.

She had previously canceled the day's experiments to give them a break after a long string of twelve-hour days. Aisha had said she was in danger of falling behind in her classes and was also taking the day off to get caught up. So, with no commitments this afternoon, Rene settled into her quiet office to get caught up on emails and other paperwork before the trial of the Witness with Owen and Yoshi this evening.

The most recent email was from Dr. Stauss's office with a terse confirmation that Rene's application to be granted privileges at the hospital had been approved. She gave silent thanks to Dr. Ainsworth for pushing Stauss to reverse his earlier decision.

The subject line on another email instantly raised alarm bells. It was from an address she didn't immediately recognize, but the subject line read, *Formal Complaint.* Then the username registered: it was from Brenda Harris, the volunteer from her original experiment who'd panicked and left the facility prematurely.

Brenda's email threw Rene. It cited psychological harm that she'd allegedly suffered as a result of the experiment but offered no specifics. The vague complaint didn't request a remedy but hinted at the possibility of future legal action.

Rene sat back, the muscles in her back tightening. That original experiment had been what, five or six weeks ago now? At the time, she'd reported the incident as required by the IRB and twice called the subject with no response. She needed to immediately verify that everything she'd done with Brenda that fateful afternoon had been by the book. It wasn't just a matter of making sure she was free from liability. With Marcella's case still fresh in her mind, she needed to reassure herself that she hadn't fallen victim to the same kind of blind ambition that Stauss had exhibited in surgery.

She frowned as she pulled out her file from that experiment, but thankfully, Brenda's signed consent form, including permission for a video of the experiment, was in her notes. Rene found the relevant video file on her hard drive and watched it through twice, taking a critical look to see if there were any mistakes or flaws in their actions. She exhaled a sigh of relief: everything they'd done followed protocol and was totally professional.

Still, she was rattled that Brenda's aborted experiment was coming back to haunt her. She forwarded the woman's email and a copy of the video to the foundation's attorney, asking for advice as soon as possible.

—

Rene was in the break room brewing a fresh pot of tea to calm her nerves when her cell phone buzzed.

The caller was the assistant to CRINR's director. "Dr. Elder, Dr. Ainsworth needs to meet with you as soon as possible today."

Rene frowned. "What's this about?"

"I'm sorry, he didn't tell me."

Rene waited a beat. She instinctively rebelled against jumping at Ainsworth's request, especially without knowing the agenda.

"He said it's urgent," the assistant said.

The MDAP software was crucial to her work, and the institute's offer to nominate her for the Kavli Prize was such an honor that everything else she'd planned for the afternoon suddenly seemed insignificant.

"All right then, I'll come right over."

"I'll let Dr. Ainsworth know."

Dr. Ainsworth didn't bother with pleasantries. "This morning, Administrator MacKenzie and I received a very disturbing email about an experiment you recently supervised," he said, looking at her sternly. "A Ms. Brenda Harris was the subject in question. Do you know whom I mean?"

Rene's defenses shot up. "Who sent you this email? This was an experiment conducted at a separate private facility. My IRB will deal with it."

"A blind copy was sent to Dr. Stauss, who was your medical director at the time. He thought it important enough to forward it to Administrator MacKenzie, the hospital's legal department, and to me." Ainsworth's eyes bored into hers.

Shit. Stauss was in on this.

"Look," she said reasonably, "the experiment she referenced happened after I left the employ of the hospital and before CRINR granted me access to MDAP, so neither the hospital nor CRINR has any role in responding to her."

"Ah, but that's not technically true," he said, indicating a paper on his desk. "The legal department checked your personnel records. After your last day on the job"—Ainsworth referred to some notes—"you took five days of accrued vacation time before your resignation was final." He gave her a hard look. "The date Ms. Harris gives falls within your vacation time."

Damn. She'd totally forgotten that technicality. Her stomach tightened.

"The letter alleges that she had an adverse reaction to the experiment, and that your research may endanger participants by altering their perceptions of reality," Ainsworth continued, his eyes narrowed. "Is it true?"

"Ms. Harris did become upset and left abruptly without completing the experiment." Rene spoke confidently, meeting his eyes. "The Human Subjects Committee cleared this experiment. We followed all the study protocols to the letter. And Ms. Harris signed the consent form."

"Be that as it may, Administrator MacKenzie is now involved, and he's talking with the hospital's legal counsel."

This could be big trouble. The legal department had a reputation for being very conservative. "Let's just take a moment here." She tried to remain calm through her rising panic. Brenda had rushed out, leaving Rene with no way to pursue Brenda's reactions in the moment; still, she could understand why the woman had been surprised by the unexpected and mysterious perceptions that popped into her awareness. Rene knew from firsthand experience how very disconcerting the Witness experience could be. "Why don't I meet with Ms. Harris and see if we can work through this together? I may be able to talk her through her fears and head this off."

"It's too late for that. Administrator MacKenzie has already decided to handle this as other recent investigations have been handled."

Rene's anxiety jumped another notch. "What does that mean, exactly?" The only other investigation she knew concerned Marcella's death and Dr. Stauss.

Ainsworth's eyes narrowed. "We're requiring you to suspend any further experiments using the MDAP software until we can get to the bottom of what happened."

Damn. Owen and Yoshi would be doing their trial run later this evening. "I truly think that's an overreaction," she said with all the reasonableness she could muster.

"Sorry, Dr. Elder, the legal department wants six weeks to study the situation more formally." Ainsworth used the tone of finality that Rene recognized from her previous meeting with him and Stauss.

"Six weeks?" Her growing outrage crept into her voice. "As you well know, I'm on a deadline to complete a complex case study, and I'm in the middle of some very important experiments." She sighed in exasperation. "Can't we work out some kind of compromise so I can keep moving forward?"

"I'm sorry, but if there's a chance that harm is coming to human subjects, then your research takes second place to their safety," he said, glowering.

"No one should ever doubt my commitment to protecting

anyone's safety. I was the whistleblower on Marcella Lopez's case, remember?" As Rene paused, a new realization began to take hold. "You know what? This decision to delay my work for so long smacks more of hospital politics than actual concern. Dr. Stauss is advising MacKenzie on this, and Stauss also has a pending investigation about the Lopez case. Sounds like a conflict of interest to me."

Ainsworth broke eye contact. "Be reasonable, Dr. Elder."

"This is an intentional roadblock," she said angrily. "It shouldn't take more than two weeks to thoroughly investigate this kind of vague complaint." She paused, daring Dr. Ainsworth to meet her steady glare. "Stauss talked with MacKenzie, who then put pressure on you, right?"

Ainsworth squirmed in his chair and continued to look down. "Just put the research on hold. Then we'll see what happens."

Rene clamped her mouth shut to avoid saying anything she might regret.

"You need to suspend use of MDAP, effective immediately, or risk losing our support altogether," Ainsworth continued with a grimace, still not meeting her eyes. "Agreed?"

She had to say *something*. "Understood," she said, with disdain dripping in her voice. She stood up. "May I go now?"

"Yes." Ainsworth didn't rise to see her out.

Rene resisted the urge to slam the door as she left. Striding back across the hospital campus, she considered how to deal with this unexpected development.

The administration's overblown reaction to Brenda's complaint did trigger layers of worry: there might be serious repercussions not just for her work, but also for Owen and Kyle.

—

After the disastrous meeting with Ainsworth, Rene headed home rather than going back to the office, feeling the telltale signs of a migraine creeping into her awareness. She was scheduled to meet with Owen at seven this evening to conduct his test run of the Witness; she needed time to clear her mind and determine if Ainsworth's prohibition would force her to cancel.

Her rose garden was her sanctuary, where she went for both solace and inspiration. The roses mesmerized her as she stepped into the garden under a cool, overcast sky; she was entranced by the colors, the smells, and even the velvety sensation of the petals. The headache symptoms began to subside as she allowed herself the guilty pleasure of gently touching a few of them.

Ever since her first trip to the Portland Rose Garden as a child, Rene had loved roses. She'd been adding to her collection of rosebushes ever since moving into this house six years ago, and generally tended them with loving care. But she was falling further and further behind in her weeding without Rob around to help.

Humboldt nosed the ground as Rene knelt on foam pads to reduce the strain on her knees. With a strong grip and a yank, she extracted satisfying fistfuls of weeds from the moist ground.

How in the world could CRINR halt her research for six weeks? It couldn't possibly take that long to investigate the report of one disgruntled research subject.

"The delay is outrageous!" She stood and wielded her clippers like a weapon. "How dare you restrict my work!" she muttered, vigorously clipping atrophied blossoms, sending them toppling to the ground.

"This is for you, Ainsworth!"

"Take that, Stauss!"

She'd have to cancel dozens of study volunteers who'd filled her ambitious schedule of experiments.

Snip!

Snip!

Then there was the backlog of data to analyze with MDAP.

Damn!

She emptied her spoils into the green waste container. Retrieving her rake, she walked along the perimeter of the garden, clearing the debris that had accumulated under the bushes.

Foremost on her mind was her immediate obligation to Owen. How could she justify going forward with this evening's trial if it meant violating the new restrictions?

After the stretch of gardening had tested her muscles and rested her mind, she headed inside for a shower. As the warm water washed her clean, she had an idea that might allow her to exempt the night's experiment from Ainsworth's prohibition.

While it was true that CRINR was providing the MDAP software, it was her foundation that had independently funded the research. She was both sponsor and researcher, which meant that CRINR didn't have total control over everything she did, just over the use of their software for data analysis.

The purpose of this trial was to explore Owen's reaction to the Witness experience and assess his ability to have a genuine dialogue with Yoshi. She didn't need MDAP for that analysis.

She and Aisha had previously experienced the same type of personal Witness connection that Owen and Yoshi might undergo. The same approach could suffice this evening. If she recorded their physiological responses with her own software, but didn't run the data through MDAP, she wouldn't be violating Dr. Ainsworth's prohibition.

Stepping out of the shower with renewed commitment, Rene dried herself and headed into the bedroom for some fresh clothes. Moving forward with Owen would give her research a focus while her other work remained idle. Besides, the possibility of improving Kyle's quality of life was looming larger in her priorities.

She studied herself in the mirror while slowly brushing her hair. She'd been naive to assume her resignation would free her from all the politics surrounding Marcella's death. But improving the well-being of someone like Kyle was an opportunity to cancel out the ugliness she still carried and provide a much-needed healing for *her*—and for Owen and his family.

Renewed, Rene led Humboldt downstairs into the garden where she collected an array of fresh blossoms to take with her to the office. There was just time for them to have their dinners before heading over to the foundation to meet Owen and Yoshi.

CHAPTER 21

Owen arrived at the Carl Elder Foundation office precisely at seven that evening. He couldn't imagine what this Witness experience would be like, even after Rene's detailed explanations. It was one thing to watch Spock do a mind-meld on *Star Trek* and quite another to do it yourself.

Rene greeted him at the door and walked him down to her office, where Yoshi was down on one knee, playing tug with Humboldt. As he stood to greet Owen, Humboldt jumped up, nearly knocking Yoshi over.

"Enough," Rene said firmly to the big pooch, who immediately went to his bed and lay down.

Rene and Yoshi exchanged grins. Yoshi blushed as they held eye contact. Owen smiled, hopeful for the man who'd been painfully alone since Kimi died.

"Before we start, I better update you." Owen filled Rene and Yoshi in on Kyle's unexpected return to the hospital earlier that day. "I can't believe this turn of events. The doctors are optimistic that he'll survive this pneumonia, but I'm worried sick. Kristen is beside herself."

"I'm so sorry," Rene said. "Are you sure you're up to going through with the trial run tonight?"

"Absolutely," Owen said, forcing himself to sound confident. "The more information we have, the better we'll be able to deal with whatever happens."

"Maybe what we learn tonight will help us know how to advise Kristen next," Yoshi added.

"Let's hope so," she said, closing Humboldt in her office with a new chew toy to keep him occupied. "Let's get started."

They went into room 3, where they signed the informed-consent paperwork and handed over the photo Owen and Yoshi had selected; Rene had requested that they find a photograph that captured just the two of them in a situation that provoked fond memories.

Owen tried to keep a lid on his fears as Rene began to orient them. He had to make this work for Kyle.

"You may sense that someone is listening to what you're thinking," she said, prepping them from the notes in the procedure manual. "But the Witness cannot alter your thoughts, make decisions, or have any control over you; each of you will just 'witness' what the other is aware of in their internal experience at that moment."

"So I shouldn't freak out that Owen is trying to take control of my mind, right?" Yoshi said, winking at Owen. Owen offered a slight smile, not feeling as jovial as his best friend.

"Exactly right!" Rene said, smiling. "OK so far?"

Owen and Yoshi both nodded. Owen was glad Yoshi sounded so relaxed and confident. Owen, on the other hand, had choked down a few bites of a cold packaged sandwich he'd grabbed from the hospital cafeteria, and so was suffering from an uncomfortable burning in his stomach.

"OK, on to some specifics." Rene resumed her instructions. "In order to reduce distractions, you'll both wear VR goggles, showing the same image or images. You'll wear headphones, and I'll pipe in identical auditory input. That way, your two most dominant senses will be engaged in the same way at the same time."

Owen paid close attention and calmed a bit as her confident presentation went along.

"Once you're settled in with a backdrop of sights and sounds from nature," she continued, "I'll align the frequency of the two ultrasounds. I'll sustain it for a while to allow you to adjust, and then I'll bring up the photo you brought in. As you focus on the picture and the memories it evokes, you can explore how to communicate with each other."

"That's it?" Owen asked. Maybe this wouldn't be so bad after all.

"Yes, that's all you have to do. After you spend some time with the photo and conversing, I'll reverse the process by taking the frequencies out of alignment. OK?"

He nodded, impatient. As nervous as he was, he couldn't wait to find out if this would work.

"OK. I'll be monitoring your physiological responses with the pulse oximeter and blood pressure cuff." She handed each of them a palm-sized gadget about the size of a car fob. "If you want to pause the alignment to get oriented, just push the button. It's better to take the time to get oriented than try to push through, so don't hesitate to use it."

"Yup," Yoshi said, with a grin and a thumbs-up.

"Got it." Owen gained a burst of confidence just from seeing Yoshi's relaxed attitude.

"OK, let's get going. Owen, I'll start with you, then I'll get Yoshi set up." Yoshi turned his smile toward Rene, though she didn't seem to notice.

Once Owen was seated in the recliner, Rene helped him don the headset, VR goggles, headphones, and monitors, calmly wrestling with the tangled wires. He admired how she placed the various devices and monitors with practiced precision.

"OK, now you're fully connected." Rene handed him the fob and patted him gently on the arm.

"I think I'm attached to more devices than when the astronauts take off for the moon." He tried to make it a joke, but all the heavy paraphernalia on his head made him quite uncomfortable.

"You're not far off," Rene said, then added, "I suggest you lean all the way back in your recliner—with all that equipment, you'll be a lot more comfortable."

Owen eventually found a relaxed position to support his head. Still, the headset, headphones, and VR goggles made his head feel ten times bigger than normal. Maybe he'd get used to the strange appendages as they went along.

He heard Rene making similar movements at his side and talking Yoshi through the same process he had undergone. Owen's leg, his only body part that wasn't tied down with wires and sensors, jiggled wildly. What if he couldn't connect with Yoshi? He should have taken something to settle his stomach.

Finally, Rene finished the preparations. "I'll be monitoring everything from the data center," she said before leaving the room. A couple of minutes later, her voice came over the intercom. "OK, you're cleared for liftoff. Anything else before we get started?" She sounded relaxed, and Owen released a breath he didn't know he'd been holding.

"I'm ready." Yoshi's enthusiasm came through loud and clear.

"Let's do it." Owen tried to sound confident as he broke into a sweat. He wiped his palms on his pants before resting his arms on the armrests. With the fob in his right hand, he took a few slow breaths as he began to hear faint ocean sounds.

He relaxed into the rhythm of the gently breaking waves. After a bit, the pitch-black of the goggles gave way to a faint glow revealing a horizon at sunrise. A long unending beach, with small waves breaking along the shore, became visible as the sun rose over the ocean. The water was clear turquoise and the foam from the waves a crisp, bright white. The perfectly smooth sand was unmarred but for the tiny footprints of a few shore birds who dabbled along the edge. The beach extended to a row of palm trees that swayed gently in the breeze. An occasional gull swooped and cawed as the sun's rays brightened the scene.

Owen drifted along, the breeze cooling his sun-warmed skin, the smell of salt water filling his nostrils. The warm water lapped over his toes as the waves came in, and he beamed with pleasure. For the first time in weeks, Owen was free of worries. He took in the cloudless sky and reveled in the ocean's power before him.

As he sat quietly on the beach, he sensed the gentle companionship of his best friend. He grinned, feeling a warm response within. Yoshi was sitting next to him on the beach. *He's right here with me.*

Hey! This is amaz—hey, no—wait—weird—OK—relax—no! All

at once, his mind filled with words he hadn't thought. They came from out of nowhere, creating a weird jumble of his own and another's thoughts in a mixture he couldn't decipher. *Owen—it's—no wait—don't be—what—stop!*

He mentally tried to swat away the invader words, as if they were bees at a picnic. He writhed in his seat and almost spoke out loud. *Get out—of my head.* His heart was beating triple time, and he tried to slow his ragged breathing.

O, it's me. Owen identified the calming voice of his best friend.

Yo? he thought.

It's me came an instantaneous response.

Hearing voices.

And as quickly as he thought those words, Yoshi's response immediately arrived. *Freaky—fun!*

Bizarre—going crazy. The room was spinning.

Not crazy, this is what—

*Can't figure out—words aren't—don't—*Stop*—spooky—you—*I'm*—No—wait—*

His body recoiled, rejecting the mental intruder. Nausea came on fast, his stomach reacting as if to spit out the invader, taking over when his brain was unable to evict the foreign mind.

He gasped for air. His heart rate soared. He was sweating profusely.

Yoshi remained silent.

I'm not OK, Owen finally sent when he began to relax.

Yeah, I can tell—just take it slow.

Whoa—spinning again—stay quiet.

Yoshi remained still. Owen stretched his fingers, gradually releasing his death grip on the arms of the recliner, careful not to drop the fob. *I'm OK when you're silent, but every time I hear your voice in my head, I get disoriented.*

I like it—but I can sense your fear, Yoshi responded.

Can't get my balance, spinning out of control. Owen's malaise spiked again. He was failing at this trial. Sweat dripped down his face.

He couldn't go on. He reached for the button to cancel the trial. *I have to bail—like a super hyper Tilt-A-Whirl—can't tell what's up, what's down—oh—shit.* The nausea surged again. *I just can't do this.*

Wait, Owen, wait. Let me try a meditation technique.

Owen gritted his teeth to hang on a few seconds more.

Try concentrating on my emotions, Yoshi said. *You can ride this out through me.*

Yoshi's thoughts slowed, then stopped. Feelings of calmness, even enjoyment, emerged in the background of Owen's perceptions. He mentally grabbed for them like a drowning man reaching for a life preserver.

Owen allowed Yoshi, the professional musician, to fill his mind with a light, lilting melody that became a lively, fun ditty full of playful enthusiasm. His body resonated with the refrain that emerged in his mind, and he could breathe easier.

Isn't this fun? Yoshi said, inserting a few words into the calmness. *Like we're dancing with our minds. Relax and let me lead, OK?*

Yeah, OK. Owen focused his attention on the incoming emotions, welcoming Yoshi's confidence and enthusiasm into his awareness and absorbing them as his own. His body responded to the input. *Hey! I feel better, a little lighthearted. How'd you do that?*

I'm meditating, just letting our minds play together as they will came Yoshi's response.

Owen let his friend's adventurous spirit flood through him. His fears faded and the nausea disappeared. He exhaled deeply and moved around in the recliner, carefully stretching his legs to relieve the stiffness.

After a bit longer, his energy increased, fueled by Yoshi's excitement. He was ready to move on. *OK, I'm finally getting the hang of this!* Owen smiled as he was drawn even further into his friend's easy enthusiasm. *My god, this is really working! We can really think a conversation!*

Yoshi's agreement was immediate, and their compounding exhilaration gave him an intoxicating rush.

OK, I'm going to concentrate on the beach scene again, Yoshi thought. *Just stay with me. Oh man, what a glorious view—*

Um—yeah, gorgeous.

They were silent again, Owen enjoying the beach next to his best friend. Once again, they were relaxing in the soft breeze and the warm sun.

The magnitude of the discovery left him astonished. They were reading minds!

Doing OK now? Yoshi asked after a bit.

As long as you keep flooding me with fun vibes, yeah. I think I can do this.

The ocean scene faded as the photo they'd brought in gradually appeared in front of them.

Dr. Elder had been brilliant to prepare them with a beach scene, as the picture was from a time when Owen and Yoshi had been at the beach together. They were about ten years old. Owen grinned. They'd selected this photo because it had been such a wonderful time of childhood freedom, with none of the cares that Owen took on after his parents died.

Again, Yoshi got the hang of it first, and began flooding Owen's mind with his happy memories of that day. Soon Owen was sharing his own memories, the two of them playing on the beach with the abandon of the children they'd been then. Owen closed his eyes, no longer needing the visual stimulus of the photograph, relying instead on the shared images they each contributed.

Remember that sandcastle we built—

Oh, yeah! They patted the warm sand into place on their fort as the tepid salt water washed up around them to challenge the stability of their work.

Each had memories that the other didn't, and when Yoshi recalled chasing the birds on the beach, suddenly Owen was right next to him, laughing as they splashed along in the surf. Yoshi's memories added a new depth and context to his own, making them seem as real as if they were living them for the first time.

Their connection grew deeper as they remembered the same moments but from two perspectives, like a memory experienced in stereo.

Yeah, and then I buried you in the sand—

And there he was, lying in the wet sand, letting Yoshi plop big scoops over his torso and around his legs until he was just a head sticking out from a mound of sand, and then Yoshi's mom and dad came over, and they were all laughing, laughing so hard, and Owen's mom, pregnant with Kristen, took a picture—

Mom. Kristen. An unexpected stab of heartache pierced him: his parents' deaths; a vision of the day he'd delivered the devastating news to a teenaged Kristen. Owen's pain reverberated into Yoshi's mind a millisecond later, then instantly ricocheted back into his own mind, compounded by Yoshi's own grief at the loss.

Overwhelmed by the emotions, he again considered pushing the pause button. But Yoshi began recreating the triumphant strains of another calming symphony, seeking to raise Owen's emotions from torment to fulfillment with the musical masterpiece.

It worked; he felt uplifted again as he followed Yoshi's emotional guidance. For the moment at least, he released the painful memory.

Soon he was ready to proceed. Again, there were the two of them romping in the surf, playing Frisbee in the waves.

Then Owen experienced an odd new sensation, as if he was no longer immersed in the memories of the day at the beach but was instead disconnecting from them. Their shared perspective gradually moved from the Frisbee game to a farther vantage point. Their new view was from above, making them objective observers of their game rather than participants.

It filled him with wonder. This experience was far beyond what he'd imagined. *How amazing is it to step back like this? I guess this is why Dr. Elder calls it the Witness,* Owen said to Yoshi as they observed themselves playing, like watching a movie.

Yes, wow, what a perspective—how are we doing this? Yoshi, too, sounded amazed.

Uh-oh, I'm getting a little queasy again.

Stay with me, Owen. Nothing to fear.

Owen took some deep calming breaths and once again focused on the direct input from Yoshi.

Their observation point continued to move farther and farther away until they could have been observing any two boys playing in the far distance.

And then they left their thoughts and memories behind altogether—just as they'd already left behind the two men sitting in the recliners and the two men enjoying the sunrise at the beach, they left behind the two boys playing Frisbee.

Suddenly the boundary between them vanished, and then there was OwenYoshi. Not two, but—one. Their identities blended, creating a fresh openness, joyful in newfound freedom to behold what lay even further beyond—yet deeper inside—

    a sudden flash of insight
    revealed
    spacious, pure awareness
    floating,
    buoyant, as if carried on an ocean of warm salt water
    there was only
    eternal witness
    everything
    everywhere
    all
    one
    wonder
    bliss

    exaltation

CHAPTER 22

Rene's eyes were the only part of her that moved. The rest of her body was frozen in place while her gaze shifted constantly between the readouts of Owen's and Yoshi's physiological status and the view of their motionless bodies in the recliners.

She'd almost ended the experiment when Owen's heart rate exceeded 160 beats per minute, but it had since slowed to normal. In fact, the men's heart and breath rates were synchronized and had been for several minutes. She was well aware of research that showed sometimes physiological measures of people engaged in a task together did find a common rhythm. This finding convinced her that the men were experiencing a meaningful connection through the Witness.

Rene jumped at an unexpected sound, causing her to knock her clipboard to the floor with a clatter. She heard Humboldt tossing around one of his toys in her office across from where she sat in the data center. She would need to take him outside for a break soon.

She picked up her clipboard, checking her notes. It was time to bring the men out of their experience. She began changing the frequencies to take the TCU equipment out of alignment.

The joined mind OwenYoshi slowly drifted back to Rene's lab as if parachuting down to earth from a high distance, basking in the peace of Oneness, perceiving all life-forms on earth, seeing each entity as an individual glowing presence.

Sensing the essence of thousands of beings in the proximity of Portland.

Narrowing focus, distinguishing individuals in a restaurant, in the library, exiting a building.

An ever-shrinking view, nearing Rene's lab; people sitting in motionless cars, a dozen or more people milling about. A wandering dog. Someone riding a skateboard across the parking lot. Three people in the business next door. A skunk outside the office complex. Humboldt moving around in Rene's office. Rene in the data center, picking something up off the floor.

Their own bodies in the recliners.

As abruptly as a lightning bolt, Owen was back in his chair, detached, alone, his five senses trapped once more in the here and now. Disoriented, frantic.

"Yoshi?" Owen ripped off his headset, barely remembering where he was. "Yoshi, where are you?"

By the time Rene got down the hall from the data center, the men had escaped from the confines of their equipment and were embracing in a long hug. There was a kind of spell between them, and she stayed quiet, reluctant to disrupt the moment.

When they finally stepped apart and acknowledged her, Owen's eyes were glistening. Yoshi was flushed. What the heck?

Rene quickly rolled her chair around from behind the computer desk to sit in front of them and leaned forward, intrigued to begin the debriefing.

The men sat in the adjacent recliners and began talking before she could say a word. The interview questions she'd crafted immediately fell to the wayside.

"Rene, you can't imagine—"

"It's amazing, there aren't words—"

"I've never been so—"

"I know, right? It was like—"

The men were leaning toward each other, looking back and forth, occasionally glancing at Rene, completing each other's sentences. There was a palpable connection between them, like trees swaying together in the breeze.

Rene rubbed the muscles in her neck. She itched to interrupt, to force them to focus, but held back. There was something important here that she needed to let run out, uncensored. These first impressions might hold some valuable clues. The video was still running, documenting everything.

"Go on, guys."

"Being able to converse without talking was amazing enough, but then we got even deeper into the Witness, and then—"

"That's when we were just blown away," Owen finished. "It was some kind of out-of-body experience. Right, Yo? You felt that too, right?"

"Yeah, it was like I was myself and part of Owen at the same time," his best friend said, his eyes gleaming.

Rene struggled to understand. "Would you say it was a kind of meditative state?"

"Not exactly. I mean, I've had peaceful moments during meditation, but nothing this profound. At some point," Yoshi continued, closing his eyes, "I became very, very calm. I lost . . . it's hard to describe. I lost a sense of being an 'I.' I wasn't Yoshi anymore."

What? This wasn't what she'd expected.

"That's it exactly. Owen and Yoshi didn't exist anymore." Owen picked up where Yoshi left off.

Yoshi nodded vigorously, looking at Rene, eyes wide.

Rene's blood ran cold. Their descriptions alarmed her. Had the Witness technique triggered some kind of delusional episode?

Yoshi paused. "There was just—One—an openness, a wide-open awareness." His eyes were bright, his voice enthusiastic. "The entire universe opened up to us, I—we—saw it all, immense, everything interconnected."

"Yes! We're all just part of this one big . . . cosmos . . ." Owen's voice went soft, almost reverent.

"And there was no perception of time, it's like it's all one past, present, and future, all rolled into . . . now." Yoshi waved his arms in an expansive gesture.

"And the vastness of it all, huh, Yo? I've never been so peaceful in my life. Now everything makes sense." Owen grinned.

She pushed back in her chair and regarded the two men carefully. Were they each experiencing some kind of psychotic break? She worked through a quick assessment of their demeanors. Many mental health crises were marked by distress, but neither man seemed traumatized. Both were rational and grounded in the moment. In fact, they were effusive, even joyful.

She ruled out psychosis, but she still had no clue as to what they'd experienced. Their descriptions were so far removed from her own concept of the material universe that they were making her agitated.

"It was like the perfect ending to a symphony performance," Yoshi gushed. His eyes closed again, his face serene. He moved his arms as if he were conducting an orchestra. "When the ensemble hits that final note in a perfect blending of the instruments, the sound reverberates for a moment of sublime beauty. Being in the Witness was like that—sublime. But with music, the sound fades away. With the Witness you could just rest there forever, in complete harmony . . ." He held his arms out, perfectly still, his eyes still closed, as if he were reliving that perfect moment in the concert hall.

"We were joined with all beings, all One, like Yoshi described," Owen said. "Then just before we . . . got back . . . the One separated into many separate . . . beings . . . individual people, even animals. At the end, we saw you and Humboldt here in this building, and then, pop! I was just me, back in my chair again."

Their descriptions of a mystical experience were running roughshod over the fragile framework of theories she'd assembled to explain the Witness. Rene was torn between her respect for the men and the concept they were forcing her to consider.

Yoshi nodded. "You've stumbled on something amazing here, Rene. The whole experience seems . . . profound . . . you know? And it wasn't just me—Owen experienced exactly what

I did. Our connection was absolute." Yoshi locked eyes with her. "I'm filled with awe."

Rene froze. She stared at Yoshi and suddenly was looking at Gramps. There was that same soft look in Yoshi's eyes, the familiar gentle voice, that unassuming confidence in the truth of a profound but private experience.

"How can that be?" Yoshi asked. "How can something occurring between two people's brains be . . . both . . . universal . . . and then so very detailed?"

She snapped back into the present as the men looked at her expectantly. She was unprepared for any of this, off-balance emotionally and intellectually. She ran her fingers through her hair. "I don't know. Not yet anyway."

As she hesitated, Owen and Yoshi again turned to each other. Their interaction gave her a reason to escape. "I'll leave you alone for a few minutes," she said as she rose and moved to the door. "I need to take Humboldt out."

"Dr. Elder, wait!"

She turned back to Owen.

"Be careful with Humboldt. There's a skunk outside."

"Say what now?"

"Yeah, we saw . . . no, that's not the right word. Um, well, I guess you could say we *know* there's a skunk nearby."

"You mean you saw one when you drove in?"

"No, no, we *know* it from just a couple of minutes ago, while we were . . . together . . . in the Witness. Right, Yo?"

"Yes. It was snuffling around the dumpsters."

This was too much. Rene couldn't help but roll her eyes.

"It happened as the sense of Oneness faded and our view scattered into awareness of . . . separate beings."

"OK, you say you . . . *know* . . . there's a skunk outside. What else do you . . . know?" she asked, struggling to keep the doubt out of her voice.

Owen closed his eyes. "Well, there's a big traffic tie-up at the intersection. There may have been an accident . . ."

"I remember someone on a skateboard riding across the parking lot," Yoshi said.

"Oh, and three people left the office next door."

"And we saw you in the other room picking something up off the floor."

A cold chill went through her. There was no way they could know that. "This gets more interesting by the moment," she said, trying to remain calm. "I'll be back in a few minutes."

Humboldt whimpered urgently as she grabbed his leash and led him through the break room to the side door. The dog froze as soon as the first whiff of air came in through the opening. A second later, Rene caught the acrid smell of skunk and slammed the door shut. "Holy shit."

Humboldt whimpered more fervently and looked up at her.

"Let's try going out the front." Rene walked her dog down the hall, through the reception area, and very cautiously opened the front door. The stink was present, but only faintly. Humboldt pulled her toward the grass area on the front edge of the parking lot, well away from the dumpsters.

As her friend took care of his business, Rene took some deep gulps of the cold air and looked around. Her eyes were pulled to the flashing red lights of an ambulance and fire truck arriving at the intersection. She saw lines of stalled cars up and down the street, blocked by the accident. How could they have known?

Her thoughts seized, her rational mind paralyzed. A gust of

wind rattled the nearby trees. She stood there, empty, motionless, as the cold air breached her sweater, raising bumps on her arms.

Eventually, Humboldt nudged her hand, returning her attention to the present. So much of what she'd heard in the last few minutes was . . . unbelievable. And yet . . . She shook her head, trying to clear her thoughts. The men's reports of a universal consciousness and their bizarre awareness of outside events were serious findings she'd need months to unravel.

But in the meantime, she couldn't allow their unexpected accounts to overwhelm the original intention of the experiment: to determine if Owen could use the Witness to have a dialogue with Kyle. She compartmentalized her cascading questions into a mental box to be scrutinized later. For the moment, it was time to get back on track.

The men looked up at her expectantly as she returned to her seat in front of them.

"Yes, there was a skunk and an accident," she said, trying to sound matter-of-fact. "And I'll be looking into all aspects of your report thoroughly. But right now, let's refocus on the person whose quality of life depends on tonight's exercise: Kyle."

She immediately had their full attention.

"Remember that our goal was to explore having a dialogue marked by the kind of clarity and depth Owen might need to converse with his nephew."

Both men mirrored her serious demeanor.

"So what was your experience in that regard?" she asked.

Owen took the lead. "I had a rough start. After that, we had a very clear conversation." He closed his eyes. "First I'd receive a kind of . . . gestalt . . . understanding of what Yoshi had at the forefront of his mind, and then, through his thoughts, he helped crystallize the idea."

Rene began making notes.

"Sharing within the Witness is richly textured, full of nuance and subtlety," Yoshi said, his brow furrowed. "Talking like we are now seems terribly flat and one-dimensional, prone to misunderstanding."

"Kyle's intellectual capacity may be diminished from the accident," she said. "Just how effective do you think the Witness might be, in the worst case?" She paused in her note-taking to observe Owen carefully.

Kyle's uncle returned her serious look. "Transferring the essence of our meaning between us was effortless. The Witness provides so much depth and substance without words that even if Kyle's verbal skills are limited or even nonexistent, some kind of communication with him through the Witness should be possible."

Yoshi nodded.

Their assessment sent a thrill up her spine. "Well, gentlemen, you've demonstrated monumental success: you're the first to hold a meaningful conversation using mind-to-mind communication thanks to the Witness." She flashed a triumphant smile.

Owen and Yoshi grinned and exchanged high fives.

"So let's talk about where to go from here."

Before calling it a night, Rene agreed that Owen should bring Kristen up to date on the Witness: her approval to use the technique with Kyle was mandatory, and there was no reason to delay.

After talking through the details, Rene walked the two men out to the front door. Owen draped his arm around Yoshi's shoulders as they headed to their cars. Something important had happened between them.

"Take care, guys," she called after them.

Back in the data center, Rene's qualms about the men's reports surfaced with a vengeance. Yes, they'd verified that it was possible to have a meaningful conversation through the Witness, a tremendous accomplishment in and of itself. Their accounts of a shared transcendent experience were startling. But their knowledge of things happening inside and outside her office while they were confined to their recliners was absolutely confounding.

Perhaps one of them had seen the skunk when he drove in and didn't register it consciously until just before she'd ended the test. Perhaps the traffic had already been snarled when Owen arrived, and he later assumed there'd been an accident. Or maybe the men heard the distant sirens while they were still in the Witness.

But there was no way they could know she had knocked the clipboard onto the floor.

If she could prove that the Witness gave rise to a transcendent out-of-body awareness beyond the five senses, then she would have to seriously consider the possibility of a universal consciousness.

But her observations about the skunk, accident, and clipboard wouldn't carry any credibility in scientific circles. She needed the kind of proof that anyone could analyze and even replicate.

What else had the men seen? Someone on a skateboard, three people leaving next door. She racked her brain. Ah! The security cameras the landlord had positioned all around the complex.

She pulled up the website and selected views showing the side of the building, parking lot, and front door of the office next door, then rolled the time stamp back to a few minutes before she'd ended the experiment.

The first motion she noticed was a dog sniffing at the dumpsters by the side door. The dog suddenly flinched, then turned and ran full speed out of the frame. Had it just been skunked?

Shortly thereafter, the front door of her neighbor's office opened, and Samuel, the accountant, walked out with a man and woman. Samuel turned and locked the door, then waved goodbye to the couple as they walked to their respective cars.

She almost missed the quick shadowy blur zipping across the upper corner of the frame of the parking lot. She rolled the tape back and after a few tries was able to freeze a view of . . . a pair of feet and lower legs on a skateboard.

She double-checked the time stamps just to be sure. All the views from the security cameras were recorded while the men were lying quietly in their recliners.

So there it was. Objective proof that for these two subjects, using the Witness triggered out-of-body awareness beyond the five senses. She'd found the men's reports of a transcendent experience perplexing, but this verification of what they had seen outside was deeply unnerving.

The data center was chilly, but she was sweating, oddly dismayed by the latest twist in her research. Their descriptions of the loss of identity, the experience of Oneness, a sense of peace and something universal threatened to upend her world. Those were terms used by people who joined cults.

Universal Oneness? What the hell?

She'd never had such a visceral reaction to the result of an experiment. She was at once intrigued by their reports, yet deeply distressed at the implications for her career. The CRINR's board would never nominate her for the Kavli Prize if she presented her careful scientific research with reports of . . . what . . . nirvana?

Suddenly furious, Rene hurled her notes across the room, scattering them over the floor. Leaving the papers where they landed, she retrieved Humboldt, turned off the lights, set the alarm, and strode to her car. What the hell had she gotten herself into?

CHAPTER 23

Rene woke in a haze well before dawn. Her thoughts immediately snapped back to the previous evening's experiment with Owen and Yoshi. Throwing back the covers, she stumbled to the shower and tried to wash away her angst over the disturbing results.

The men's subjective reports of a transcendent experience were remarkable in and of themselves. Coupled with the images from the security cameras, the findings became . . . unbelievable. What could account for it?

Was it possible they'd encountered an objective reality, some kind of universal consciousness? The prospect both intrigued and terrified her.

She drove through the drizzle to arrive at her foundation office a good hour before her usual start time. Humboldt tagged along as she moved through the building, turning the lights on and the thermostat up until the heater kicked on.

The results of her outburst were still evident in the papers strewn across the floor of the data center. She picked up the mess and reorganized her notes, still simmering with the unease of the night before. Perhaps a second opinion from Aisha would ease her discomfort.

She brought up the video file of her interview with the two men and the footage from the security cameras. She'd have Aisha look at all the information fresh, without providing any prologue that might skew her reactions. Maybe the young researcher would have a different interpretation or find something that Rene had missed.

Back in the break room, she prepared a strainer with her strongest black tea, poured the boiling water into her favorite glass mug, and submerged the infuser.

She was still ruminating over her beverage when Aisha came through the front door. After a brief stop in her office, the research assistant joined her in the break room. "Morning," she said, smiling.

"Morning," Rene answered.

"You're here early."

"Yeah, I didn't sleep well, so I came in to get started. What are you going to work on today?"

"The procedure manual, of course," Aisha answered. "It's a never-ending project."

"Indeed. Well, maybe I can offer a reprieve. I've got another task for you if you don't mind."

"Sounds great," the young woman said with a smile, taking a seat across the small table from Rene. "What's up?"

Rene returned the smile, determined to behave as normally as possible. "Yesterday evening I conducted a Witness experiment with Owen Nichols and his friend Yoshi," she began.

Aisha's eyebrows shot up. "Oh?"

"I thought you might enjoy looking at their interview and reviewing the physiological data." She kept her voice neutral.

"Sure. Is there anything special you want me to watch for?"

"No, nothing in particular. We'll talk about your impressions afterwards."

"OK," she said with a shrug. "Where do I start?"

"The video is cued up at the point when my interview began."

"You've really piqued my curiosity," her assistant said with a grin. "I'll get my notebook and get started."

"Don't get too excited," she said, trying everything she could think of to avoid contaminating Aisha's raw reactions. "But have at it."

After Aisha headed off to the data center, Rene focused on looking for new leads in the work of other researchers.

Nearly an hour went by before Aisha returned to Rene's office and sat down quietly in the chair across from her mentor.

"I listened to your interview twice and I was deeply moved by their reports," she said without prompting. Her voice came out with a little quaver, and her eyes were glassy. "My gut reaction is to believe them, that they actually were in touch with something universal. Their reports were so spontaneous, so genuine. And they said exactly the same thing."

Rene just nodded.

"Tell me they were having a shared delusion," Aisha said.

"Is that what you think happened?"

"I've never heard of ultrasound causing delusions, have you?" Aisha asked.

"No."

"This has never happened before?"

"None of this has ever happened before."

"Ah." Aisha looked out the window at the trees and clouds.

Rene waited.

"The Witness phenomenon provides the ability to observe, but not to alter, another's perceptions, right?" Aisha finally said.

"Agreed."

Aisha closed her eyes, her brow deeply furrowed. "So if one person was having a delusion," she continued, "the other would observe it, but their own perceptions of reality would remain unaltered." Aisha nodded to herself. "So even if both men were delusional simultaneously, their delusions would still be separate and unique."

"Yes."

She sat opposite Rene, disbelief written across her face.

Rene just nodded.

The younger woman remained frozen in place with her hands knotted in her lap, her eyes narrowed. "There's more?"

"Now watch the security tape. Then tell me what you think."

Aisha abruptly stood and strode out of the room. Rene returned to her computer.

It wasn't long before Aisha, somehow looking smaller, again returned to Rene's office. She started to say something, then stopped. Shaking her head slightly, she walked over to the book-shelf, where she stood for a long moment with her back to Rene.

Rene waited. She forced herself to stay quiet so as not to taint the assistant's impressions.

Finally, the younger researcher turned to face her mentor. Rene maintained her silence, watching Aisha closely.

"I reviewed the footage from the security cameras."

Rene remained still.

"It's *impossible*."

Rene kept her face impassive. "They knew I dropped the clipboard," she finally shared. "And I personally confirmed their accounts of the skunk and the accident."

"Those things really happened?"

"Yes. After Owen and Yoshi left, I pulled up that security footage and found proof of the other events they described."

Aisha sat down hard on the chair, then leaned forward onto Rene's desk, holding eye contact with her supervisor. "Doesn't this all strongly suggest that the Witness could actually let people share a universal consciousness?"

Rene held Aisha's eyes for a long moment. "I honestly don't know what to think," she said, shaking her head. "Frankly, I'm struggling to accept what happened, let alone propose a hypoth-esis to explain it."

Aisha sat back, her eyes wide. "It was beyond belief when we stumbled on the thought-sharing with the two volunteers a month ago," she said softly. "Now that seems almost . . . mundane."

She paused and again stared out the window into the dis-tance. "I go to yoga strictly for the exercise," she explained, her gaze returning to the room and making eye contact with Rene. "But there's a spiritual component to the practice. Serious adherents say they can get in touch with what they call cosmic consciousness." She paused again for a beat. "That's what came to mind as I listened to Owen and Yoshi talk."

Rene's chest tightened at the need to draw on a spiritual tradition to understand the Witness. She remained committed to grounding her work in the natural sciences.

"Remember"—Rene hastened to add—"we only have this one dataset. Once I settle on a hypothesis, we'll have to run a lot of experiments before we can prove it true or false."

Aisha was wide-eyed. "I'm really excited, but I'm also kinda freaked out." She stood to leave, then stopped and turned back to her mentor. "Dr. Elder, can I ask you a question?"

"Of course."

"Is there a reason why you didn't schedule me to help with last night's experiment?"

The question caught Rene by surprise. "Why do you ask?"

"What you've stumbled on here is just . . . unbelievable . . . groundbreaking." She hesitated. "I hope this doesn't sound too pushy, but frankly, I want to be here for it all. The more I can learn, the better. Besides, maybe I can be of help."

Rene smiled, tickled yet again by the younger woman's enthusiasm. "Well, your insights have already been very useful, so yes, I promise to include you in future experiments." She made a mental note to eke out enough funding from her budget to offer Aisha a full-time position when she graduated. "I look forward to it."

Aisha broke out in a big grin. "Thanks, Doc." Her eyes got big. "Oh, I'm so sorry—Dr. Elder." She corrected herself, looking abashed.

Rene laughed. "No worries. How about you write up your reactions while they're still fresh. We'll talk more later, OK?"

Aisha smiled and left the room with a little bounce in her step, leaving Rene alone with her thoughts.

Aisha's impressions of the events from last night mirrored her own, save the information about yoga. In some respects, she was disappointed that Aisha hadn't come up with an alternative explanation. But the fact that their perspectives were consistent suggested they were on the right track.

She swiveled her chair and let her gaze drift out across the trees into the backyards bordering the business complex. Large cumulus clouds cluttered the late morning sky; their menacingly dark undersides promised rain later in the day.

It had only taken Aisha a few minutes to associate the subjects' reactions with one of the world's oldest spiritual practices. The possibility that others might make similar religious connections from the men's descriptions made her uneasy.

Rene had no interest in spiritual research. The very idea of a universal consciousness left her cold. She imagined publishing her results and the subsequent headlines asserting that she had proven the existence of God. Or that she was a dangerous heretic attempting to disprove God. Religions might take advantage of her findings to promulgate their belief systems or vigorously reject her research out of hand. What if new religions sprung up based on her data? She cringed at the thought that her results might sound like something from a religious cult. She imagined the death threats.

Even more worrisome, the findings threatened to uproot her personal and professional concepts of the universe. Her perspective was firmly entrenched in the physical attributes of a material world. She was unsettled, off-balance at being forced to deconstruct her deeply held understanding of the fundamental nature of the universe.

And what of Owen and of Yoshi? She'd seen in both of them a serenity she found compelling. Instinct told her they were solid, grounded individuals not prone to flights of fancy. Yoshi, who had seemed more affected by his experience, reminded her so much of Gramps.

The high winds morphed the clouds as they moved quickly across her field of view, never holding the same shape for more than a few seconds.

Could she put aside her own biases and objectively analyze this startling new information? Would Yoshi's and Owen's reactions lead her to a new view of the universe?

Her doubts were many but her faith in the scientific method deeply ingrained. As a researcher, she was committed to exploring phenomena in depth and letting the data take her where it would.

It wouldn't be easy to overcome her qualms, but as always, science gave her a clear sense of direction. Heading into the break room, she brewed herself another cup of strong tea and got back to work.

CHAPTER 24

Owen awakened at dawn, more refreshed than he'd been in weeks. Qwerty lay next to him, curled into a tight ball within a nest of covers. He smiled as she roused with a yawn; took a long, languorous stretch; then jumped off the bed.

The afterglow of his amazing experience in the Witness the previous evening carried into the new day: Owen overflowed with optimism. He'd found a way to communicate with Kyle! He couldn't wait to update Kristen.

He knew Kristen would visit Kyle before heading to work, so he quickly dressed, fed Qwerty, and drove to the hospital to meet with her as soon as possible.

She hadn't arrived yet, so he entered his nephew's room and quietly greeted him, brushing his thin hair back from his forehead and pulling the light blanket up from where it had slipped. Kyle's skin felt cooler, and the color was back in his cheeks. Owen nodded with relief; the boy seemed to be improving.

Now that Owen had learned how the Witness could bridge

two minds, his nephew's frail body seemed like a mere shell. Hope lightened his thoughts. How incredible it would be to wear Dr. Elder's headsets and be in direct connection with Kyle. He couldn't wait!

Kristen came in a few minutes later, accompanied by the attending physician. Owen stepped aside to let the doctor examine Kyle and watched his sister unobtrusively. His heart ached: her clothes were rumpled, and her hair was badly in need of a touch-up. Perhaps his news would lift her spirits as much as it was lifting his.

"He's turned the corner," the physician said as they exited and stood outside at the small window looking into Kyle's cubicle.

Owen sighed with relief.

"We'll be moving him to the neurology floor later today, though it may still be a week or so before he's ready for discharge."

Kristen was teary. "I can't thank you enough, Doctor," she said, before the physician strode off to check on the next critically ill patient.

"Great news, eh?" Owen said, bouncing a little on his toes.

Kristen only managed a slight nod.

"How are you?" he asked gently as they moved to the nearby waiting room and settled on plastic chairs in the corner.

She sighed deeply and met his eyes. "I don't know if I can take much more. Seeing him so sick on top of everything else . . ." Her face was gray, her shoulders slumped.

"Yeah," he said softly. "I get it." They sat silently together, Owen waiting for the right time to broach his news.

Finally Kristen refocused. "You aren't usually here so early. Is something up?" she asked.

He'd been thinking how best to share his Witness experience

with her. Kristen would be very skeptical about anything experimental. He would have to proceed carefully.

"Remember last week when you said to bring you new technologies only if I find something that's been proven?" he started.

Kristen rolled her eyes. "Proven and safe. This better be good, Owen."

He held her gaze. "I promise this is worth your attention," he said. "There's actually a way we can communicate with Kyle. It's called the Witness."

She leaned forward, instantly alert. "Seriously? I could talk with Kyle?"

"I know what I'm about to say might sound far-fetched at first," he began, filling his voice with as much confidence as he could muster. "Just hear me out, OK?"

She nodded tentatively.

"The Witness allows two people to communicate their thoughts back and forth, without ever talking out loud. Since Kyle can't speak, this would be the perfect technique to connect us with him."

"What? Say again? You talk without . . . talking?"

"Yes." Owen nodded. "Exactly."

Kristen sat back, frowning. "Don't mess with me, Owen."

"I'm not fooling around, Kristen. I tried it with Yoshi, and it worked, so there's every reason to believe—"

"Wait! You and Yoshi tried this . . . Witness thing?"

"Yes, yesterday evening. Dr. Elder set us up with a trial run to—"

"A *trial* run?" Her eyes narrowed. "Are you telling me you were the first person to try this—whatever it is? That doesn't sound like something that's already been proven safe."

"A few other volunteers have tried it before, but we were the first to attempt to have a conversation." He kept his voice positive, upbeat. "I needed a partner to 'talk' to, and Yoshi agreed. We just sat in our recliners, wearing headsets, and Dr. Elder adjusted the frequency to activate the Witness and—"

"How could you two take such a risk? Shooting—rays or whatever—into your brains? What the hell were you thinking?"

"I'm fine. Don't worry. I'm OK."

"Are you sure? What about side effects?" She sounded panicked as she looked deep into his eyes.

"No, no, I'm absolutely fine." He smiled. "No side effects at all."

"Jeez, Owen, you took a colossal risk. I know you want to save Kyle, but how could you use yourself as a guinea pig?" She sat back with a groan, biting her lip. "What if something had happened to you guys? I can't risk losing you or Yoshi. What if you'd both suffered brain damage?"

"I guarantee we're both perfectly OK." He hadn't anticipated her fears for his safety and needed to refocus the conversation. "The important thing is how this technique could help Kyle communicate with us."

He paused, finally sensing her readiness for him to move on. "As I was saying, we just sat there, and Dr. Elder adjusted the ultrasound frequencies. That's all there was to it. We exchanged our thoughts and had a discussion without ever speaking out loud. We showed that the Witness works, and we're both just fine." He watched her carefully. "We've proven this works and is safe, just like you wanted."

"This trial run of yours really isn't what I meant by 'proven and safe,' and you know it," she said. "I'm looking for something that has a significant, documented track record." She frowned. "I mean, really. Mind reading?"

"It's true, Kristen. Yoshi and I had quite the conversation, just my thoughts sent directly to his mind, and vice versa."

"That sounds . . . absolutely bizarre," she said, shaking her head.

"There's a scientific rationale for all this. Matt thinks this will be a very important breakthrough. And after experiencing the Witness myself, I'm convinced of its value."

"I don't know. You got me really excited for a minute there, but this is sounding more and more like something out of a cheesy movie."

"Kristen, I'm your brother, not some mad scientist. I wouldn't bother you unless I was convinced it was valuable."

"I know that. But I also know you're frantic to find something to help Kyle. And while that's incredibly noble of you"—she put her hand across his—"I don't think I can follow you into this fantasy."

"I know it sounds like science fiction, but it's actually a revolutionary new technique that could open up the world for Kyle and for you," he said, squeezing her hand. "Think of how amazing it would be if you could communicate with him—what a tremendous improvement it would make to his quality of life, to be free from his prison of isolation. And what a relief it would be for you to be back in touch with him."

Kristen's face softened. "Of course, that would be wonderful . . ." Her eyes lost focus and she looked over his shoulder while he waited. "I don't know . . ."

"Maybe it would help if you talked with Dr. Elder your-self," Owen continued. "I think you'd find that this isn't hocus-pocus—it's grounded in science—real science."

She frowned, her expression alternating between hope and skepticism. "You're really serious about this, aren't you?"

"Absolutely." Owen held himself motionless—she might be on the verge of relenting, and he didn't want to break the spell.

"You said Yoshi and Matt agree?" Maybe she was coming around.

"Yep. Look, if you aren't ready to meet Dr. Elder, how about if you just call Yoshi to hear what he has to say?" Kristen valued Yoshi's opinion; he might provide the extra push she needed.

"All right, all right," she said, though he could still hear a note of hesitation in her voice. "I'll call him. But if I decide to talk with Dr. Elder, I'll meet her alone, on my own terms."

Owen exhaled with relief as she relented to contacting Yoshi. "Whatever you need to feel comfortable." She was the decision-maker here, after all.

"No guarantees, Owen. OK?" Her look bored into him.

"Of course," he responded. She wasn't convinced, but at least the door was open a crack.

"I've got to get to the office." Kristen stood, gathered her things, and started to walk away, then turned back. "Are you sure you're OK?"

Owen smiled back at her. "I'm absolutely sure. I'll check in with you later."

After she left, Owen walked back to the window looking into Kyle's room, pondering the gaunt, motionless frame of his be-loved nephew. What if he was wrong? What if he were to con-nect with Kyle only to find his brain totally scrambled? Or that he was incoherent, just a mess of disjointed feelings with no abil-ity to reason? What if he was mentally deranged, or insane—be-yond understanding or logic?

Thinking about what might go wrong made him nauseous.

What if there was no Kyle anymore?

What if there was *no one* in there?

CHAPTER 25

Rene arrived at the coffeehouse where Matt worked on Thursday morning. Yoshi had called earlier and asked to further debrief his Witness experience from two days before.

She'd found herself unexpectedly eager to accept his invitation; on a professional level, it was an opportunity to further explore his reactions to his Witness experience. But she was also excited on a personal level, because . . . well, she really liked the man.

She'd been keenly aware of Yoshi observing her Tuesday evening in that certain way people do when they are attracted to someone and don't think they are being noticed. His romantic vibe enticed her, though she still felt raw from her breakup with Rob.

The coffeehouse was crowded with couples chatting at small tables and individuals hunched over laptops. She spotted Yoshi waving and smiling from a secluded spot by the window. A tingle went through her as she returned his wave before getting in line to make her selection.

The smell of roasting coffee beans and a hint of fresh pastries tempted her. She smiled as Matt took her order.

"We've got a fresh batch of poppy seed muffins in the back," he said as he rang up her breakfast. "I'll snag one for you while they're still hot."

"I like having a barista as a friend," she said and left a generous tip in the jar.

She balanced the scalding hot pot of steeping oolong tea leaves on her tray and wove among the tables toward Yoshi. She carefully set the pot and cup on the small round table and ditched the empty tray nearby. Finally, she was seated and settled.

"How are you after all your adventures Tuesday evening?" she asked once they'd exchanged greetings.

"I haven't been able to think about anything except the Witness since then," Yoshi said. His face was flushed, eyes wide. "It was such an incredible experience. I still can't fully grasp it."

She nodded. "I barely slept myself. I've spent every waking hour of the last two days totally immersed in reviewing the results."

"Tell me you've got this all figured out," he said, looking at her seriously. "I could use some help processing what I experienced."

"I've made a little progress," she said, "but trying to unravel this complex mystery . . . it's a major intellectual challenge."

"I admire your expertise," he said. "I'm totally out of my element in your world. You must have worked exceptionally hard to get to this point."

"It's been a long journey, yes," she said, smiling. His recognition gave her a warm rush. It was flattering to have her accomplishments recognized by him, even though he was a layperson.

Matt arrived with Yoshi's beverage and her pastry. "I was just about to go on break," he said. "Would it be OK if I joined you for a few minutes?" He hesitated. "Dad told me about his experience, and I'd love to hear your thoughts."

Yoshi nodded.

"Sure," she said. "Pull up a seat."

Matt maneuvered an empty chair from a vacant table as Rene and Yoshi edged their seats closer to make room. Yoshi's knee briefly rubbed against hers and she enjoyed another little thrill.

"I was telling Matt that my time in the Witness left me with a deep appreciation for the . . . majesty . . . of the universe," Yoshi said. "It's such a powerful feeling. . . . No, it's not just a feeling, it's more *knowing* . . . what we're all a part of." He looked into the distance for a long moment.

Waiting quietly, Rene poured her steeped tea into the cup. It was still too hot to drink.

"I was raised a Buddhist," he abruptly went on, continuing to stare across the room.

"Oh?" She kept her voice neutral, but her jaw tightened at the reference to yet another religion.

"Some sensei share an analogy that goes something like this," he said, the faraway look remaining on his face. "We are all a part of a large ocean, and each of us is but a wave. A wave can be clearly identified, but after it crashes on the shore, the wave is gone, though the water remains." He met her eyes. "That's how I've started thinking about my experience with

Owen. For a short while, our waves merged back into the water, where we experienced the depth and breadth of the ocean. Then our individual waves rose again, and we returned to our sense of being distinct individuals."

"That's useful," she said. "It helps me understand what you've been trying to describe."

"Tuesday night I called it 'sublime,' and I think that's still the best word for the feeling." He stared at her, as if willing her to understand the nature of his experience. "I wish we were in the Witness right now, so you'd really understand what I'm trying to say," he went on, crumpling his napkin. "Words are just so damn inadequate."

"And I wish I had more of an explanation to offer," she said, smiling ruefully. "You and Owen were breaking new ground. It's going to take a while to sort it all out."

"Did you find anything in the hard data to support their descriptions?" Matt asked Rene, inching his chair closer to the table.

"Actually, I did. And it's quite remarkable." Rene smiled. She kept her voice low. "Your dad and Owen described specific events that they said happened outside my office while they were still sitting in their recliners. I was able to verify several of them." She turned to Yoshi. "Then, after you and Owen left, I checked the tape from the security cameras. I saw three people leave the office next door, and I saw the skateboarder ride through the parking lot."

"Just like we said. Unbelievable."

Matt's eyes got wide. "Seriously?"

"What does all this mean?" Yoshi asked, pausing with his cup halfway to his mouth.

"I'm not sure yet. But it does lend itself to the interpretation that what you reported wasn't a delusion, but rather a demonstrable event, with some elements that can be measured objectively."

"It's good to know we aren't crazy." Yoshi's eyes smiled at her over the cup.

"Is there any theory that might explain what happened?" Matt persisted, looking earnest. "I mean, this whole thing sounds unbelievable."

"I've been poring over the work of scientists who presented at the Science of Consciousness conference. One theory postulates something called panpsychism."

Matt looked puzzled.

Yoshi sputtered his coffee. "That's a thing?"

"It's the theory that the universe itself is conscious in some sense," she continued, squinting her eyes to capture how her thinking had evolved since Aisha had reviewed the men's results. "Some think that consciousness flows from the larger whole to the smallest atomic particles; others believe the opposite, that particles endowed with consciousness collectively build and together create the larger awareness."

"Wow." Matt's eyes were wide. "Either theory would upend a lot of what my professors were teaching just last year." He paused. "I bet some of them would have a stroke if they heard about this."

"Remember your NDA," a solemn Yoshi said to his son.

"Yeah, of course," the younger man said. "OK, let's assume that panpsychism is true, and there is some sort of universal consciousness out there. What's the connection between that theory and what Dad experienced?"

"I've drafted a working hypothesis, but bear with me, it will take a moment to explain."

The men looked at her with rapt attention.

"If we assume that a conscious awareness is inherent in the universe, then it's possible that through the process of evolution, human brains are slowly developing the capacity to connect directly with each other, and perhaps even with the universe itself."

She closed her eyes, trying to summarize all that had whizzed through her mind in the last few hours. "But evolution takes thousands of generations to make significant changes. At this point, according to this hypothesis, humans have only evolved far enough to create our individual experience of self-awareness. But we haven't progressed far enough to connect our individual consciousness with that of anyone else, much less with the universal awareness itself." She opened her eyes again. "So we still live confined inside our own skulls, pending further evolution of the species."

"Does that mean your technology didn't create Dad's extraordinary encounter with Owen or with the universe," Matt asked, his brow furrowed, "but it allowed him to . . . tap into . . . something that's already present? Sort of jump-starting evolution?"

"Yes, I think that's the implication of this hypothesis."

Yoshi nodded. "That sounds right."

She focused herself, preparing her final summation. "The logical extension of this idea is that the Witness is the ability of the universe to be aware of itself."

Matt sat back, looking stunned. "Holy shit."

Rene nodded solemnly and locked eyes with the young man.

With his background in biology, he could appreciate the significance of her proposal.

"Those concepts would have profound implications for all of
science, even for religion," Matt concluded, looking wide-eyed.
"They're just astonishing."

She nodded, her heart racing. Hearing someone else articu-
late the implications gave them even more gravitas. This could
be the discovery she'd dreamed of—and more.

"This sounds more revolutionary every moment," Yoshi
said.

"My head is spinning," Matt said, looking pained. "Damn,
I hate to leave, but my boss is waving at me to get back to work."
He stood and found an empty tray to pick up some dirty dishes
from another table. Then he turned back. "Thanks, Dr. Elder—
you're amazing. Later, Dad."

Rene smiled and nodded as the young man rose. "He's going
to make quite the researcher," she said, motioning toward the
boy's retreating back.

"I wish he could get a foot in the door somewhere. I'm encouraging him to put in more applications, but his highest priority is spending time with Kyle."

"He's a very loyal friend. I'm sure it means a lot to them
both."

Yoshi nodded and took a sip of his latte. "Kristen called me
after she talked with Owen. I tried to explain the Witness, but I
got a very flat response. I think I sounded a little too woo-woo."

Rene set her steaming cup on the table. "I'm meeting her
tomorrow afternoon. Do you have any advice for how best to
approach her?"

"Well, she's an attorney, but when it comes to Kyle, she's a mother and her gut feelings about his welfare might overrule any logic you can offer. I think you should focus on her as a parent, an average person—like me," he said and laughed softly, then got more serious.

Yoshi had a light in his eyes as he stared off over Rene's shoulder, watching Matt at the espresso machine. Rene observed him discreetly over the top of her cup. He seemed so serene; she couldn't see any worry lines on his face, just some laugh lines around his deep brown eyes. It was nice to spend time with someone so relaxed.

"You should know that Kristen's a fiercely independent single mother," he said, resuming his description. "She went it alone right from the start, even though Owen's been a big help. If she has to, she'll go it alone with this decision as well."

"I can relate to an independent woman."

A small smile played at his lips. "So can I."

Another thrill went through her as she met his eyes. She blushed and hurried to get the conversation back on track. "That's insightful background. Thanks."

"No problem," Yoshi responded. "Say, have you gone to visit Kyle since he's back in the hospital?"

"No," she said carefully. "I don't plan to visit until he returns to long-term care."

"Oh? Can I ask why?" Yoshi's face was open, friendly.

Painful memories of Marcella Lopez turned her upbeat mood more solemn. "I've found that getting too close to patients can have painful results, especially if things don't work out," she said. Not to mention that she also needed to avoid running into Dr. Stauss, who was again consulting on Kyle's case.

"I'm guessing you learned that the hard way?"

His gentle manner made her feel safe. "Yeah, I had a traumatic experience when I was doing patient care." She took a small bite of her muffin while deciding how much more to reveal.

He raised his eyebrows but didn't press her.

"One case in particular was the final straw," she said after working through her bite. "A three-year-old girl. She'd wandered into the driveway. The father backed the car out of the garage and the bumper hit her in the head."

"Oh, God. How tragic."

"It was a gruesome injury. Doc—the surgeon called me in to observe." Rene took a drink of her tea, hoping to dissolve the growing lump in her throat. It was a relief to talk about this with someone impartial. "She died on the table."

Yoshi remained quiet, attentive.

Rene had to take another sip before continuing. "The parents were devastated, of course. The father was overcome with guilt. They soon divorced, unable to survive the pressures."

She gazed into the man's eyes, allowing him to see that her own had filled with tears. Rob had tired of listening to her, and she still carried unresolved feelings that needed release. Yoshi seemed able to absorb her pain, willing to hear the worst.

He held her eyes with a gentle gaze. "You don't have to tell me if it's too painful."

"Afterward, I started losing sleep and having other physical symptoms."

"I'm so sorry. I forget that patients can affect their doctors so strongly."

"Some are better at staying objective than others, I suppose," she said, sighing. "I went over the surgeon's head and reported his decisions. I had to participate in a formal interview about what happened. They cleared me of any wrongdoing." She brought her hands together to keep them from shaking. "But I still feel guilty that I wasn't able to prevent her death."

"Perhaps there was nothing more you could have done."

"Maybe there was, maybe there wasn't—I don't know. I've asked myself that question a thousand times." She studied the depths of her teacup. Should she trust him, let it all out?

Yoshi reached out and lightly touched her hands. His warmth traveled through her, a wave of kindness that unraveled her resolve to never speak the details.

Everything came out in a rush. "We were in the middle of emergency surgery, for God's sake. The girl was hanging on by a thread, but she had a genuine chance to make it. Then Doct— the surgeon started implanting electrodes deeper into her brain so he could later gather more data for his research. In the few moments before I could object, her vital signs went from critical to dead. The anesthesiologist began administering lifesaving drugs, and the surgical team put on a full-court press, but their efforts to save the child's life were in vain. It was completely reckless of him."

Yoshi squeezed her hand.

"I was even more outraged when he ducked responsibility. He had the audacity to direct me to inform her parents." The pent-up emotions came pouring out. "I calmed myself and went out to the waiting room to deliver the bad news. The parents were sitting in the corner, huddled next to each other. A priest was sitting on a chair facing them. Their heads were bowed in prayer, and I stood there for the longest time, silently fuming, before they finished and noticed me."

Rene took a drink of her tea. A knot in her gut relaxed as she released feelings that had been bottled up for so long.

"They didn't blame God for not answering their prayers," she continued. "They blamed me. I had to endure a barrage of verbal abuse that I didn't deserve. I struggled to stay professional, even though I silently agreed that the surgeon had made mistakes."

"How awful for you." Yoshi held her hands tightly.

"The parents had given him authority," she continued, unable to stop the torrent of grief from pouring out, "but it was obvious to me that she was far too vulnerable for his procedure. I think she died because he went too far, all to further his own career. It was horrible, it was unethical, it was immoral. I will never again trust Dr. Stau—" She stopped in her tracks.

A stony look of realization replaced Yoshi's kind expression. He hadn't missed the crucial point. "Dr. Stauss," he finished for her.

"Oh, damn. Look, I've said way more than I should. I need to go." Rene got up abruptly, embarrassed for letting down her guard. "I've really overstepped. Please forget what I said."

She rushed out of the coffeehouse, leaving both her muffin and her conversation with Yoshi unfinished.

CHAPTER 26

Sitting at the table in the foundation's break room, Rene absently watched a plume of tea steep into the water of her glass pot as her thoughts drifted to her emotional talk with Yoshi the previous day.

Pouring out the details about Marcella's death left her feeling lighter. Rob hadn't been interested in the dynamics of her workplace, and lacking a willing and appropriate confidant, she'd held her anger inside for months. Yoshi's warmth had caught her by surprise as the emotional pressure broke through the dam of her reticence.

She closed her eyes and replayed the conversation in her mind. There was something about how he spoke of his Witness experience that had stayed with her. Yoshi's eyes, his face, his choice of words, all reminded her of Gramps when he had talked about feeling awed in church. The two men couldn't be more different. Gramps had been a boisterous extrovert. Yoshi was reserved and soft-spoken. Yet they both emanated the same joy as they spoke of their spiritual experiences. Her intuition told her there was something meaningful in that insight, but the significance remained elusive.

After a few moments, she shifted her attention to the task at hand. Kristen wasn't unlike other parents she'd counseled about treatment plans for their injured children. In previous situations, she'd describe the pros and cons of available alternatives and, only if asked, would offer her recommendation.

But there was nothing familiar about this encounter. For the first time in her career, Rene wouldn't be a neutral advisor discussing options with a desperate parent. Rather, her mission was to advocate for one procedure and only one procedure: Rene's very own Witness Project.

There was such potential for the Witness to transform Kyle's life. Yet if Kristen agreed, Rene would also benefit directly; positive results with someone in the boy's rare condition would advance her own research and give her a chance at the Kavli nomination.

The situation posed a clear conflict of interest that left her deeply unsettled. She vowed to tread very carefully and keep Kyle's well-being at the forefront of her every decision.

Pulling the tea strainer out of the pot, she placed it on the tray along with the glass cups and carried them into her office, lost in thought.

Rene's reverie was soon broken by the doorbell. She walked to the entrance and offered Kristen her hand. "It's good to see you again," she said, smiling up at the tired-looking woman, who stood a good four inches taller than her.

"And you," Kristen replied, looking around curiously as she entered the sparsely furnished reception area.

Kristen, as one might expect, looked every bit the attorney dressed for court. Rene was momentarily off-balance as she compared her slacks and casual sweater to the other woman's attire. But this was Rene's home turf, and she quickly regained her confidence.

"How about a tour on the way to my office?" Rene walked into room 1, prepared to repeat the detailed explanation she'd given Owen several weeks ago.

Kristen's stiff bearing signaled discomfort, however, as she stopped in the doorway, taking in the recliners, the computer, and the array of medical equipment in a single swift glance. "This setup looks like something out of a Frankenstein movie," she said. "Hooking up to all these electronics and then zapping your brain? Just the thought makes my skin crawl." Her face went pale, and she quickly stepped back into the hallway.

"Then how about we just sit in my office and talk?" Rene amended. With a sense of foreboding, she ditched the rest of the tour and escorted her to her office.

Kristen settled in one of the overstuffed armchairs and accepted the cup of tea that Rene offered. She took a moment to center herself as Kristen got situated. The visit had gotten off to an awkward start, and she needed to regroup. "I understand you want to talk about the techniques we're developing and how they might be useful in Kyle's situation," Rene said. "Where would you like to start?"

Rene saw the deep worry lines on Kristen's face and the dark circles lurking under her eyes and warmed in sympathy.

"Owen and Yoshi urged me to meet with you. They speak

highly of you and your work." She sent Rene a piercing look. "But I need to form my own opinions."

"Of course," Rene said.

"Owen says that he and Yoshi had some kind of conversation in their minds without actually talking?"

"Yes. Sounds unbelievable, doesn't it?"

"It sure does." Kristen's eyes narrowed. "It sounds like a circus act, frankly."

Rene was determined not to get defensive. "Well, what they experienced wasn't magic, nor smoke and mirrors. This phenomenon falls completely within the laws of biology and physics. It's just that we don't fully understand those laws yet," she said, adding what she hoped was a confident smile.

"Look, I'm an attorney, not a scientist. I'm not interested in getting into the weeds about experimental medical procedures." Kristen's face remained rigid, suspicious. "I just need to hear the layperson's version."

"Of course." It was a challenging request, given the highly abstract nature of the science that made the Witness possible. "I'll do my best, but let me emphasize that there's still much we don't know."

Rene looked over at the vase of roses on her desk to calm herself. Everything depended on the next few minutes. "Bear with me for a minute while I suggest an analogy that seems to describe our limited data." She leaned forward, warming to her subject. "You've heard that old saying that every snowflake is unique?"

"Yes . . . ?" Kristen blinked, looking puzzled.

"It's true, they're all unique," Rene continued, "but when snowflakes melt, the drops of water they form are indistinguishable from each other. In fact, they easily merge to become larger drops—a pool, lake, or ocean. Right?" She paused, checking to ensure her guest was following along.

Kristen inclined her head, but her eyes had narrowed again.

"In a similar way"—Rene picked up where she'd left off— "we're all unique. We could say that each of us is our own snowflake of consciousness—but our individual snowflakes can also melt back into a larger ocean of universal consciousness. That's what I call the Witness."

Kristen stared at her without speaking, so Rene kept going.

"This technique brings our personal snowflake a bit closer to the 'melting point,' if you will, allowing us to share our consciousness with others." Rene stopped to see if her analogy was making sense to her guest.

"So that's what happened with Owen and Yoshi? The technology allowed their consciousnesses to . . . melt . . . together?"

"You could say that, yes."

"That sounds dangerous. Couldn't it change their brains? Turn them into freaks?"

The woman's fear was palpable, and Rene hurried to correct her misconceptions. "No, this ultrasound technology has been safely used for years; I'm just applying it in a new way."

"Huh."

Rene plunged on. "My hypothesis is that our process takes advantage of unique properties of the atoms in one brain and allows them to interact with atoms from another brain without being in direct contact. It may be related to the phenomenon of quantum entanglement."

Her guest scowled. "You're getting too far into the weeds, Doctor."

"Sorry."

The mother's eyes pinched to pinpoint intensity. "So what's the bottom line when it comes to Kyle?"

Rene held Kristen's gaze. "Based on Owen's and Yoshi's reports, as well as my other successful experiments, I believe it's possible to open a direct channel of communication with Kyle," she offered. She left it at that, short and sweet.

"I've heard promises from doctors before," Kristen said as her face clouded. "I've had my hopes dashed more than once."

Rene struggled to find the right approach. "I'm definitely not making any promises, Ms. Nichols," she said quietly. "All I can say is that I'm very optimistic about the possibility of helping Kyle express himself."

Kristen gazed out the window and off into the distance. Her shoulders slumped; her face seemed older. Rene waited silently.

Finally, Kristen sighed loudly and returned her attention to Rene. "Dr. Elder, here's an analogy of my own. Kyle is being held indefinitely in solitary confinement in a maximum-security prison, tormented every second by an inescapable life sentence with LIS." Her face contorted into a grimace. "I'm the warden who can keep him confined or free him from this sentence." Her jaw was set, her voice defiant. "I'm not about to add another element of torture."

Rene swallowed hard and leaned toward the woman. "I believe that this approach might actually help you relieve his torture," she said, matching Kristen's urgent tone.

"Look, I'm sure you're sincere," the boy's mother said, a new note of cynicism coloring her tone. "But you also stand to benefit from having someone like Kyle test out your new ideas."

Rene sat back in her chair. Kristen had posed a fair question: Was she going too far in encouraging Kyle's mother to try the Witness with her disabled son? Was she in danger of making the same mistake for which she had so criticized Stauss—putting her research above the needs of the patient?

No. The tendril of doubt quickly wilted. In contrast to Dr. Stauss's methods, her techniques could cause no physical harm—doctors had safely used TCUs for years. It might turn out that they couldn't communicate with Kyle, but they wouldn't hurt him by trying.

Her confidence held firm as she scooted forward to the edge of her chair, once again leaning closer to Kristen. "Ms. Nichols, every new breakthrough in medicine requires that some people be the first to try something, not for themselves, but for what researchers might learn to help others in similar circumstances." Her voice filled with passion. This was her mission in life. "There are literally thousands of people suffering from various brain injuries and diseases who could benefit from the outcomes of this research. Someone has to go first."

Kristen went rigid.

Rene instantly regretted her approach. Of course the boy's mother would focus on the well-being of her own child, not on some abstract appeal to the greater good. She sat back in her chair, realizing she'd made a misstep.

This time, Kristen was the one who leaned forward. "Let me tell you something, Dr. Elder," she said, her voice strained. "A few years ago, I supported a dear friend with terminal cancer. Kimi was so desperate to survive that she subjected herself to a clinical trial that gave her an experimental drug with horrible side effects. Ultimately, Kimi said she'd made a huge mistake by letting herself be a guinea pig." She sat up ramrod straight, her face tight. "Her regrets haunt me, now more than ever."

Rene didn't shy away from Kristen's gaze as she absorbed the outpouring. It was the story of profound disappointment that she'd heard from many other patients as their options ran out.

"Failed clinical trials are terribly hard on everyone."

"I learned from my grandmother about coming to terms with death. She told me that death can bring great peace. And if you hold on too tightly, life itself can become unbearable."

"It's not my intent to pressure you into something that's not right for you and your family. I respect whatever decision you make." Rene spoke gently, her gaze still locked with Kristen's. Reaching out, she squeezed the other woman's hand.

Kristen squeezed back as tears began to leak from her eyes. They were just two women sitting together, talking about the most important things of all—life and death.

They sat quietly for a few moments. Kristen's emotions had been all over the map. What would come next?

"Give me a minute, OK?" Kristen finally asked in a quavering voice. "Could I have more tea?"

"Of course." Rene rose and went to the break room, where she slow-walked the preparations of a fresh pot. Kristen had just revealed the beliefs that governed all her decisions about Kyle: the importance of avoiding suffering, the willingness to accept, even welcome, death. Rene's hope for helping Kyle battled with her empathy for the woman sitting in her office.

"Thanks for sharing all that," Rene offered as she returned and gave a steaming mug back to Kristen.

"I'm embarrassed I got so emotional. I didn't mean to unload on you," Kristen said, stuffing a crumpled tissue into her purse.

"Please, don't apologize. Now I have a better understanding of where you're coming from."

Kristen set the cup down on the end table without taking a sip. She closed her purse with a snap. "When all is said and done, Dr. Elder, despite all your assurances, I still have a visceral revulsion to anyone experimenting on my son's brain." She was the most composed she'd been since arriving.

Rene tried not to let her disappointment show on her face. Kristen was preparing to leave, and the chance to help Kyle was evaporating. It was a letdown, but she had one more idea. "Ms. Nichols, if I may, there's something else I could offer that might affect your decision." Rene held herself still, waiting for Kristen to give her permission to continue.

Kyle's mother gave the slightest of nods.

It was a long shot, but Rene decided to try. "A direct experience with the Witness would inform your decision more than anything I can ever say. You could know for yourself what it's like to communicate through your thoughts." Rene smiled with confidence. "I'd be happy to set up a session for you whenever it's convenient. Owen could be your partner and guide you through it."

"Thanks, but no thanks, Dr. Elder," Kristen said, rising to her feet and starting toward the office door. "Bottom line, I don't want to be a guinea pig either. Honestly, I get freaked out at the idea of triggering a meltdown of my consciousness." She threw her scarf over her shoulder before leaving the room. "I want to keep my mind solid and intact, just the way it is."

With that, she was halfway to the exit before Rene could get up to see her out.

—

It was early Friday evening. Before settling in to watch the Mariners game, Owen called Kristen to find out about her meeting with Rene. As he learned the details of their discussion, her stubborn refusal to try the Witness with Kyle filled him with frustration.

"I wish you'd stop badgering me about this," Kristen said after she made her reactions clear to him. "I said I'd meet with Dr. Elder, and I did. But one look at all the equipment in her lab gave me the heebie-jeebies. When she offered to let me try it myself, I couldn't get out of there fast enough."

"If you don't believe me when I say it's safe, and you don't believe Dr. Elder, then who would you believe?" Owen asked, trying to keep his voice calm.

"Owen, the only doctor I trust at this moment is Dr. Stauss," she said firmly. "He saved Kyle."

"So if Dr. Stauss agreed to try the Witness with Kyle, then you'd go along with it?"

"If Dr. Stauss gave me the green light, I'd be willing to consider it further. Consider it, not agree to it."

Owen waited a beat. "OK, then. We're meeting with him for a patient conference on Monday. How about if I bring it up then?"

"You're driving me crazy with this, Owen." Kristen huffed. "If I agree to this and Dr. Stauss doesn't approve of her technique, will you promise not to bring it up again?"

Owen paused for a moment to consider. Dr. Stauss's approval was his last hope to get Kristen on board with the Witness. If he was opposed, that was the end of the line, and further discussion wouldn't change anything. He had nothing to lose. "I promise."

"Seriously? You'll drop this?"

"I said I promise. But, if Dr. Stauss does support it, then you have to promise to try the Witness with Kyle. Deal?"

"OK. Whatever. Now I'm going to crash out with a glass of wine and watch reruns of *Dancing with the Stars*. Bye, Owen."

As Kristen disconnected, Owen felt an ember of hope. In light of the NDA, he would have to be extremely careful to only speak in general terms about his own experience, making sure not to say anything to Dr. Stauss about Rene's technology or methods. Still, he recalled from his earlier research that Dr. Stauss and Rene had coauthored a couple of papers together. Surely that indicated a collegial relationship that ought to work in his favor.

Launching his weekend on this hopeful note, Owen grabbed a beer from the fridge and settled back into his armchair to watch the Mariners game with Qwerty.

CHAPTER 27

Not surprisingly, Dr. Stauss's face registered incredulity as Owen described his Witness experience. Still, he didn't expect the doctor's next reactions: a loud guffaw followed by a hearty laugh.

"She's convinced you it's possible to read minds? You've got to be kidding me," Stauss chortled.

Owen frowned. To Kristen, this physician walked on water, so if Stauss gave Elder's work a green light, she said she'd consider it further. If not, then that option was dead once and for all.

"Like I said, I tried it myself, Doctor. I can testify the technique works," Owen said.

"Yes, well, you call it testimony. I call it magical thinking," Stauss said to Owen. "I see it all the time," the physician said, turning to Kristen. "A loved one is so desperate to find a magic cure that they fall into some charlatan's trap and buy their snake oil remedy," he said with a rueful smile, shaking his head.

"Now wait just a minute." Owen's voice rose. "How dare

you suggest that I'm deluded, or that Dr. Elder is a quack. We came here in good faith, expecting you to give us a thoughtful, professional response. I won't be—"

"Owen's got a point," Kristen said to the doctor. "Don't insult my brother or discount his perspective. I met Dr. Elder myself, and I'd hardly call her a snake oil salesman." She gave Stauss a pointed look. "I do hope you have more substantive comments to offer."

Dr. Stauss erased his smirk and adopted a more formal demeanor. "All right then, let me approach this differently," he said. "There are some excellent reasons I won't approve of trying this technique with Kyle, and why you shouldn't spend any more of your precious time on her so-called discoveries."

Owen sat back and tried to hear the man through his rising anger.

"First, I'm familiar with the conceptual framework that underlies Elder's research. After over thirty years studying the brain, I can tell you that her theoretical constructs are total bunk." He jabbed at the air. "Her premise that noninvasive techniques can help patients regain the ability to communicate doesn't hold up to decades of meticulous research."

"She's breaking fresh ground, Doctor," Owen said, desperation rising as the discussion got away from him.

"Owen, let him finish," Kristen said to her brother, giving him a warning look. "Go on, Doctor." Kristen kept her eyes on the man she credited with saving her son's life.

Owen bit his cheek to keep from intervening again.

"Elder coauthored a couple of papers with me, but no one

in the scientific community has yet replicated her more radical approach. That alone should give you pause."

"I suppose." Kristen slowly agreed.

"A crucial part of her support comes from the Columbia River Institute for Neurological Research," Stauss said, continuing his litany of objections. "You may not know that CRINR recently suspended that assistance; a lawsuit filed by a volunteer alleges she suffered serious harm from participating in one of Elder's experiments." He paused and stared directly at Owen. "Wait till I tell Director Ainsworth what utter nonsense she's been up to," Stauss added with a bitter laugh.

Owen squirmed. This allegation was news. Was Rene keeping something from him? "You just told us that she worked through a private foundation, so how do you know about this supposed lawsuit?"

"Because, Mr. Nichols," Stauss said, with thinly veiled condescension, "she was still an employee of the hospital at the time. I was brought into the discussion because of my role as Dr. Elder's medical director"—he narrowed his eyes and paused for a beat—"before she resigned in disgrace."

"What?" Kristen sounded alarmed.

"She was involved in a surgery in which a severely injured child died." Stauss sat back, looking smug.

"Oh, Owen." Kristen turned to him, looking shocked.

He didn't know what to say. The accusations didn't ring true, but then again, he hadn't known Dr. Elder all that long. He'd check into all these allegations as soon as he could, but for now, he had to defend his own position. "I'd never put Kyle, or anyone, in any unsafe situation," he said, a fiery defiance growing in his belly. "It's not like you've come up with any other alternatives. Dr. Elder is working right here in Portland, and you didn't even tell us about her. Who knows what else you've kept hidden from us."

Stauss glared at Owen, his lips tightly pursed, then turned to Kristen once again. "It may interest you to know that I may soon be restarting a research study of my own that could benefit Kyle. I'm still getting the final clearances from CRINR. I'll keep you posted when that happens if you're interested."

"Now you tell us," Owen said. "Thanks a lot."

"It doesn't matter, Owen," Kristen intervened, sounding peeved. "I'll say it to you both, one more time: I'm opposed to Kyle becoming a guinea pig, even for you, Dr. Stauss. I won't do that to Kyle."

"I understand, Ms. Nichols," Stauss said, backing down quietly.

Owen struggled to think of another line of argument, but Stauss moved on.

"While you're here, Ms. Nichols, I need to revisit a difficult discussion we had some time ago. Within a week or so, Kyle's recovery from the pneumonia should be sufficient for him to safely transfer back to Rockridge. I do need to let you know that you are once again coming up against a deadline for moving Kyle back to long-term care." Stauss paused. "Unless, of course, this time you select the option of a gentle death by ending his life support."

"Oh, shit," Owen groaned.

Kristen rose brusquely. "As a matter of fact, that option is very much on my mind, Doctor," she said, her voice quavering.

"I'll decide soon. Thanks for your input. Come on, Owen, we've taken up enough of his time."

As they walked toward the elevator, Kristen turned to him. "Well, I think we learned a thing or two about your Dr. Elder, wouldn't you say? I liked the woman, but she's certainly not the miracle worker you thought she was."

Owen clenched his jaw and stayed silent. He needed to have a hard conversation with Dr. Elder—and soon.

CHAPTER 28

"That's not at all what happened according to what Rene shared with me," Yoshi said emphatically when Owen reported that Stauss said that Rene had resigned in disgrace. The two men sat in a popular Pearl District coffeehouse the morning after Owen and Kristen met with Stauss. "But she told me the details in confidence."

"Stauss said some really harsh things," Owen said. "I need to meet with her as soon as possible and sort all this out."

Yoshi smiled at him expectantly.

"Want to join?" Owen asked.

"You bet." His friend blushed.

"You've got a thing for her, don't you?" Owen grinned.

"It shows?" Yoshi, always a bit shy, seemed embarrassed.

"I picked up a bit of a vibe from you the evening we did the Witness." Owen reached over and playfully hit Yoshi on the arm.

"She's pretty amazing, I think. I'm getting mixed signals, though." Yoshi sounded a little discouraged. "She was kind of distant when we met, at least at first. Then she gradually told me what happened at the hospital."

"Sounds like she felt safe talking to you." Owen had always found Dr. Elder to be strictly professional, so she must have been quite comfortable if she opened up to Yoshi.

"Maybe, but right after that, she kind of freaked and left all of a sudden. I think she might have said more than she intended." Yoshi sounded serious, then perked up. "Still, I haven't been this drawn to anyone in a long time."

Owen smiled at his best friend. Nothing would please him more than seeing Yoshi have a chance at another relationship. Still, at the moment, he had a serious agenda and needed to change the subject. "I'll call Dr. Elder and see how soon we can get together. I want to get this crap from Dr. Stauss straightened out as soon as possible."

"You told Stauss *what*?"

Rene had been about to leave home for work when Owen called and explained his need for an emergency meeting. She'd immediately changed her plans and was sitting with him and Yoshi in the coffeehouse.

"How dare you." Rene slammed her fist down on the table, rattling the cups on their saucers. "You signed an NDA." The couple at the next table looked over at her.

"I didn't reveal anything specific about your technology. I only told him the basics about my personal experience. Besides, he's Kyle's doctor. Everything I said is covered by doctor-patient confidentiality, right?"

"Everything about Kyle is covered, because he's the

patient," she fumed, "but not anything about you and not my research."

"I assumed that since you worked with Dr. Stauss at the hospital, you were trusted colleagues . . ."

"Well, you assumed wrong. He's absolutely the last person I would tell about the Witness," she said with a snort. No telling what Stauss would do with this information.

Owen seemed to shrink in size. "Jeez, I didn't realize. I was so focused on finding a way to persuade Kristen—"

Rene glared at him. His intentions may have been good, but he'd put her entire project at risk. She rubbed her hand across her face, trying to move on. "So what else happened? Go on, get it all out."

"He spouted all kinds of allegations."

"Such as?"

"Here's the big one: he said you allowed a child to die on the operating room table, and then you resigned in disgrace."

"*What?* That asshole." She ran her hands through her hair. "He's going way out on a limb making false allegations like that. Did he happen to name the surgeon, the one who made the decision that led directly to the girl's death?"

"Uh, no, but he implied it was you."

She addressed Owen with absolute conviction. "No, it wasn't me. It was Stauss himself. I was observing a difficult surgery; he made the decision."

Yoshi nodded, having heard this revelation a few days earlier.

"Seriously?" A look of astonishment took over Owen's face. "It was *his* fault? He gave us the distinct impression that you were to blame for the girl's death."

"No way." Her blood was boiling. "My interview with the

hospital administration nailed Dr. Stauss's poor judgment. I was cleared of any wrongdoing. It's Dr. Stauss who's in deep trouble. CRINR put his research on hold until the investigation is concluded." She paused for emphasis. "He's clearly trying to get even with me for calling out his actions in the first place."

"I can't believe he's allowed to keep practicing after something like that." Owen almost knocked over his cup. "I mean, he was on Kyle's case from the beginning. What if he'd . . ."

"No, Owen, don't go there." She had to give credit where credit was due. "Dr. Stauss is genuinely excellent at patient care, and he's done right by Kyle. I'd have said something immediately if I believed otherwise." She let that sink in. "But his ambition about his research gets the best of him. Plus, he's got deep connections in the hospital administration, and they approach someone with his reputation with kid gloves."

"Speaking of that, he said he'd let us know when he was able to restart his own research," Owen said. "He implied that it was a bureaucratic holdup, not an investigation."

"You're kidding. He told you about his own research?" A fresh wave of outrage flooded through her. "Dr. Ainsworth expressly forbade him from even mentioning it to any prospective patients." Ainsworth wouldn't be happy about this; it might be a small point of leverage she could use against Stauss if she needed it.

"What can I say? Kristen didn't bite on his offer, thank goodness." Owen fiddled with the zipper on his jacket. "I hate to say it, but he said something else that didn't sound right either."

It was best if Owen got everything out on the table, once and for all. "Go ahead, just spill it."

Owen squirmed in his chair. "He said there was a lawsuit against you, from someone who had a bad reaction to participating in an experiment."

"That *bastard.*" She got another annoyed look from the nearby table. Stauss had obviously used his meeting with Kristen and Owen to do as much damage to her reputation as possible. "There has been a *complaint,* yes. But the claims are spurious. The IRB and the legal department are investigating." How dare Stauss characterize it as a lawsuit. "I didn't tell you about it because it's supposed to remain confidential."

"Stauss's insinuations hit Kristen really hard." Owen sighed. "By tarnishing your reputation in her eyes, he destroyed our last hope of working with Kyle."

"I understand why it would sound bad to her, especially with the way Stauss spun things." Rene was reaching the end of her rope. *Please let there be an end to this barrage of revelations.*

"Rene, you don't have to defend yourself to us." Yoshi spoke up for the first time, his voice calm. "We've experienced the quality of your work firsthand."

"Thanks, Yoshi." Rene shot him a grateful look. "But I can't believe he said all those things just to sabotage my credibility with Kristen."

"Sounds like he's out to get you." Owen looked down again. "He threatened to tell the director of CRINR."

Oh, no, no, no. "Dr. Ainsworth? He said he was going to tell Ainsworth?" A jolt of panic shot through her.

"I think that was the name, yeah."

"Damn it." Rene's eyes shot darts at Owen. "Stauss and I have research projects that are in direct competition for CRINR's

support." Rene struggled to hold her anger in check. "You should have talked with me before sharing anything at all about the Witness with Stauss." This could backfire on her big-time.

"I never thought there would be so much backstabbing in a hospital," Yoshi said.

"Medical research is intensely competitive." Filled with anger, Rene had to force herself to speak less emotionally. "Dr. Stauss is nearing the end of his career, and his current research is the capstone to all his work. He sees my approach as an assault on his reputation because I'm breaking ground in new areas that he's never even considered." She paused. "My Witness breakthrough is likely to overshadow all his contributions to the field. It's no wonder he's targeted me."

"God, I'm so sorry, Rene. I really blew it by talking with him." Owen fiddled with his zipper again.

Rene shook her head curtly, not ready to forgive him.

"So now what?" Yoshi asked quietly into the silence.

"The least I can do is have another talk with Kristen and clear up the crap Stauss fed her," Owen said. "She needs to know how badly he lied and misrepresented your work to us."

Rene shook her head. "Stauss is never going to let you try the Witness while Kyle is still in the hospital."

"Maybe not, but when Kristen realizes how Stauss tried to play us," Owen said, "maybe she'll reconsider. If I can get her on board, we'll have some genuine leverage over him." Owen stood. "I'll keep you posted."

Rene stared into the remains of her tea, still too angry to meet his eyes.

"Owen screwed up big-time, huh?" Yoshi asked after Owen left the building.

"I'll say," she said, shaking her head. "Look, I get how important this is to him, of course. It's just . . . well, never mind that right now," she said, sighing as they stood.

She put on her jacket. "Look, I want to apologize for rushing out the other day." She met Yoshi's eyes. His smile was kind. "I guess I was embarrassed by everything I said. I didn't mean to unload on you."

"No worries, Rene. That's what friends are for." Yoshi reached out and touched her lightly on the arm.

There was a light in his eyes, and the warmth of his hand shot through her. Flustered once again, she gave him a quick nod and walked out the door without another word.

Rene drove from the coffeehouse to the foundation. She walked down the hall toward her office, deeply worried about Stauss's comments. If her adversary repeated what Owen had revealed to Dr. Ainsworth, he'd undoubtedly spin it in the worst possible way.

As she walked by her intern's office, Aisha called her over. "That woman from CRINR's IT department is here. She and her assistant are working in the data center."

"What? Mai Cheng? I wasn't expecting her today. Did she say what's up?"

"No. She did the MDAP installation, so I assumed it was OK to let her in. She said it was important. Is there a problem?"

"Not that I know of, but I'll find out." It had been five weeks since Mai had overseen the installation of the software, and she'd never once arrived without an appointment. Rene hurried down the hall, an uneasy feeling nagging in her gut. Startled, she found Mai's assistant hunched over her computer in the data center.

"Hey there, what's up?" she asked, annoyed. She hadn't been notified of software maintenance.

"Um, just cleaning up your hard drive, ma'am. We just finished the uninstall," the fellow mumbled as he quickly flashed an ID badge and continued working at her keyboard.

"Uninstall? What the hell are you talking about?" Something was very wrong here. The techie remained silent but continued to work, fingers flying over the keyboard.

"What the hell are you doing with my files?" Rene could see him moving files to a flash drive he'd inserted. "Stop working," she demanded. "I need to approve what you're doing."

The young man ignored her and continued to type.

Rene was reaching to grab his flash drive and pull it out of her computer when Mai walked in.

"What's going on, Mai? You need to tell this fellow to stop whatever he's doing while you explain." Rene was boiling mad, her face flushed, her hands trembling.

"Sorry, Dr. Elder. We got an urgent directive from Dr. Ainsworth's office to uninstall the MDAP software immediately and transfer any related files," she said, shrugging her shoulders. "I'm sorry if no one notified you, but that's not my job."

"You've broken into my computer system and are accessing my files without my permission. That's not acceptable." Rene was ready to call the police.

"Dr. Elder, there's fine print in the license you were granted that says access could be revoked at any time at the discretion of CRINR. We were sent here to remove the application," Mai said brusquely.

"Revoke the license? Why?" Rene feared a link between Owen's meeting and Stauss talking with Ainsworth.

"No idea. Sorry." Mai averted her eyes as the young tech pulled the flash drive out of the computer. Rene should have moved faster and pulled it out first.

"I'm done here." He rose and moved toward the door.

"Good, I've finished deleting the program from the server. We're good to go." Mai headed out the door. "Sorry."

For a moment, Rene just stood there, stunned. Then she sprang into action. She wouldn't allow this setback to stand.

CHAPTER 29

After leaving Rene and Yoshi at the coffeehouse, Owen sat in his car for a few moments, making plans. His priority was to connect with Kristen and correct the numerous distortions that Stauss had used to persuade her not to trust Rene or attempt the Witness with Kyle.

He texted his sister to ask where and when they could meet. Kristen replied that she wasn't required in court that day, so she was taking the afternoon off. She suggested they meet up at the hospital.

True to the doctor's word, Kyle had been moved back to the neurology floor. Owen found Kristen helping Lorena change the boy's position in bed, a regular requirement to prevent bedsores.

He nodded to the nursing supervisor, once again impressed by the accomplished ease with which she maneuvered Kyle's inert body without tangling the various tubes that sustained him.

Lorena looked up as she finished. "Good to see you again, Mr. Nichols. Sorry about the circumstances."

"Thanks once again, Lorena," he responded, smiling.

Kristen greeted him with a quick nod.

Owen walked over to Kyle's bedside. "Hey, dude."

"I'm surprised you had time to come over this afternoon," Kristen said to her brother as she combed the boy's hair, her gaze loving.

A fresh stab of anguish hit him at the tenderness with which she touched her only child. He refocused on his mission. "Well, there's a Mariners game on soon, and it'd be fun to listen to it with Kyle. The pregame is already on," he said, addressing the boy. "How about if I get that started, and then your mom and I can talk for a minute."

Kristen gave him a quizzical look as he picked up the remote and found the channel.

They settled in a private corner of the waiting room. Owen relayed that he'd met with Rene, and she'd countered every negative thing Stauss had said about her.

She sat rigid, her fists balled up. "Owen, I'm absolutely sick and tired of talking about this Witness thing. You promised you'd drop this if Dr. Stauss didn't approve."

He persisted, needing Kristen to hear the details. "I know, I know. You're relying on Stauss's input to debunk the Witness," he said, "but it turns out everything he said about Dr. Elder is untrue." She gave him a stony look, but he plunged on. "Stauss implied that Rene let a child die on the operating room table. That's simply false. *Stauss* was the doctor in charge." He leaned forward and let his words sink in. "It was *his* decision that led to her death." His eyes bored into Kristen's, willing her to understand. "Rene spoke out against him, and they cleared her. They suspended Dr. Stauss's research as a direct result."

"So? Dr. Elder's research is also facing a legal challenge."

"That's not true either," he said, an edge in his voice. "But in any case, no one has died from Dr. Elder's work, unlike Stauss's research."

"At this point, I don't trust either of them when it comes down to their pet projects." Kristen brushed away his update with a wave of her hand. "It sounds like they've both hidden information about the risks of their procedures. I'm done with their backroom politics."

"What does that mean?" he asked warily.

"Don't you get it? Both Dr. Elder and Dr. Stauss each have a vested interest in getting me to agree to their special experimental procedure," she said, her eyes narrowed. "They're both trying to further their own research agendas. Maybe some people are willing to put their loved one through that, but I'm not."

Owen started to sweat. "But Dr. Elder's Witness procedure is noninvasive, so it's much safer than what Stauss is proposing," he sputtered. "And I've tried it, for God's sake. Yoshi and I were the guinea pigs to make sure it was safe for Kyle."

"Honestly, I think you two were foolish to take such a chance with your brains." She wagged her finger at him. "You might be injured in ways you haven't noticed yet. You might have even sustained long-term damage that won't turn up for a while. Why?" She pounded her fist against the arm of the chair. "Because you're both healthy," she said, her voice rising, "but Kyle is not—that's the crux of it. His brain is severely damaged.

Trying the Witness with Kyle might cause him additional harm, and we wouldn't even know it." Her arms and hands went limp against her sides and her body sagged back into the chair.

Owen took her hand, squeezing tightly.

"This bout with pneumonia has changed my thinking," she continued, her eyes pleading for understanding. "The doctor says he's more vulnerable than we had realized; he could face another incident at any time." Her face crumpled, and she wiped at her eyes. "That just adds exponentially to the torture he already faces every single day. And the fact that he had to go back into the ICU after such a short time at Rockridge? That definitely doesn't fit my definition of 'quality of life.'" Her face went pale as a tear rolled down her cheek.

Owen slumped as the conversation slipped away. A pit of despair grew in his belly.

Kristen paused. "I can't tell you how hard it's been to see Kyle's body slowly deteriorate, to never see another movement, even another blink." Her voice was reedy from the strain. She wiped away a tear with the back of her hand. "But this is not about my grief. This is about Kyle."

Owen was desperate to console her. It was taking every last bit of courage she had to make this decision.

"I remember that last afternoon I spent with Nana . . . when she told me that she was ready to die," she said after regaining a bit of composure. "She wasn't afraid, and she didn't want me to be afraid either. And Mom had the courage to help her."

Owen bit his cheek, trying to be a good listener.

"Later, I remember being there with Nana's body," Kristen continued. "I was completely at peace after her death." She gulped back a quiet sob. "All that keeps coming back to me when I think about Kyle."

"I don't think the situations are comparable," Owen countered softly, knowing this would be his last chance to persuade her but not wanting to press too hard. "I worry that making this decision for Kyle is something you will come to regret."

"The only way for me to live without regret is to learn from the past. Mom is guiding me."

"Nana made a conscious decision and was able to ask Mom to help. Kyle is conscious too, so he could tell us if he wants to live—or die—he just doesn't have a way to tell us right now." He spoke as gently as he could. "But if you move him back to Rockridge and try the Witness, then he can tell us."

He silently begged her to give the boy that chance.

"What you're suggesting is a catch-22," she said as her logical mind surfaced. "In order to use the Witness to find out what Kyle wants, he needs to be living in Rockridge Place, because Dr. Stauss refuses to allow it while he's in the hospital. But even if I found out he wants to die, I wouldn't be able to fulfill his choice, because Dr. Guramurthy won't participate in ending a patient's life support. So moving him back to Rockridge Place resolves nothing."

She held his eyes, almost daring him to contradict her.

He had to concede the logic of her analysis. "But we might find out that he wants to live," he countered softly.

It was Kristen's turn to look kindly at her brother. "I think when it comes down to it," she said quietly, "you're banking on Kyle wanting to live, aren't you? Because you'll miss him so very much."

Something inside him crumbled. "Yes! Damn it, yes! Of

course, I want him to live. I need him to live. What's so wrong about that?"

"I have to decide based on what Kyle would want, not on what you want." She turned steely.

"Just because I want him to live doesn't mean my judgment is wrong. I just happen to think Kyle wants to live as much as I want him to, especially if he can use the Witness to communicate with us."

Owen bit his lip, regretful that this had turned into an argument.

"I don't know, Owen. Sometimes you act like my understanding big brother." She reached over and took his hand. "Other times you're just another guy mansplaining why I should buy into Dr. Elder's supposed discovery."

He inhaled sharply. "Well, I hope you can understand why I haven't been totally neutral," he said, pulling his hands away. "Kyle's just so important to me."

She nodded. "You must know that I don't want to let him go—I don't—but I also don't want him to live in unrelenting torture. Mom's my role model," she said, speaking with resolve. "It's time for me to give Kyle the greatest gift of all and let him go."

Owen's heart sank. There was no shaking his sister's belief that granting Kyle a gentle death was the ultimate act of her love. The absolute sincerity of her conviction did nothing to ease his pain.

"I'm sorry, Owen. It's the loneliest decision I've ever had to make," she said, her voice shaking. "But my deepest intuition tells me I know it to be right."

Her eyes withered the last shred of hope within him. He couldn't find the words to respond.

She looked at him sadly. "I guess I'm just not your baby sister anymore, Owen," she said. "Ever since Mom and Dad died, you've been my anchor. You were my guardian, you supported me through pregnancy, you agreed to be Kyle's male role model. You counseled me on every big decision. You nurtured me, provided safety, stability."

He nodded. She'd leaned heavily on him, especially when things got tough. He'd willingly surrendered a lot of his own freedom to sustain her over the years.

"But not this time."

He gulped.

"This time, we just can't find common ground about what's best for Kyle, and I have to go my own way."

"Are you breaking up with me?" he asked, trying a wry smile but not really joking.

She didn't return his smile. "I guess you could say that. Yes."

He went cold as his world shifted. He'd prioritized her needs for nearly two decades. Nurturing her and Kyle was his primary purpose in life. Shaken, his throat was tight as he met her determined gaze. There was nothing to do about it now, things had gone too far. "So be it," he said with a heavy sigh.

"The hospital plans to move Kyle back to long-term care tomorrow afternoon," she said. "I have to act quickly—I've talked with Dr. Stauss." She closed her eyes and took a few deep breaths. "He's kept the ethics department informed all along, and they've given their approval. So I've arranged—" Her voice broke. "I scheduled the appointment with Dr. Stauss—for nine tomorrow morning."

His throat tightened, and he barely maintained his

composure. He didn't want to make it worse for her, though his own grief threatened to spill out.

"I want us to get there about eight so we can have some time with him—you know—before—" Kristen stopped. She didn't need to finish.

He reached out of his misery to take her hand.

"I've never felt a pain like this before, Owen." She took another series of deep breaths. He was afraid she would hyperventilate. "When I go back into his room now, I'm going to tell him, so he has time to prepare himself."

His throat was painfully tight. Kyle was trapped, unable to respond to his mother's announcement of his death sentence. Would the boy feel complete relief or abject terror? They would never know.

"Please say you'll be there tomorrow, Owen." She met his eyes with a pleading look he'd never before seen. "He would want you there, you know. And I need to have you there too."

A chill went through Owen's body. He clamped his jaw shut to maintain his composure. He needed to stay steady for now, for Kristen, but there would be no holding back the dread once he was alone. Owen slowly nodded his assent. "Of course I'll be there" was all he could whisper.

They held each other's eyes for a long moment. Leaning forward, she placed her hands on his shoulders and gave him a soft kiss on the cheek. Then she stepped back and walked away, leaving him wondering if he would ever be able to forgive her.

CHAPTER 30

Furious at Mai Cheng's intrusion into her facility to uninstall the MDAP software, Rene drove to the hospital and strode into Dr. Ainsworth's suite.

"I'm sorry, you don't have an appointment, and the director is in a conference," his assistant informed her blandly. "I can schedule something for tomorrow if you'd like."

Rene wouldn't be put off. If Cheng could show up at her office unannounced, then she could do the same to Ainsworth. "Tell the director that he can either interrupt his conference, or I will barge right in and interrupt it for him. Got it?" Rene's blood ran hot, and she made no attempt to hide her outrage.

After a moment's hesitation, the assistant said she'd see what she could do.

Rene had to cool her heels for another ten minutes, but she eventually got entry to Ainsworth's office, where she stood looking down at the dispassionate bureaucrat sitting behind his desk.

"Doctor." Rene had never heard this cold, hard tone of

barely controlled anger escape from her own mouth. "What the fuck is going on?"

"Now, Dr. Elder," Ainsworth began. His dismissive tone further inflamed Rene. He pointed to a chair, but she refused to sit, preferring to loom over his desk.

"Don't you 'now, Dr. Elder' me. Your IT staff raided my facility, deleted the MDAP software, and stole files from my computer." Rene clenched her fists in frustration. "This is absolutely unacceptable."

"We exercised our right to revoke your license after the hospital received a copy of a lawsuit filed by Brenda Harris," he announced with an edge of disdain. He leaned back in his chair, adding some distance between them. "I spoke to you about her complaint once before," he continued. "Well, now she's hired an attorney, and they're seeking damages for the psychological problems she experienced subsequent to your experiment. They're asking for a considerable amount in penalties."

The news shocked her. She remembered that Stauss had told Owen and Kristen about a lawsuit—she'd assumed he'd misspoken, but apparently not. "Seriously? If there's a lawsuit, then why haven't I seen it?"

"She's suing the hospital, not your foundation. They've chosen to go after the deepest pockets."

Curbing her anger, she took a seat in front of his desk. "Look, Dr. Ainsworth," she said, forcing herself to use a more reasonable tone. "Ms. Harris signed all the required consent forms. I even have video that validates the professionalism with which we carried out the experiment. My careful documentation protects the hospital from spurious claims." She spoke with conviction. "And you should have my back," she added ruefully.

"Look, I know you got approval from the Human Subjects Committee," he said, matching her more professional tone. "I know that there's evidence that transcranial ultrasound is physically safe. But there's no way you can guarantee that there was no psychological damage."

It was one thing for Brenda to be upset by the unexpected intrusion of someone else's thoughts into her mind; that was entirely understandable. But that was very different from claiming permanent psychological damage from an experience that lasted but a few brief seconds. "If this young woman is claiming psychological damage," Rene countered, "then it's possible she had psychological problems before she agreed to take part in the study. Besides, she seems highly litigious. Has the legal department done any investigation into her status or motivations?"

When Ainsworth didn't respond, she abruptly realized that no one from the hospital had ever followed up with her about the complaint. "They haven't done anything, have they?" she said, as the truth hit home. "I'm doubting that there was ever any intent to conduct such an investigation."

"Don't go there," Ainsworth said curtly. "The hospital is being targeted and this lawsuit asks for a bundle."

Rene's fury returned full force. "That is the exact reason you should fight it tooth and nail. The hospital is being blackmailed into paying her off with no regard for the reasonableness of her claim or the importance of my research."

"Look," Ainsworth responded, "the bottom line is that Administrator MacKenzie has already reviewed this entire situation and made his decision. The hospital will make a modest payout to this woman rather than take on the expense of defending your work. Your experimental approach is just too far out for them to have confidence that we could win in court."

Rene shook her head in disbelief. "I can't believe he's caving in."

"MacKenzie can't take any chances." The director's eyebrows arched as he glared at her.

"But why remove the MDAP software? The program wasn't even installed when Ms. Harris volunteered. It has nothing to do with her complaint."

"The hospital developed and owns the software. I granted you use of the software under the auspices of CRINR's license," Ainsworth said, "but MacKenzie is distancing the hospital from your research to avoid the possibility of additional untenable legal costs from future lawsuits."

"This just keeps getting more outrageous."

"Just so you know," Ainsworth said, "I was prepared to argue that you keep the MDAP license. But we also received information that you continued your research surreptitiously even after I gave you a directive to suspend use of MDAP during the investigation. Knowing you violated my goodwill, I concurred with MacKenzie's decision to deny you further access."

Livid, Rene came half out of her chair, put her hands on the edge of Ainsworth's desk, and bent toward him. Their faces were but a foot apart. "I swear I haven't used MDAP since we talked." She'd been very careful not to activate MDAP when she'd worked with Owen and Yoshi. "The techies can look at the files and see when I last accessed the program. That's a straightforward way to prove my innocence."

Ainsworth just shook his head.

The connection became clear. "OK, I get it. Stauss got to you and MacKenzie. Again." Rene sat back. This was a disaster of the highest order. Without MDAP, her methodical research plans would slow to a snail's pace for months or years while she worked with a vendor to design what she needed. "How am I supposed to complete a quality case study by CRINR's deadline without this software? It has sophisticated algorithms like no off-the-shelf program."

"I'm afraid that's your problem," Ainsworth said.

So it was as she first suspected. Ainsworth didn't really care if she was able to present a credible case study. Her inclusion in the process was just window dressing to make it look like CRINR wasn't automatically favoring Stauss. "What hypocrisy. First you tell me I'm being considered for the Kavli nomination because my approach is so innovative, then you cripple my efforts at every turn for the same reason."

Ainsworth just stared at her, eyes narrowed, lips pursed.

It was time to go on the offensive. She might have a slim chance of influencing the director, but she had to pull out all the stops to save her work. "Dr. Stauss has a big conflict of interest, wouldn't you say? Look, if you want to know what's actually been going on, you should know that Dr. Stauss offered his research to the family of Kyle Nichols, a patient I'm working with, in direct defiance of your directive." She stood up straight and ticked off her complaints. "He's behaved unprofessionally in numerous ways. He led them to believe that I was responsible for Marcella Lopez's death. He misled them about why I resigned, and he maligned my research efforts."

"Forget Stauss. Let's talk about that research that you say was maligned." Ainsworth leaned forward across his desk. "I understand you've been pitching Ms. Nichols a ridiculous notion about mind reading with her severely disabled son." His voice dripped with disdain. "You dare not make a laughingstock of CRINR by presenting a case study that makes that kind of preposterous claim."

Damn it! Owen had absolutely screwed this up. Ainsworth must have gotten an earful from Stauss after he and Kristen spoke with him. Rene glared at him across his desk.

"Are you saying that the board is officially withdrawing my work from contention for the institute's nomination without even hearing my case study?"

Ainsworth hesitated. "No. The institute's board has no knowledge of the lawsuit or that MacKenzie is severing the relationship with your foundation; those are confidential personnel matters within the hospital."

"I thought not. And you know damn well that if that participant's false claim leaks to the board, I'll have grounds for a defamation lawsuit."

Ainsworth's jaw muscles tightened, but he remained silent.

Rene pushed on. "Admit it: the real reason you're keeping me in contention is because of how it would look to the Kavli judges for the younger, more visionary researcher to get bounced out of consideration without being given a formal review of the experimental results—especially since she's a woman." She stood again, staring down the director. "My techniques may be unorthodox. The results may sound outlandish to you. But my research is meticulous and well documented. The board will be impressed, and you'll rue the day that you undermined my breakthroughs."

"Believe me, you're lucky the hospital isn't countersuing you and your foundation," Ainsworth said. "You might think this is bad, but things could still get so much worse."

Rene stood stock-still as it all became clear. The internal politics, the backstabbing, her own ethical dilemmas, and the potential conflicts of interest. It wasn't who she was, and the price of fame wasn't worth it. "I see. Well, then I'm going to take this opportunity to formally withdraw my work from the competition for the Kavli nomination. I won't allow my goal of helping people regain their voices get mired any further in the muck of this incestuous bureaucracy."

It only took a moment for Rene to walk out and slam the door.

CHAPTER 31

After Kristen left, Owen sat in shock. Kyle's life support would be turned off the next morning. Everything was happening too fast. His grief morphed into panic. He was frantic, desperate to do something, anything, to keep Kyle alive and give him a chance.

His hands shook, his adrenaline ran high. There was yet one more thing he could try. He pushed forward, his nerves sizzling. Vaguely aware that he was acting irrationally, he plunged on recklessly.

Rene sat at her computer, deeply engrossed in a search to identify a qualified software developer to replace the MDAP application.

Her concentration was broken by two people talking in the hallway. Aisha's voice and that of a man approached her office door, which suddenly burst open.

Owen strode in first, with Aisha right on his heels. "Mr. Nichols," Aisha said, "you can't just barge in—"

"Dr. Elder, I need you to help me," Owen said as soon as he crossed the threshold. The man was so disheveled and dispirited that Rene barely recognized him.

Rene motioned to Aisha that she was OK with the interruption. Frowning, Aisha moved back into the doorway, keeping a watchful eye.

Owen's words came out in a torrent. "Kristen's arranged for Kyle's life support to stop tomorrow morning. He's not going to get a chance to tell us what he wants," he said, breathing heavily. "I believe he wants to live, but we'll never know unless I can connect with him through the Witness first." He leaned forward, his fingers gripping the edge of her desk. "You have to help me. Please."

His urgency washed over her; she dared not let it invade her thinking. "Owen. Both Kristen and Dr. Stauss have vetoed it."

"But what if . . ." He hesitated, then blurted, "What if we smuggled your equipment into his room? With your help, it would just take a few minutes for me to connect and find out directly from him what he wants."

Rene tried to keep her voice gentle despite a rising frustration. "I told you from the beginning that I wouldn't go forward without their approvals. Your scheme is totally off the table."

"I trusted you, Rene," he said, leaning over the desk toward her.

Rene stood and glared at him. "It's Dr. Elder, and don't try that on me, Owen. I'm far more torn up about this than I can express. But there's no way in hell I would try a stunt like that."

Owen's face was getting redder by the minute. "How can

you leave me hanging like this? More importantly, how can you abandon Kyle?"

Rene's voice rose a notch, her anger overruling his desperation. "Don't pull a guilt trip here, Owen." Her fist landed with a loud thud on her desk. "Remember, you're the one who violated your NDA. You're directly responsible for my research getting sidelined." Her voice carried a sharp edge. "You screwed me royally. So forget it."

Owen stood stony-faced.

Rene stared back at him, her body rigid.

He glared at her for a few long seconds. Then abruptly, he broke eye contact. His shoulders slumped as he collapsed in the chair that faced her. "I'm so sorry," he said quietly. "I shouldn't take this out on you." He sighed. "It's just that I know you're right—Kristen and Dr. Stauss hold all the cards."

"Yes, they do." She kept her tone even but stern.

"I totally lost it there. I'm so very sorry I tried to railroad you."

Rene slowly nodded, and she returned to her own chair. She glanced at Aisha, still observing the scene from the doorway. "It's OK, Aisha," she said. The younger woman hesitated for a few seconds, then moved down the hall toward her own office.

"I can't bear the thought of Kyle lying there, fully aware of what's about to happen," he continued. "You and I know how to reach him"—his voice broke—"but we can't."

The sad reality of his statement deflated her anger. "It's a tragedy, Owen. There's just no other word for it." She bit her lip. "We were so close," she said softly.

He sat, staring vacantly over her shoulder. Finally, he stood, and she and Humboldt walked with him toward the exit.

"You know this means the end of our work together," he said, turning to face her at the door.

Tears sprung to her eyes. This wasn't the way she wanted things to end. "I hope for the very best for Kyle. And of course, for you and Kristen as well."

Owen reached down and gave Humboldt a last pat on the head.

"Goodbye, Owen," she said to his back as he walked away.

CHAPTER 32

"I can't believe we're about to lose him." Yoshi stood at the patio door, staring out at the dark backyard.

Owen slouched on the couch at his friend's home later that evening. Kristen was exhausted and had asked him to deliver the news to Yoshi and Matt on her behalf. She asked that they both join her at Kyle's bedside the following morning.

"There's got to be another way." Matt was near tears. "I'm not ready to give up."

Owen sighed, weighed down by fresh humiliation from Dr. Elder's rebuke on top of his mountain of grief. "We've reached the end of the line. It's over." Kyle's best friend would have to find his own way through this tragedy.

Yoshi sat and put his arm around his son.

"There has to be something else you can do. It can't be over. You can't just give up on him now," Matt persisted.

"I'm not giving up," Owen shot back. "I've already done

everything I can think of. Besides, what right do you have to tell me if it's over or not?"

"Screw you. Kyle's my oldest friend. You aren't the only one who thinks the Witness will help him. And I don't want to give up."

"Hey, guys. Matt. Owen." Yoshi's tone stopped the others in their tracks. "Chill."

"Sorry," Owen said. "I get it, Matt," he said as gently as he could, "but we have to face the fact that there just aren't any more options."

"If you say so," Matt said. "I'm going over to see him now." His tone was still edgy. "Are you two coming?"

"I can't bear it right now. I don't think I can be there without breaking down," Owen said.

"You go, Matt. You can have some private time with him," Yoshi said.

Owen didn't look up as Matt stormed out of the room, slamming the door as he left the house.

"This is bringing up all his grief about losing his mother," Yoshi said quietly.

Owen hadn't anticipated how the news would pack a double whammy for Yoshi and his son. "I'm sorry. I don't know how to make it any easier."

Yoshi nodded. "I keep trying to hold on to that sense of Oneness we shared with the Witness. It gives me great comfort."

"Thanks, I need that reminder. I'm really spun." Owen paused. "Besides hearing Kristen's decision, I screwed up big-time with Dr. Elder this afternoon."

"Oh? How so?"

"After hearing Kristen's decision, I got this idea that I could convince Dr. Elder to bring her Witness equipment into Kyle's room without anyone knowing. Then we could find out Kyle's wishes for certain and go from there."

"You actually proposed that to her?"

"Yeah, I did. God, this is embarrassing. I stormed into her office unannounced and, well, demanded that she help me." Owen shook his head. "I got really angry when she refused. I said some ugly things."

"Oh, Owen."

"It was awful. I calmed down and apologized, but I still just feel like shit."

"Give yourself a break. You're under tremendous stress."

"Yeah, I guess." Owen stared off into space, then turned to his best friend. "You know, once Kyle is gone, I won't have any reason to stay in touch with her. So we said our goodbyes at the door."

Yoshi's sad expression turned even more crestfallen.

"I'm sorry, Yoshi."

Yoshi was slow to reply. "Well, let's just get through tomorrow, OK?"

Owen nodded and rose to leave. "Yeah. I better get home and try to get my head on straight so I can be strong for Kyle."

Yoshi walked him to the door, where they hugged. "Good night, my brother," Yoshi said as Owen turned to leave.

It was almost ten when Owen walked numbly into his condo. Qwerty greeted him as always, running from another room to circle at his feet. When Owen reached the main level, he stopped and surveyed the dark, empty space, then walked over to the dining room table. He leaned on the back of the chair that directly faced his grandmother's tapestry, once again studying the complexity of her design. He bowed his head and confessed: "My best wasn't good enough this time, Nana."

He turned and entered the kitchen. Pure habit took him to the cupboard where he stored the cat's food. He grabbed a handful of dry food from the bag and dropped it in the cat's dish. No canned salmon treat. No rubs or playing before dinner on this night.

As Qwerty munched, Owen slouched back against the wall, sliding down until he was sitting on the cold tile floor next to the cat. His mind was blank, his emotions heavy.

The morning would mark an ending to Kyle's journey and the beginning of their life without him. Those remaining behind would face repercussions that would ripple long into the future. He fretted that ending Kyle's life support might permanently scar Kristen. How would making such a fateful choice change her?

And what about their relationship? Earlier that day he'd betrayed his beloved sister. "Betrayed." That was the only word for it. He'd plotted to override her decision and try the Witness against her will. Yes, Kristen had "broken up with him" as her caregiver and taken an independent stand, but he had no right to go behind her back to try to nullify her wishes.

He could never tell her of his failed coup, but the secret itself would create a distance between them.

Kristen had forced him to look at the truth: more than anything, he was desperate for Kyle to live. His pursuit of the Witness was driven by his own desperate need for Kyle's survival; his conclusion that Kyle wanted to live was in fact a projection of his own need.

The chance to have an active role in Kyle's life had filled the emptiness from losing his own son so early in Carol's pregnancy. That void in his life reopened, big and menacing. In a few hours, the center of his existence would collapse.

Qwerty stopped chewing long enough to look up at Owen. As their eyes met, a searing realization pierced him: his pet had more ability to move, to eat, to enjoy life, even to communicate, than his beloved nephew. He groaned, slumping over on his side, and curled up in the fetal position.

For long minutes he didn't move; the hard floor held him safe and stable. The cold tile soothed his fevered cheek. It all came down to accepting the truth—Owen was out of options.

Kyle was going to die.

CHAPTER 33

It was ten fifteen when Rene sat down on the chaise lounge under the eaves. A layer of clouds passed in front of the full moon, darkening the view before her. Many of her roses had bloomed, and the entire garden was in need of trimming.

The last two days had been among the worst of her professional life. No matter where she turned her attention, another disaster presented itself. Brenda's lawsuit had struck a colossal blow. Owen and Kristen's conversation with Stauss had backfired big-time, locking in Ainsworth's opposition. Rene's relationship with CRINR had gone up in flames, taking her access to the precious MDAP program along with it and prompting her withdrawal from the Kavli competition. Then Owen had turned up with a last-ditch appeal that was totally out of bounds, leaving her both angry and sad at their failed collaboration. The early warning signs of a migraine nagged at her awareness.

She couldn't get Kyle's tragedy out of her mind. In Marcella's case, Stauss had moved so quickly that there was nothing she could do to save the child. But the tools to rescue Kyle were in her hands. And she'd refused to use them.

A small ray of warmth crept into her gloom when her cell phone chimed with a call from Yoshi. The one pleasurable thing that had come out of this mess was her growing fondness for this gentle man.

"Rene." A mournful tone replaced his usually friendly, up-beat voice.

"Yoshi," she answered softly.

"I'm sorry to call so late, it's just . . . I wanted to talk . . . I guess you already know Kristen's decision and the plan for to-morrow morning."

"Owen told me earlier." Poor man. Yoshi loved Kyle as much as Kristen and Owen did. "You must be devastated."

"I'm heartbroken, honestly. I'm to meet them at the hospital at eight. I can't imagine how we're all going to get through this."

"Damn it. I was so optimistic after you and Owen tried the Witness." She winced as her neck muscles spasmed. "I'm so saddened at the missed opportunity. This entire tragedy makes me ill."

"Owen's at his wit's end. I've never seen him so crushed." He paused. "He told me he came to you with a bizarre proposal."

"I wasn't going to mention it, but yes. He was quite inappropriate."

"He said he feels horrible about it."

"Did he ask you to call me?" A faint wave of nausea swept through her.

"Oh, no, no. No. I'm calling because, well, he also said the two of you said your goodbyes, and I—I—I'd like to stay in touch—with your research. I found the Witness session to be very profound. I'd jump at a chance to try it again. I mean, the longer Owen and I were in the Witness, the deeper the experience became. I regret that you brought us back so soon."

Rene paused. "Say that again?"

"Well, we didn't connect with this universal consciousness right off. Our experience progressed over time before we got to that transcendent point. I sense there's much more to be learned during an even longer session."

There was something important about Yoshi's comment, but she couldn't put her finger on it.

"So anyway, let me know if there's ever a chance to try it again."

"I will," she said. "Thanks for offering."

"Um, well, to change the subject, I wonder . . ." Yoshi paused. "If it's not unethical for you to fraternize with one of your volunteers . . . would you be interested in going for coffee—or tea—some time?"

The unexpected invitation brought a burst of warm relief to her tense body. She smiled. "I'd really like that, Yoshi."

"Great. Let me get past tomorrow and then we can plan a time."

"Of course."

"Well, it's late and I need to get some rest. I'll call you soon."

"Thanks, Yoshi. I look forward to it." She waited a beat. "And I'll be thinking of you tomorrow. Take good care."

After the call from Yoshi ended, Rene sat outside for a while longer. Her mood was lighter, and the symptoms of migraine began to subside. But something was nagging at the back of her mind.

Though it was late, she felt compelled to go to her home office and see if she could surface whatever it was.

Not sure where to start, she rummaged through her papers until she found the transcript of her interview with Owen and Yoshi after their Witness experience. Flipping through the pages, she found Yoshi's haunting comments:

> *It was like the perfect ending to a great symphony performance. When the ensemble hits the final note in a perfect blending of the instruments, the sound reverberates for a moment of sublime beauty. Being in the Witness was like that—sublime. But with music, the sound fades away. With the Witness you could just rest there forever, in perfect harmony . . .*

She closed her eyes and recalled Yoshi saying these words, his face serene, a faraway look in his eyes. She replayed her memory of him in the coffee shop, the peaceful tone of his voice, and the wonder in his manner as he reviewed his experience.

Spontaneously, her mind transposed her grandfather's face over Yoshi's. She was cuddled up next to Gramps in the church pew, smelling his musty jacket, absorbing that sense of awe he'd exuded, a feeling she'd longed to capture ever since she was that child.

The images of these two men snapped together like interlocking puzzle pieces.

She desperately wanted to experience this state of awe for herself. But there was no one she trusted enough to be her Witness partner. She rejected trying another thought-sharing experience with a relative stranger like Aisha—it was far too intimate. Maybe someday with Yoshi . . . but at this point she barely knew him. She threw down her interview notes with a thump that woke Humboldt.

She strode to the window. The clouds had passed, and the full moon stood high in the sky, so bright she had to squint. The rosebushes in her garden cast distinct shadows on the lawn. Unable to resist, she opened the window just a crack and reveled in the burst of frigid air that raised goose bumps across her arms. She lingered at the open window, letting her thoughts roam freely. Did she really have to find a partner? Wasn't there some way to have a solo Witness experience?

Yoshi's comments about the impact of time on creating their transcendent experience suddenly triggered a new line of thought. What if he was right that it was the length of time spent exposed to the TCU that created the connection with universal consciousness?

"Oh!" She shut the window and rushed back to her computer.

Her fingers flew as she typed out a new hypothesis: two different influences, two different impacts: a connection to another person was created by identical ultrasound *frequencies;* a connection to universal consciousness was triggered through *exposure over time.* That meant that a single individual, given sufficient exposure to the TCU, should be able to contact Oneness directly.

Yes!

It was finally time to try the Witness and find out for herself.

CHAPTER 34

Eventually Qwerty got bored with Owen lying motionless on the kitchen floor and moved to her favorite spot on the back of the couch to look out the window.

A few minutes after eleven, Owen pulled his stiff body upright. Standing at the sink, he forced himself to eat a bowl of cold cereal before heading up to his bedroom.

Failure permeated his every cell. He'd tried and failed to find a route into Kyle's thoughts. Kristen had admonished him. Dr. Elder had rejected him. And Matt, his dear godson, had nailed him for his failure, calling him out for giving up. Owen hadn't run out of the willingness to act; he'd run out of things to try.

Owen put his phone on Do Not Disturb. No calls, no texts—nothing. He needed to be alone. As he lay down on the bed, the Witness sprang unbidden into his awareness. Grateful, he surrendered to the transcendence he'd known with Yoshi. Then, exhausted, he fell into a dreamless sleep.

—

Nearly four hours later, Owen woke. He turned on his side, faced the window, and caught sight of the full moon.

In no way did he discount what Kristen had gleaned from Nana's and Kimi's deaths. But did those insights apply to what Kyle wanted? Surely there were as many ways to approach the quality of life and the quality of one's death as there were individuals. Kyle's unique experience and perspective should govern what happened next: not Nana's, not Kimi's.

Whether Kyle would live or die wasn't Owen's decision.

But it wasn't Kristen's either.

It was Kyle's.

He sat upright.

He was seized by an overriding, moral imperative to allow Kyle to voice his own decision. The Witness offered the only portal through which his nephew could render his own final verdict. Dr. Elder's unwillingness to participate left Owen as the sole person willing to allow Kyle to control his own destiny. The early morning appointment with Stauss was looming, so empowering him without delay was of paramount importance.

He stopped, startled by an inspiration.

What if he . . . ?

Could he . . . ?

He closed his eyes tight, visualizing Aisha's office and the sticky note hanging from the doorframe. It came back to him readily: the first digits of the formula for pi: 314159.

OK, that should get him into the foundation office—if Dr. Elder hadn't changed the code in the meantime. Could he pack up the Witness equipment, get to the hospital, connect with Kyle, and find out his choice all before Kristen and Stauss showed up? It was a long shot at best. But still, didn't he have to try?

He paced around the room, working through the angles. The risks associated with his scheme made him cringe. Going to jail for burglary, for example. But his worst worry was that he could permanently damage his relationship with Kristen.

He'd already betrayed her during his attempt at convincing Dr. Elder to subvert his sister's decision. And he was hatching an even more radical maneuver with this plan. Would Kristen hate him if he tried the Witness against her express wishes, an action he had no right to take? Was that a risk he was willing to take to give Kyle his rightful choice?

He stopped at the window, finding the moon high above the nearby town houses. He leaned his forehead against the cold window, trying to stay centered, thinking deeply.

His resolve crystallized as he stared at the bright moon. It was time to act.

CHAPTER 35

It was just after three in the morning when Rene pulled on jeans and a sweater. She drove through the deserted streets to the foundation office and headed directly into room 1, where she donned the TCU headset and arranged the controller so she could easily adjust it from her recliner. She set the timer on the controller for the same length of time that Yoshi and Owen had been exposed.

She sat quietly and let herself settle, lured to this late-night quest by Yoshi's sublime experience, by the chance to resolve the mystery of Gramps's awe. If there was something greater than herself out there, she had a visceral need to feel it for herself.

She programmed a photo from the Portland Rose Garden to gradually be revealed in the virtual reality goggles. Then she cued up a favorite piece of music in the headphones—a lengthy classical piece that she often relied on to relax, and let the music take her away.

A breathtaking close-up of a pale-yellow rosebud gradually revealed itself within the light of dawn. The view slowly widened to include a glowing yellow blossom on the adjacent bush, then another, this one tinged pink orange along its furled edges.

The view expanded along the row, each new flower a deeper shade of pink orange than the last, until a flaming orange-red blossom dominated her view.

The image gradually pulled back to encompass dozens of bushes and hundreds of flowers of all hues.

A memory from the garden came to life. Her four-year-old self stood several feet away from her grandfather. She glimpsed him bending deeply into a profligate bush bearing dozens of the brightest yellow roses in the entire garden. Gramps closed his eyes, a look of pure serenity on his face as he buried his nose among the petals. She reveled in the glorious view of him and his halo of blossoms.

Once again, she was—

aware

memories and ambitions floating off

a tsunami of relief washing through, the past evaporating

the frozen water of identity dissolving

into the eternal now

merging with everything

every atom and cell

every plant and being

everyone

linking in a golden chain of love stretching around the

    universe—

vowing

to keep her link bright and strong

to be kind and gentle to every living thing

to protect those who are weak

so that all might attain this perfect peace

as immense as all existence

after a time

the chain of being dispersing into an endless array of individuals

the view narrowing to her city, her building

two people moving around in an office at the opposite end of the complex

Then suddenly, once again she was Rene sitting in her recliner, filled with courage.

CHAPTER 36

Grounded in his moral center, Owen was ready to put his plan into action. His first step would be to get Matt on board. He'd considered asking Yoshi for help, but he didn't want to risk the possibility that this gambit would cause a problem between him and Rene.

Would the young man even answer his call after the angry scene between them earlier? *He thinks I've let him down. No, even worse. He thinks I've let Kyle down.* He desperately needed Matt's help but feared he'd already alienated him.

After several rings, Matt answered.

"What the hell? It's not even four."

Owen struggled to keep his voice calm. "Look, I want to apologize for not respecting how much Kyle means to you. I was self-centered not to acknowledge how much you've been helping him."

A slight grunt from the younger man.

"I'm truly sorry. I wish I'd been more sensitive."

"Yeah, me too. Can I go back to sleep now?"

"I need to ask you a big favor. I'm going to see Kyle early this morning. I'd like you to be there with me." He couldn't operate the Witness equipment alone. He would bring Dr. Elder's procedure manual; he hoped Matt would be able to help him figure out the controller.

There was still a tinge of bitterness in Matt's voice. "So now you want me to be there to watch him be . . . terminated? Is that it?"

"No, no. That's not it at all. Despite what I said last evening, I'm not giving up." He raised his voice. "I. Am. Not. Giving. Up."

"Then what's going on?" Matt sounded intrigued.

"Matt, if you can be at Kyle's room, say at six forty-five, I'll fill you in then." He didn't want to tell him that he was about to commit a crime and make Matt an accessory.

Matt hesitated.

"Please, Matt. I need you to trust me on this. This is for Kyle."

"OK, OK. If you tell me this is something Kyle needs, then I'll be there, but I don't understand why."

Matt didn't sound convinced, but Owen trusted that he would keep his word and show up as promised. He sat back with a tremendous sigh of relief. The risks were obvious. But deep down, his commitment was solid.

Moving on, Owen called the nurses' station on the neuro floor to leave a message for Kyle's night nurse that he'd be coming by early, before visiting hours, to have a meditation session with Kyle. He asked that they not be disturbed.

Nervous but focused, he showered and dressed carefully. Later in the day he might have to witness Kyle's last moments. He dressed to match the solemnity of the moment: slacks, starched shirt and tie, suit jacket.

Owen dug out his gym bag and dumped the contents on the bed. Then he added three bath towels to cushion Rene's equipment, a flashlight, and a large handkerchief he could use as a blindfold.

In a moment of panic, he considered wearing a hoodie, ball cap, and sunglasses to disguise himself during the burglary. Owen winced every time the word "burglary" came into his mind; his plan was still illegal, even if his motives were noble. But no, he decided to wear no disguise and let the security cameras identify him, just to clarify that neither Rene nor Aisha had anything to do with this escapade.

He'd already made his peace with whatever legal and personal consequences came his way.

CHAPTER 37

Rene sat unmoving, allowing her senses to gradually return to the present as she sat in the recliner in room 1. The air was cool against her skin; the comfy chair holding her stable.

She'd finally experienced the sublime moments that Owen and Yoshi had described, the awe that Gramps had exuded, inspired by his faith. The anticipation that had been building for a lifetime had been fulfilled far beyond her hopes.

Eyes still closed, she appealed to the new voice within for guidance. It wasn't a voice, not really. It wasn't a feeling either, not in the usual sense. More of a *knowing:* a knowing that was absolutely familiar despite having just been revealed to her. She conceived it as a voice only because after the knowing came the need to translate the knowledge into the words she would need later.

Foremost in her mind was the vow she'd just taken to protect all who were weaker than herself. It was a vow in complete harmony with the other oath she'd taken years ago—to first do no harm.

Both oaths led her to one person: Kyle Nichols.

Her heartbeat remained steady. She told herself she alone had the tools at hand to liberate this young man from his personal hell, to reunite a devastated mother with her only child, and to assist a devoted uncle in his dual quest to support his sister and rescue his nephew. She sat up.

It was more than guidance that she'd discovered within; rather, it was validation that the route she'd previously considered unthinkable was now, obviously, the perfect path.

The only path.

She didn't ask for courage, but it came bubbling up, unbidden. She welcomed it; the risks suddenly seemed insignificant. Her spirit was light and her resolve fierce.

Stretching, catlike, her breaths came slow and easy as she carefully freed herself from the monitoring wires and headgear. Her next moves were clear.

It was ten minutes before five, and traffic was still light. Rene broke her rule against using a cell phone while driving and placed a call to Aisha. *Aisha, c'mon, answer, please.*

After several rings, Aisha answered. "Dr. Elder?" She sounded surprised and groggy.

"Aisha, sorry. I know it's early, but this is urgent. Do you remember when you asked me to include you in all my future experiments?" Rene didn't wait for an answer. "Well, I'm going to be doing something very important in a short while, at the hospital, with Kyle Nichols. I'd like you to be there."

Aisha sputtered for a minute. "Wait, what?"

Rene urgently updated her on Kyle's current situation and described her plan.

"I could really use your help, Aisha," Rene said. "If you do this, I promise I'll take full responsibility if there's any blowback. But your involvement is totally voluntary. Seriously. You don't have to do this."

"Screw the blowback," Aisha said. "I want to help. I'll be there as soon as I can."

Relieved, Rene quickly gave her instructions.

Next, she placed a call to Owen.

Please answer, Owen. Please answer.

He didn't.

She left a brief summary of her plan on his voicemail.

CHAPTER 38

Charged with purpose, Owen arrived at Rene's facility right on schedule at five a.m. It was unlikely that either Rene or Aisha would be at work this early, but he double-checked anyway. Neither of their cars were there. The parking lot was empty save for an unattended van parked at the curb at the far end of the complex.

His nerves started to fray. There were so many things that needed to go right in order to get to the hospital with Rene's equipment. He clung to his checklist and struggled to keep his mind on the tasks at hand.

More than any other item on his list, this next one would make or break his plan. He closed his eyes, visualizing that all-important sticky note with the first digits of pi. Yes! He was positive: 314159.

Still, it was always possible that Rene had changed the code since his visit, which would stop him dead in his tracks.

His hand shook as he pushed the buttons, anxious that he

might enter a wrong number and trigger an alarm. He heaved a sigh of relief when a green light appeared on the panel, approving his entry on the first try.

He opened the door into a pitch-black foyer and fumbled in his gym bag for the flashlight. Casting it around, he found the light switches for the reception area and hallway. The building lit up.

He knew that locating the green procedure binder could take some time. Aisha had been working on the protocols when he was there before, so he walked directly to her small office.

Swiftly scanning the desk and shelves, he didn't see the binder.

This was a major stumbling block. He started sweating. Matt would never be able to operate the device without it. Frustrated, Owen decided to move on and look for the manual again later.

He went into room 3 and began studying the layout. Owen immediately recognized the TCU headset and followed the wires back to the controller. His experience with electronic equipment made this the part of the plan where he was most confident.

Aha! The green procedure manual was in full view on the desk next to the computer. Of course. If you're going to have a procedure manual, you're going to keep it where you need it most, in the testing room itself. Relieved, he stuffed it into the bottom of his gym bag.

He stopped and thought for a moment, then opened the camera on his phone and took a couple of selfies with the equipment. Then he turned and waved at the security camera in the upper corner of the room to document that he was there on his own.

Back on task, he carefully unplugged the controller from the outlet and detached the wires that led back to the computer setup on the desk. After using his cell phone to photograph where the headsets fed into the controller, he disconnected them and carefully wrapped each in one of the towels he'd brought along for this exact purpose.

Engrossed in securing the device, he jumped when the door suddenly burst open. Panicked, he almost dropped the delicate controller, just barely managing to ease it into his bag before looking up.

His heart was hammering so loudly he could hardly think. Two very serious men in blue uniforms were blocking his exit.

Damn it. Caught red-handed.

Rene mustered her most officious, surgeon-like demeanor as she exited the hospital elevator on Kyle's floor, carrying her purse and the satchel with the TCU equipment from room 1 packed carefully inside.

Her plan was simple. Just the day before, Owen had pleaded with her to do a surreptitious Witness session with Kyle, so she knew he was on board with the scheme. She intended to set up the equipment in the boy's room with help from Aisha, who was on her way. When Owen arrived—assuming he got her urgent voicemail—they could help him connect with Kyle, and then she'd make herself scarce before Kristen and Stauss arrived.

She strode by the nurses' station. It was too early for visitors, but if she was lucky, the night nurses wouldn't stop her.

She wasn't lucky.

"Can I help you, ma'am?" the nurse called out.

Her jaw tightened at the challenge, even as she tried to exude professional confidence. Many of the nurses on the night shift were strangers to her, and she didn't recognize this woman.

"Yes, I'm Dr. Rene Elder," she said. "I'm consulting on the Kyle Nichols case. I'm here to check on him prior to a procedure this morning." She started boldly down the hall, displaying all the authority that her role as a physician carried.

The nurse looked at her skeptically. Rene realized that she hardly presented the look of a physician tending to a patient; her jeans, sweater, and tousled hair would make any responsible staff member question her intentions.

"I'm sorry, no one ordered a consultation," the nurse said firmly. "And it's five thirty in the morning."

Rene smiled with a confidence she didn't feel. "Sorry about that, it was rather last-minute. I know his room. Thanks."

"Ah, I'm sorry, ma'am. For security reasons, we do have very strict protocols for visits after hours." The nurse was apologetic but firm. "Can I see your badge?"

"I guess I must have left it in my office," she mumbled, embarrassed.

"I'm afraid I can't allow you to go to the patient's room," the nurse said, moving closer to the phone. "Perhaps you should wait for Dr. Stauss or a family member to escort you."

"I do understand, thanks." No point arguing any further; that would just draw more attention and give the nurse a reason to call security. Still, time was of the essence, and her anxiety spiked.

"Dr. Stauss is expected to be here this morning," the nurse said.

"Thanks." Rene managed a small smile and pointed toward a small waiting area near the elevator. "I'll just wait for him over here and make some calls," Rene lied. In fact, she planned to disappear well before then to make sure she didn't run into him or Kristen.

She selected a seat where she could see if the nurse left the station untended at some point. But when a second nurse joined her, the chances of sneaking down the hall unnoticed vanished.

Rene checked her phone: nothing back from Owen. *Damn!* Her plan stalled, she left him another urgent voicemail and sent a text. If she didn't connect with him soon, they'd lose this opportunity, and Kyle would be lost to them forever.

She couldn't shake the hopelessness that descended upon her. Kyle's lifeline sat in her satchel at her feet. He was a mere thirty yards away, but she could only sit there, helpless.

Owen froze and reflexively raised his hands in the traditional *you caught me* pose. The two men in blue uniforms considered him grimly.

Despite his careful checklist, Owen hadn't planned a cover story in case he got caught. His mind spun wildly, searching for what he might say to avoid being arrested.

He steadied a little as a plan formed. Owen straightened his coat and tie and tried to look official, glad that he'd dressed professionally and hadn't worn the hoodie and sunglasses that he had jokingly considered.

"Oh, man, you guys scared me!" He laughed reassuringly as sweat rolled down his back.

"Hey! What's going on? Who are you?" the older man asked.

"My name is Owen Nichols," he explained gamely, nodding at the men. "I just started working here. I'm going to demonstrate this equipment at an early meeting at the hospital across town."

He noticed a vacuum cleaner standing in the hallway behind the men. These were the janitors, not night security. That must have been their van he'd seen at the end of the building—they probably cleaned all these offices in the complex. What bad luck to be here when they arrived to service Rene's suite. His heart was racing, and he had to act quickly.

"Excuse me, please." He smiled and with a burst of braggadocio moved to walk on by, hoping they would allow him through.

They didn't move.

"Did Dr. Rene say you could take her equipment?" the older man asked, apparently the one in charge. The younger man deferred to his elder, perhaps his father.

Owen took their measure. The men weren't tall, but they had the look of people who did physical labor for a living. The man who took charge was stocky, with streaks of gray in his dark black hair. The other, perhaps his teenage son, was young and lanky. They were stubbornly blocking the exit and showed no signs of moving. He couldn't bluff them and there was no way he could get by them. Shit. What was he going to do?

The older man pulled out a cell phone. "I'm calling the police," he said, looking Owen in the eye.

Owen pulled out his own phone, hands shaking. Dare he call Rene and tell her he'd been caught stealing her delicate medical equipment? It might be his only shot at getting out of this and not being locked up in jail when Kristen ended Kyle's life support.

"I'm calling Dr. Elder," he said to the men.

The older man nodded but watched Owen carefully.

As Owen rushed to place his call, he realized his phone was still on Do Not Disturb. He'd adjusted the phone's settings several hours ago, and there were notifications of several missed voicemails and texts, all from Rene. *What the . . . ?*

Scanning the texts, he learned that Rene was several steps ahead of him. She was already at the hospital with her own set of TCU equipment!

The lead janitor continued to watch him closely, looking increasingly annoyed and checking his watch.

Owen urgently tapped the icon to return Rene's call, hoping with all his might that she would pick up. He gasped with relief when she answered.

"Rene, it's me. Look, I'm—"

"Owen? Thank goodness. I've—"

"I'm in your offices at the foundation. I'm picking up—"

"What? You're in my facility? How the hell—"

"Never mind that now, Rene, just *listen*. Please. Yes, I'm in your facility," he repeated. It was an impossible act to pull off. He was frantic to brief her, but he still had to sound absolutely businesslike in front of them. "The janitors came in and found me here. I need you to verify that I have your permission to—"

He gulped, not quite sure what to say to her. He was sure panic was written all over his face. He faked a cough, then tried again. "Rene, as I was saying, I came to the facility to get the equipment for our demonstration at the hospital this morning." He was desperate, improvising, struggling to keep his voice steady, and praying she would get the gist and be willing to play along.

"The janitors came in and they're about to call the police," he continued. "They're trying to do the right thing, but can you please explain to them that I'm here at your request?" He put just the slightest emphasis on "at your request."

Now everything depended on Rene's ability to follow his scant cues and her willingness to be complicit in his actions. If she was angry at him for breaking in to her facility, as she had every right to be, then the police would come and arrest him. He'd spend the night in jail. Not only would he lose the chance to use the Witness with Kyle, but he'd miss being there for the boy's last moments.

He gave the janitors a small smile to emphasize that this was just a simple misunderstanding. The younger fellow didn't look as if he was buying it.

Owen tried to look casual as he ran his fingers through his hair to hide a drop of sweat that threatened to run down his cheek. "Sure, Owen. Put me on speakerphone." Amazingly, Rene sounded perfectly calm. "Hey, Jackson, Marcus? Are you there?"

The two men who'd been blocking his exit signaled their recognition of Rene's voice. The older man stepped closer to the phone.

"Oh, hi, Dr. Rene. We've never seen this guy before, so we thought he was breaking in."

"I'm so sorry, guys, I should have warned you that Owen would be in so early. It was good that you challenged him. Thanks for being so careful." Rene's response impressed him; she spoke with a confidence that belied the fact that she, too, was making this up on the fly.

"OK, thanks, Dr. Rene," the man said into the phone. "We're so sorry we bothered you."

"No worries. Thanks again. Owen, I'll see you at the hospital as soon as you can get here."

"On my way," Owen answered. "Thanks, Rene," he added quietly.

Looking chagrined, the older man approached Owen and offered a handshake, which Owen warmly accepted, hoping his clammy hand wouldn't seem suspicious. He wouldn't feel safe until he was driving away.

"You guys did the right thing," he said, trying to sound gracious, as if he had somehow been wronged. "Sorry for the inconvenience."

The younger janitor carefully scanned Owen up and down, still seeming unconvinced, but his father was satisfied, and they moved on to begin their work.

Owen picked up his gym bag and walked out of the building, carefully placing his bounty on the back seat of his car. He settled behind the wheel and let out a loud sigh. That had been way too close. His damp shirt clung to his torso. He leaned his head against the steering wheel until he steadied.

Now came the hard part.

CHAPTER 39

Rene sat quietly on the plastic seat in the hospital waiting area with her equipment safely tucked in the satchel at her feet. It was eerily quiet on the neuro floor in the wee hours of the morning. The lights in the patients' rooms were dimmed, while the nurses' station was well lit. The two nurses chatted quietly before turning to their computers.

Rene had been there on early morning rounds many times before to check on her patients and then move on. But she was sitting alone, idle, even as Kyle's death sentence marched toward a nine-o'clock deadline.

She shook her head in amazement at the call from Owen. What audacity he had to break in to her lab! She'd installed a high-end security system—how the hell had he gained access? She reluctantly gave him credit despite her anger. He'd given her enough clues that she'd been able to help bluff the janitors. She'd deal with him when everything was said and done. But at least for the moment, she and Owen were on the same page, and he was on his way to the hospital.

She tried to imagine what it must be like for Kyle, knowing they would soon turn off his life support, believing that these were his last moments of life. Was he grateful for the chance to escape a future of imprisonment, or desperate to beg for a reprieve? If Owen didn't get there soon, no one would ever know.

She repeatedly checked her phone to see how much time remained. Every minute that ticked by meant they'd have less time to connect with Kyle. And every minute meant a greater chance that either Kristen or Stauss would bust her.

Just after six, the elevator door opened and Owen rushed out, a duffel bag over his shoulder. Rene sighed with relief.

Owen marched right to the counter and spoke with the nurses, one of whom then motioned toward Rene. She got up from her seat and gave the nurse a small wave. Since Owen was here, he could accompany her to Kyle's room without further question.

Rene met Owen in the middle of the corridor, where they stood face to face. So much had happened to her and to Owen since their collaboration had dissolved. It would take a serious conversation to straighten it all out, but this wasn't the time.

"I'm so glad to see you, Rene," Owen said as they strode down the hall together. "And I'm deeply grateful. But you don't have to do this if you don't want to. There are still very real risks to you. I've asked Matt to help, and he'll be here soon. I brought the procedure binder." Owen indicated the duffel bag he'd packed at her office.

Rene shook her head. "Matt's a smart guy, but it wouldn't be wise to have an untrained person work the controller. Besides, Aisha's on her way. I'll leave after she arrives."

"What changed your mind?" he whispered as he stopped just outside Kyle's door.

"I tried the Witness myself. Until now, I didn't truly accept what you guys reported about your experience." She shook her head. "But let's just say I had an epiphany, OK? Now everything just adds up differently." She met his eyes. "You know."

"Yes," he said. "I do know."

Rene held out her hand to Owen to seal the deal. As they shook, Rene placed her left hand over both of theirs. "It's OK, Owen. I know what I'm doing."

A solemn look passed between them, and their relationship shifted. As their lives intersected in the deserted hospital hallway, they became comrades on a sacred crusade.

Owen returned a look of appreciation that warmed her. Newly bonded, they walked into Kyle's room to face unknown risks and an uncertain ending.

"I'll set up while you brief Kyle," Rene said.

Owen carefully set his duffel in the corner, then moved to his nephew's side and rested his hand on the boy's shoulder. "Hey, Kyle. I'm here with Dr. Elder. We're here extra early, even before your mom arrives. Time is short, so I'm going to say this really fast. I know that your mom told you that your life support will be turned off later this morning." Owen almost choked on the fateful words. "She loves you with all her heart, and she truly believes that is the best way to release you from this disability. I don't doubt her commitment to you, not for a second," he said, his voice quavering. "But I believe you should be the one to decide to live or let go. You're an adult. It's your right to choose."

He took a few more breaths, and his emotions began to settle. "Obviously, the challenge has been finding a way for you to communicate your wishes. That's where Dr. Elder comes in."

"I'm standing right over here, Kyle, setting up the equipment on the table," Rene said as she unloaded her equipment.

"Do you remember a few weeks ago, when Dr. Elder stopped in and mentioned her research?" Owen said. "It turns out she's found a way for you and me to communicate with each other! Yoshi and I tried it, and it really works."

Owen pulled a chair up next to the bed, taking Kyle's hand. "Dr. Elder is going to help you and me connect, and then you can let me know your decision." He squeezed the boy's hand. "I hope you'll trust me with this. I promise I'll support whatever decision you make, but it must be *your* decision."

Owen sat back, thoughts racing. Was Kyle excited at the last-minute chance to communicate? Or would he be terrified by the unexpected intrusion into his mind? His nephew remained still as a stone. There was only the rhythmic sound of the ventilator and the colored lines on the monitor to confirm that he was even alive.

It was just past six thirty when the door to Kyle's room abruptly opened. Owen jumped, afraid that Kristen or Stauss had arrived early.

Instead, Matt entered, then stopped dead in his tracks. Yoshi, following immediately behind, almost knocked his son over. Owen hadn't asked Yoshi to come early but was immediately grateful to see his best friend.

"You're kidding me," Matt said, his eyes sweeping the room

and assessing what was happening. "You're trying the Witness with Kyle *now*?"

"Yes," Owen said. "And if you've got a problem with it, then you should just leave."

"I'm just surprised is all," the young man responded. "Kyle, this is super news, man." He went to Kyle's side and shot Owen an approving look. "Dude, now you get to tell us what you want." Matt looked at Owen. "You asked me to be here, so what do you need me to do?"

"Originally I thought that you'd work the controller," Owen said, "but Dr. Elder will do that until Aisha arrives."

"Aisha has a long drive, even with no traffic," Rene said as she expertly untangled the wires from the various devices. "It's getting near seven, and you'll need as much time with Kyle as possible. We shouldn't wait."

Owen appreciated that she was giving firm directions.

"Then I need you to stand by the elevator and keep an eye out for Kristen," Owen said to Matt. "Stall her if you can."

"Will do," Matt answered. "Go for it, dude," he said to Kyle before leaving the room. "This is your best chance."

Owen was suddenly worried that he wouldn't be able to fulfill his part of this connection. What if he couldn't push through without Yoshi to help? A trickle of sweat rolled down his back. He took off his jacket and rolled up his sleeves.

Rene finished setting up her equipment. She remained unemotional and laser-focused. Her professionalism at this critical moment exuded the confidence he needed. She swiftly placed the headset across the boy's forehead, all the while calmly talking him through exactly what she was doing.

Yoshi stood nearby while Rene completed her tasks. "I've

tried this myself, Kyle, and I'm totally convinced it's a safe way for you to let us know what you want," he said in the soothing way that Owen so valued in his friend. "It may feel really strange at first, but just relax into it. Try to stay calm, and things will clear up as you go."

Owen squirmed in the hard plastic chair next to Kyle's bed, trying to get comfortable. "It would be just like Kristen to get here early," Owen said, looking at the clock. It had taken more than twenty minutes for Rene to get set up.

Rene adjusted the second headset across his forehead. She suggested a series of hand signals by which he could let her know how things were going. A thumbs-up would mean *all is well*, a flat hand would mean *hold steady*. A thumbs-down would mean *slowly retreat*. A hand across the throat would mean *back off immediately*. "We don't need the VR glasses to create the Witness effect," Rene said to Owen. "So I brought blindfolds for each of you, to eliminate extraneous visual input."

He nodded his understanding, then rolled his shoulders, trying to ease the backlog of tension.

"Yoshi, please turn down the lights." Rene was all business, keeping things moving. "Owen, let me know when you're ready."

Equal parts anticipation and dread alternated in waves through his muscles. At last, after weeks of uncertainty, unfulfilled hopes, emotional turmoil, and family conflict, Owen was about to connect with Kyle.

But what if Kyle's brain was so scrambled that he had no rational thought? What if the emotional impact of the LIS had already led him to insanity?

One way or another, Owen was about to find out.

CHAPTER 40

The first moment of connection with Kyle was a force of nature. Raw, untamed memories flew through Owen's mind: a shocking jolt as he missed the deer, full-on terror exploding as the car rolled once, twice, three times, landing upside down. Body crumpling, excruciating pain, then nothing. Eyelids pulled up, awakening to swirling images of nurses, doctors, fading in and out. Pain. Mom weeping. Eyes defying his orders to look at her. More pain. Trying, trying, trying, but unable to turn toward her. Crying out. Waves of rage. He couldn't do it. An unseen someone said he'd never move again. Mom and Owen leaning down, repeating the same words, tears falling. Trapped. Imprisoned. Terror, rage, soundless screams.

Projecting into the future: smothering decades of immobility; dreadfully lonely isolation; tyrannical dependence on others; unrelenting vulnerability to pneumonia; abject terror at not being able to breathe, unable to call for help, drowning alone on his own fluids. Dread and foreboding, bottomless sorrow for all his losses.

Kyle's visceral cascade of horror washed away Owen's sense of self, disconnecting him from his own reality. Panicking at the sense of psychological extinction, he had to save himself. Gasping, he gave the urgent signal, slashing his hand across his neck. None too soon, the sensations faded as Dr. Elder disconnected him from Kyle and he was fully himself again.

Pulling off his headset, he was dizzy, nauseated, disoriented. He kept his eyes closed and hunched over, gasping for breath, trying to regain control. Dr. Elder asked if he was OK, but he couldn't muster a response.

The overwhelming torrent that he'd just received directly from his nephew contradicted the motionless body lying in front of him. Kyle's superficial appearance—his slack face and limp body—falsely suggested that he was relaxed, resting, perhaps even at peace. In truth, that motionless shell housed the agony of weeks of torment.

Owen's eyes filled. "I'm not sure I can go on." He slumped with crushing disappointment. He'd been naive to think he and Kyle could have a dialogue about his future. This wasn't at all like the conversation he'd had with Yoshi; Kyle's mind was overflowing with a chaos that demanded release. There was a complete absence of thought or language, just a cacophony of images, emotions, memories, and fears. Kristen and Stauss would arrive soon, and there wasn't enough time to work through all the detritus Kyle had accumulated during his weeks of isolation.

Perhaps he should abandon the effort, just end the Witness

experience and let Kristen and Stauss end the boy's torture once and for all.

Yoshi knelt, resting his own hand over Owen's tight grip on the armrest. Owen locked eyes with his best friend, searching for solace. Yoshi didn't flinch at his pain. It was as if the two were again connected in the Witness, Yoshi sending him calming encouragement through the chaos. Memories of Oneness and the depth of their connection came seeping back, replacing the terror of those first few moments with Kyle.

He loosened his grip on the chair, surrendering to that place of profound calm that he and Yoshi had found, once again immersed in the compassion they'd shared. He rested there, absorbing the remembered peace.

Wasn't there value in reconnecting with Kyle again? Could he just bear witness to whatever his nephew needed to reveal? Perhaps the best way to be of service would be to simply allow Kyle to release all the horror he'd accumulated and find some solace in his final moments.

Stronger now, he vowed to give himself over to Kyle's experience and attend as best he could. This would be his ultimate gift, one that only he could offer.

He replaced his blindfold. "I'm ready to go again," he instructed Rene. "Just go as slowly as you can."

"Courage, my friend," Yoshi whispered, squeezing his hand once more before returning to his spot by the light switch.

Rene helped Owen replace the headset he'd pulled off so abruptly. Then she settled back at the table in the corner and aligned frequencies to connect him and Kyle.

It was only then that she realized the entire time her attention had been focused on Owen, Kyle's headset had remained in place and the TCU had been on. As a result, Kyle had been continuously receiving an exposure similar to the one that had allowed her to connect with universal consciousness during her own solo experience just a few hours before.

She had no way to know what impact all this was having on Kyle; she'd have to count on Owen's judgment about Kyle's status as he reconnected with the boy.

Owen braced himself for another free fall into despair as Rene reestablished his connection with Kyle. But to his amazement, he discovered the young man reveling in a sense of pure peace. Kyle had merged his identity with Oneness, and Owen's perceptions were instantly swept along as he joined with Kyle in the same profound connection that he'd known with Yoshi.

The young man's urgent need for the healing power of infinity washed through Owen, the emotional shackles of disability falling away in the timeless freedom of open perception, and the expansiveness of reality rekindling hope from the ashes of his dreams.

Like a moth to light, Owen was being drawn deeper into Oneness himself. Yet he forced himself to fight against this seduction, knowing that this wasn't the time to surrender to the sublime. Somehow, he needed to help Kyle regain his independent identity so they could communicate as discrete individuals. Kyle urgently needed to make a life-or-death decision, and Owen needed time to act on that choice.

Not sure if it would work, Owen signaled for Dr. Elder to

bring him and Kyle slightly out of alignment. Gratefully, he felt the pull of Oneness receding and his nephew's personality regaining form. He was caught up in a new swirl of the boy's emotions: freedom from the weeks of hollow loneliness, a longing to return to the peace of Oneness, gratitude for his uncle who was making all this possible.

Owen responded with his own expression of love and determination to give Kyle his rightful choice about what happened next, but he was becoming frantic. Their time together was running out. The boy had yet to think in words that could form a basis for dialogue. Rene had warned that the accident might have permanently damaged his ability to verbalize internally.

Owen had to find out. He took some slow breaths to prepare. It was time to ask his nephew the ultimate question. "Kyle? What do *you* want?"

Instantly, Owen received Kyle's memory of welcoming Kristen's decision to provide a gentle death. He'd been eager to end the overwhelming despair of his situation. Then Owen came to understand that the energy of the Oneness that Kyle had just experienced had pulled him back from the brink of despair. Fresh excitement swirled through the boy and over to his uncle, filling Owen's mind with a revived strength and vibrancy.

But Owen's impression of his nephew's desires was based solely on the sensations and emotions being transferred through the Witness; Kyle had yet to use words to capture his final intent. Owen needed to be sure that his own interpretation of Kyle's experience was accurate. He decided to summarize what he understood and then have Kyle validate or correct his version.

He carefully formed sentences in his mind, trying to accurately paraphrase what he'd perceived and to transmit it to Kyle for approval. He thought, *Here's what I think you mean. Tell me if I'm right, OK? You were ready to die to end the physical pain and the unbearable loneliness. But you're surprised by this Witness experience. It's given you an unexpected lifeline. The chance to communicate with everyone, especially your mom, opens the possibility of a life filled with love.*

He sensed Kyle was absorbing his words and was flooded with the boy's relief that he'd been understood. Owen tried to stay neutral so as not to influence Kyle's decision, but nonetheless was filled with his own sense of relief. What a joy it would be to have Kyle's personality an ongoing part of his life.

Then Owen received new feelings of confusion and uncertainty from Kyle. Stress at having to make a life-or-death decision under the intense pressure of time. There were only two options: immersion in the peace of Oneness or ongoing connection with all his loved ones. The realization of an impossible, irrevocable choice. Kyle got more and more lost as he wrestled with the implications of his decision.

Owen felt Kyle becoming increasingly panicked: he still hadn't made a clear choice. Time was slipping away.

Owen asked again, *Kyle, what do you want?*

Finally, Kyle was able to form his own words. *I need . . . to talk . . . with Mom . . .*

CHAPTER 41

Owen exhaled with an audible rush of air. As the boy's uncertainty and need to connect with Kristen flooded through him, he involuntarily responded with his own panic. Owen believed his chances of convincing Kristen to try the Witness were slim to none.

"What time is it?" he asked, unable to see the clock for the blindfold.

"It's seven forty-five; she could arrive anytime now," Yoshi answered.

Kyle instantly absorbed Owen's fears. *Oh, no, please . . . tell her I need to . . . connect with her. I don't know what to do . . .*

I'll tell her, Kyle, I will. I'll do everything I can. But your mom doesn't accept that the Witness can work. A pit of despair grew in Owen's mind as helplessness flowed between them. *I don't think she'll believe that I've actually talked with you—she'll think it's just a trick.*

Their conversation lapsed as they searched for a solution,

threads of ideas bouncing between them as they both struggled to stay calm.

Finally, Kyle hit on an idea. *Hey, tell Mom to . . . remember . . . the tanager . . . when the tanager hit the window.*

What? The tanager? Kyle lost him. *That's a bird, isn't it?* Why was the boy talking about a bird at a time like this? *I don't get it.* This was no time to go off on a tangent about a bird.

You don't know. She does. Kyle flashed images to Owen's mind like a movie being streamed on fast-forward. After a few seconds, Owen caught on as he focused on memorizing the snippets of memory as Kyle visualized a sequence of events from his childhood, accompanied by a heavy sense of remorse.

"What the . . . ?"

Owen jumped, pulled off his blindfold, and swung around to see Kristen standing in the doorway, Matt just behind her. Owen blinked furiously as she flipped on the lights. The look of shock on her face transformed into one of betrayal.

"Owen, what the hell do you think you're doing? After all we've been through? How could you?"

Her outrage seared him to the core. She might never forgive him. He considered his motionless nephew. The abrupt movement dislodged Owen's headset, and the sudden absence of a connection with Kyle left him feeling hollow. Kyle must be feeling frantic at losing his only lifeline at this critical moment.

Kristen glared at Matt and Yoshi as she took in the extent of the conspiracy against her, then stared down at Owen from across Kyle's bed, her eye twitching, face flushed and hot.

"I planned this time together so we could have a calm,

loving time with Kyle before Dr. Stauss arrives. Now you've totally ruined that for me."

Owen grounded himself in the boundless compassion of Oneness. He dug deep, summoning a calm conviction from his very core. "He needs to connect with you, Kristen. To talk about what's going to happen. He insisted."

"I suppose he told you that just now, huh, Owen? You expect me to believe that?" Her voice was loud and quaking with anger. The depth of his betrayal played out on her face as the chasm of broken trust grew deeper every moment.

"Kyle told me to remind you of the day the tanager hit the window."

Kristen shook her head, trying to ward off his comment as if it were an annoying insect. "What the hell are you talking about? Don't you dare try to distract me with irrelevant bullshit."

He concentrated on assembling the jumbled shards of memory Kyle had transmitted: being with Kristen and Matt; jumping at an unexpected sound; the bright colors of a motionless bird; feelings of surprise, curiosity, urgency, and later, shame.

"It was when Kyle was six, Matt was about twelve. The three of you were in your sunroom. I wasn't there." Kristen looked confused, but Owen plunged on. "You were studying at the computer, and Kyle and Matt were playing on his Game Boy when there was a loud thump against the window."

Kristen flinched. For an instant, her eyes got wide, then she glared at him.

He closed his eyes, replaying Kyle's memories in his own mind's eye. "The three of you went over to the window, and there was a beautiful yellow bird with black wings and an orange-red head, lying still on the ground. You called it a tanager. It hit the window and got knocked out."

Kristen's body was rigid. Her gaze shot back and forth between Owen and Kyle, as if trying to capture invisible words flowing between them.

"Matt wanted to go outside to save it, but you told the boys to wait and see if it would recover on its own. Surely you remember?"

"What are you trying to pull here, Owen?" Kristen said, avoiding his question but sounding alarmed.

"Kyle ran outside anyway. He started poking the bird with a sharp stick. He was trying to help it wake up, but he poked it too hard, and it started to bleed." She hesitated, glanced at Kyle, then back at Owen, her eyes narrowing.

"Owen, how the hell did you know about that?" Matt's comment came from across the room. "I never told you. Kristen, did you tell him?"

Kristen took a step back at Matt's question. "No, I never did," she said tersely, finally acknowledging she had a memory of the incident. "Owen?" she asked. He heard the suspicion in her tone, but was there also a tinge of curiosity . . . ?

Maybe even a note of hope?

"Kyle told me. Just now." Owen locked eyes with his sister, who had the look of an attorney cross-examining a hostile witness. He'd never seen her stare at him like this. His throat closed. This was the Rubicon. He could lose his sister forever in the next few moments. He could lose Kyle shortly thereafter. Owen struggled to keep centered despite his smoldering panic. *Keep it simple. Just lay out the facts.*

He imagined the desperation the boy must be feeling as his uncle and mother wrestled verbally for his chance to connect with her. Despite a few brief moments of direct contact with Owen, Kyle was still in solitary confinement, helpless to influence the outcome of their debate. His last chance to make his own decision dangled by the thinnest of threads. All Owen could offer the boy was a squeeze on the arm for encouragement.

As Owen waited for Kristen's next move, he considered how far he would go if she didn't come around, if Kyle never got a chance to make a final choice. Should he try to physically restrain Dr. Stauss from ending Kyle's life support? No doubt hospital security would haul him away and he'd miss Kyle's last moments. Or should he concede defeat and watch his nephew's last breaths in stoic silence, never knowing Kyle's true wishes? He dared not go there. *Stay in this moment. Concentrate on persuading Kristen to try the Witness.* It was the only way they would ever know what Kyle wanted.

"Matt, did you and Owen cook this up just before I came in?" Kristen turned to the younger man, fired up again. "Seriously, I'll never forgive you if you're messing with me."

"How could you even think something like that, Kristen?" The hurt was plain on the young man's face. "I swear, I'm hearing about this now, just like you. I haven't thought about that tanager in years."

Kristen turned to stare down Rene, where she sat at the controller. "Dr. Elder, if this is some kind of sick joke, I will go after your license, I swear."

The researcher met her gaze. "There's no trickery here, Ms. Nichols," she said kindly but firmly.

Kristen's eyes went to Yoshi. "I went through every crisis with you and Kimi," she said to him, her voice breaking. "For God's sake, you of all people, please tell me the truth."

Yoshi's eyes softened, but his voice was strong. "I've tried the Witness with Owen, and I can testify that it works. If Owen says Kyle needs to connect with you, then I absolutely believe him."

Shaking her head, she glanced around, but there was no one else to interrogate. The steely manner of the attorney evaporated. Her shoulders were slumped, her gaze clouded. "But how . . . ?"

He willed himself to stay calm; a small, hopeful note had cracked her defenses. "Kyle shared something with me that I couldn't possibly know so we could prove that he and I have actually been communicating." He let that sink in. "So I could convince you he truly needs to talk with you."

"Did he tell you anything else, Owen?" Matt asked from his station by the door. Owen shot him a grateful look for prompting more revelations.

"Yeah, he did. Kyle didn't want me to be disappointed in him for torturing and killing an injured bird, even though he didn't mean to. So you three promised not to tell me. Not ever." Owen paused. "Until now. He just told me."

Kristen stared vacantly into the distance.

Owen plunged on, driving home the details. "You sent Matt home and told Kyle to get the trowel and dig a grave under the oak tree by the fence. Then the two of you had a burial service for it."

"I didn't know anything about that." Matt jumped in again. "I assumed you just put the body in the trash."

Kristen gazed down at her son, gently running her fingers through his hair. Her hands were shaking. She spoke so quietly that Owen had to strain to hear it. "Dr. Stauss will be here soon."

"Kyle wants to connect with you, Kristen," Owen implored. "Now. Before Stauss gets here. He needs you now more than ever."

Everyone waited for her decision. Matt dropped to a crouch, staring down at the floor as he raked his hands through his shaggy hair. Yoshi stood behind Rene's chair with his hand on her shoulder, eyes closed. Rene stared out the window at the drizzle falling on the parking lot.

What was Kristen thinking? Owen stopped jiggling his foot, willing it to be still. A few seconds later, it was jiggling again. He tried some slow breathing to steady himself.

What must Kyle be feeling as his mother touched him so tenderly? Owen imagined him screaming inside the prison of his limp body, trying to communicate, stuck in absolute frustration, becoming ever more terrified as the seconds ticked toward his demise.

"Kristen," Matt said, springing straight up out of his crouch and breaking the silence, using the same urgent tone he'd used with Owen the day before. "Listen to Owen. You have to. Kyle told him our secret. You have to believe him!"

Kristen studied her hands, still visibly shaking. Slumping, she reached for the handrails on Kyle's bed and steadied herself.

"All the equipment is right here," Owen said softly. "He wants you to connect with him, to help him decide what to do." This was the moment of truth. But would she be willing to try something that she'd rejected for so long?

Kristen's gaze lingered over her son's motionless body. She

stood there frowning, tired and crumpled. Owen's heart was ready to burst as the seconds dragged on.

"I'm just too scared to try it." She looked up at him, her voice trembling, dread written on her face. "I'm absolutely terrified."

He was at a loss. What could he say to allay her fears? "Please, Kristen. I know it's safe." He spoke with all the assurance he could muster, but his answer sounded lame, even to him. Indeed, she still hesitated.

Yoshi had been standing quietly in the background, observing the debate. But he stepped forward, looking visibly moved. He reached out to Kristen, gently taking her trembling hands in his. "He's right, Kristen. There's nothing here that would hurt either of you."

His sister's posture softened as she held Yoshi's gaze; Owen could see the man's eyes were tearful.

Yoshi spoke to Kristen so quietly that Owen barely heard. "Kimi would want you to do it. This is one experimental treatment I know she would support."

Kristen inhaled sharply at the reference to her lost friend. Yoshi enveloped Kristen in a hug. Her shoulders heaved as she sobbed into his chest.

When Kristen quieted and stepped back, she first wiped her own face, then gently reached up to wipe a tear from Yoshi's. "Thank you for that," she said to him. Yoshi gave her a soft smile and held her hand as she turned to Owen. For the first time, her gaze had a glint of hope.

"OK, OK . . . I'll try it," she said shakily. "But you have to agree that if I'm not convinced about what he wants, I'll go through with my original plan." Kristen held Owen's eyes as a final test of his reaction.

Owen held her gaze, unflinching. He couldn't be sure how the boy would react to connecting with his mother, or how she would respond to the chaos of emotions she might encounter. Holding his fears in check, Owen forced himself to speak with confidence.

"Kristen, if you try the Witness with Kyle and then decide that ending his life support is still the right thing to do, I'll never bring it up again. You have my word."

CHAPTER 42

Owen watched as Dr. Elder fitted Kristen with the headset after Kyle's mother settled into the chair at the side of Kyle's bed. "We'll take this nice and easy, Ms. Nichols," she said quietly. "Just give me the signal if you want to slow down. It'll take a little getting used to at first, so just be patient."

Kristen sat and listened to the scientist describe the hand signals to use. She was still trembling, but whether it was the technology that scared her or what she might find out, Owen had no idea. Perhaps it was both.

What would happen next was out of his control. Kristen's willingness to adapt to the bizarre Witness experience was a total wild card. Kyle's ability to master his emotions enough to speak clearly to his mother through her fear was equally unknown.

He took solace in the knowledge that all was evolving as it should: Kyle, a young adult, would have a chance to confer with his mother about his fateful choice. Owen had fulfilled his roles to support them both.

His commitment that morning had been to remain stead-fastly neutral while connected with Kyle, but that responsibility was behind him. Now he could revel in the loving connection he'd just shared with his nephew. He allowed himself to hope that Kyle would choose to live. But all he could do was sit qui-etly, relegated to watching until Kristen revealed their collective fates.

Yoshi signed a thumbs-up to Owen as he stationed himself at the wall to again manage the lights. Matt stood next to him, shifting his weight from side to side, his face solemn.

Dr. Elder's face was drawn as she finished Kristen's prepara-tions. Owen met her eyes and put his palm over his heart, grate-ful for her courage.

Finally, Kristen settled, her face pale. Owen bent over his nephew to offer a few last words of encouragement before they began. "Be gentle with her, Kyle. She's never done this be-fore, OK?"

Owen positioned his chair next to Kristen's, took her icy hand, and squeezed gently. "You can do this," he whispered. She looked at him wanly. "It might seem overwhelming at first but try to go with it. You'll get the hang of it."

Then he took Kyle's hand as well, a physical conduit to fa-cilitate the mental connection between him and his mother. It wasn't much, but it was the most he could do. He took a few deep breaths to relax his tense muscles.

At last, his sister signaled for Dr. Elder to begin.

Rene remained focused. It was her responsibility to guide the mother through an experience that could be totally disorienting.

She needed to get this right: what happened next would determine whether Kyle would live or die. Rene's shoulders were tight, and she took a moment to stretch.

At Kristen's signal, Rene aligned the ultrasound frequencies ever so slowly. She struggled to suppress her anxiety. Though she'd willingly accepted the risks, there'd be hell to pay if Stauss caught her in the act of using a medical device on his patient.

She was calibrating the settings on the controller when Aisha quietly stepped in. Rene let out a small sigh. *Thank goodness.*

Taking in the scene, Aisha tiptoed over. "Dr. Elder, I've got this," she whispered.

"Are you sure you're OK here?" Despite the pressure, Rene was reluctant to give up her seat before the most crucial test of all.

"Go. Get out of here."

"I'll stay down in the cafeteria," Rene whispered. "Let me know how it goes. Good luck."

Moving as silently as she could, Rene picked up her purse and satchel. She looked back before leaving, wanting to stay and experience what was to come. But the risks were too high, and so she slipped out.

Once in the hallway, she assumed her most official posture and acknowledged the nurses as she walked past. "Thanks, have a good day."

They nodded solemnly in response.

Relieved, Rene took the elevator down to the basement. After a stop at the restroom, she headed to the cafeteria for some food and tea. She'd been up most of the night, and the excitement that had kept her going was wearing off. Having some food would help her relax and stave off a headache. There could be a lengthy wait before she'd learn the outcome.

She surveyed the cafeteria with fresh eyes. She'd been in this line a million times before, but this morning everything felt different. She barely remembered when Owen had burst into her office the previous day and she'd vehemently slapped down his desperate plot to smuggle her equipment into Kyle's room. But after her own transformative experience with the Witness, she was doing just that. And only moments before, she'd been part of a remarkable demonstration of her discovery. Her lifelong passion had been to find ways to help people with severe brain disabilities communicate, and remarkably, she'd accomplished that—and so much more.

She finally made it to the register, juggling her belongings and a tray. She was trying to get out her wallet when she was startled by a sardonic, "Why, good morning, Dr. Elder. How very interesting to find you here on this particular morning."

She recognized the voice and fumbled the bills as she handed them to the cashier. "Well, Dr. Stauss. Hello." Her adversary was standing at the next register, paying for his coffee.

She had little desire to talk with him, but it was imperative that she stall Dr. Stauss's going up to Kyle's room for as long as possible. Flustered, she ad-libbed the first thing that came to mind. "May I join you, Doctor?"

It was an unlikely request, and Stauss looked at her oddly. Her mouth went dry as she waited for his response. What if he refused?

He glanced up at the wall clock. It was 8:40. "I guess I've got a few minutes."

Now what? Rene was so rattled she had difficulty holding the tray steady, but her awkwardness gave her a few moments to think. She slow-walked Stauss to the table in the farthest corner, using up time getting seated and fiddling with her purse.

Stauss sat down heavily, his shoulders slumped. The tired look around his eyes surprised her. For an instant she was in the company of a different Dr. Stauss, the one who'd first interviewed her several years ago. And this same physician was about to end a life he'd worked so hard to save. It was a supremely emotional task for any physician—even one as jaded as Stauss.

Filled with a genuine kindness, she asked, "How are you, Doctor?"

He hesitated. "Not well, given what I have to do upstairs." Sadness and a sense of defeat crept out from behind the deepest recesses of Stauss's professional armor.

Her heart opened in the aftermath of her own recent Witness experience. "I can only imagine. I'm so sorry it's come to this." She filled with compassion, even forgiveness, as Stauss met her eyes. Once colleagues, then adversaries, they shared an instant of understanding that at his hands, their shared passion to defeat death was about to meet the limits of their profession.

Stauss's moment of vulnerability lasted only an instant before he reverted back to form. "May I ask what you might be doing here at this hour?" he said, staring at her.

She held her tongue, dragging things out, as if spreading cream cheese on her bagel required her complete attention.

"I'd like to know if you are up to some last-minute trick with the Nichols boy," Stauss continued impatiently.

"I'm just here for support," she answered, staying calm. "I've gotten to know the uncle and some of his friends, and I empathize with them." That was technically true—support could take many forms.

"You don't intend to interfere, I hope."

Rene pretended to choke on her bagel and feigned a look of shock at the brazen accusation. She wasn't interfering—she was *intervening.* The subtle difference between illegitimate and legitimate involvement made all the moral difference in the world. "That's a hell of a thing to suggest."

Dr. Stauss stared at her for a few seconds, then just shrugged and got up.

Desperate, Rene needed to buy more time for the folks upstairs. Besides, there was something she needed to say to him.

"Doctor, can I get another minute of your time, please?" she blurted.

CHAPTER 43

Owen hadn't felt so helpless since he'd first seen Kyle in the ICU. He'd done everything he could over the last few weeks to bring about this fateful moment. All he could do was hold Kristen's hand and hope.

All went quiet. Kristen's face was tight, her body rigid and every bit as motionless as her son's.

Owen willed himself to mimic their stillness, but his mind raced as he waited for any sign that his sister and nephew had joined minds. This frozen moment was the fulcrum, the point from which every life in the room would change irrevocably.

"Oh!" Kristen flinched.

He searched her face for a clue to interpret what was happening. How could such a tiny sound carry so many meanings? Disbelief? Uncertainty?

Owen chose to believe it was a sign of recognition, an indication that she'd successfully connected with Kyle.

He worried that his own emotions were transmitting through

his hands and distracting Kristen's attention from Kyle. He took in slow breaths through his nose and out through slightly opened lips, as he'd learned from his meditation lessons.

Kristen remained still as the minutes ticked along.

Kyle's fate was being silently determined by the two most important people in Owen's life. He was the odd man out, the surrogate father who wasn't the real father, the one who'd enabled this moment but couldn't be a part of it.

Kristen inched closer to Kyle, her brow becoming less furrowed. She relaxed her death grip on Owen's hand.

How wonderful it had been to communicate with Kyle, to feel his personality shine through even the darkest of emotions. That Owen might be able to connect with him again in the future, perhaps have regular, even daily contact, sent a fresh wave of hope through him.

The tension in Kristen's face seemed to ease even further. Her shoulders relaxed a little.

Encouraged, his own breath came a little easier. The possibilities offered by the Witness suddenly exploded. With the help of an assistant, Kyle should be able to dictate his thoughts to share with others. Why, he could write articles to help promote the Witness to others with brain dysfunctions. Maybe he could even attend online college classes!

After a bit, Kristen leaned even farther forward, and her expression opened. A slight smile played at her lips, which moved slightly as if she were talking. She let go of Owen's hand altogether and rested both of hers on Kyle's.

Owen allowed himself another shot of optimism. He exchanged a glance and a nod with Yoshi, who stood near the door, serious and alert, eyes on Kristen. Matt slid down into a squatting position on the floor, resting his elbows on his raised knees, head in his hands. Aisha kept watch on Kristen, her hands hovering over the dials of the controller. The room was so still that Owen's brain filled in the ticking sounds of the second hand on the hospital clock as it marked off the last few moments before Stauss's arrival.

Kristen sniffed and wiped a tear from her cheek, then gave the thumbs-down signal to indicate she was ready to disconnect from her son. Aisha made the adjustments and sat quietly at her station at the table in the corner.

Kristen put her head down on Kyle's chest and cried. Owen reached his arm around her, desperate to know what was driving her tears. Was she grieving or rejoicing?

Finally, she pulled off her headset and turned to face him, face streaked, voice ragged. She immediately grabbed the arms of her chair. "Whoa, dizzy."

All eyes were locked on her, waiting, gauging her response, fates held in abeyance.

"Being with Kyle in the Witness . . . ," she finally said, "we had such an amazing connection. It felt, I don't know . . . sacred . . . somehow." She reached out and took her son's limp hand. "I've spent hours obsessing over what Kyle has been through: now I've experienced firsthand the physical pain, the isolation." Kristen shook her head.

Then she steadied, her energy transforming before them. The strain, the tired eyes, the slouch all evaporated. Owen imagined waves of pain detaching from her body, floating into the air, and dissipating into nothingness. She sat up straighter, head high with clear purpose. "I'm so proud that your spirit has endured all this trauma," she said to Kyle.

Owen's heart beat triple time. He desperately wanted her to get to the point: *Will he live?*

Kristen paused and looked around the room at everyone who loved Kyle. The tense silence seemed to go on forever. Finally, with a kind look, she locked eyes with Owen.

"He wants us to let him go," she said to him gently.

CHAPTER 44

Her words punched through Owen, the force of the shock knocking the breath out of him.

"I never thought it would turn out like this." A muffled sob escaped from Matt where he squatted near the wall. Yoshi went over and knelt by his son. "I assumed he'd want to live," Matt said to his dad.

"Me too," Yoshi said, pulling his son in close for a hug.

Owen bowed his head. The fantasy of Kyle finding purpose, even a career through the Witness, dissipated in an instant.

Kristen's eyes teared as she surveyed the grief of those surrounding her, but her voice only got stronger. "It's very important to him that we understand why he's ready to go, and I'll do my best to share what he told me." She looked around the room at the members of Team Kyle. "He wants to make sure we know that he hasn't been defeated by the suffering he's endured. Quite the contrary. The ordeal has made him stronger."

Owen reached out and squeezed her hand.

She squeezed back and continued. "He knows that if he stays, connecting with all of us through the Witness would dramatically improve the quality of his life." She offered them a small smile.

"But his body will never be the same, and his spirit needs to heal. As he and I were embraced by the universe, we both opened to a new perspective. We went to a place at the edge of . . . *bliss*. It's where he will go . . . where we all go . . . after. I felt a serenity in him that seems unimaginable, especially after all he's been through." She looked lovingly at her son. "He found a place of boundless hope.

"Kyle struggled with the decision. In so many ways, he wanted to stay." She turned to Matt. "But he wants everyone to understand that he will be with us all, everywhere, every day. He knows that's the way the universe works. And now . . . so do I."

That truth flowed through Owen, acceptance beginning to replace grief.

"Before he goes," Kristen continued, "Kyle wants a chance to . . . talk . . . with each of you." She walked over to where Matt squatted, still looking dejected. She touched his shoulder. "Matt, Kyle would like to spend some time with you," she offered kindly.

Matt looked up, wiping his face on the sleeve of his sweatshirt. He looked shocked, uncertain. "I . . . don't want him to see me like this."

"He already knows how you feel; he's right here listening, you know," she said with a small smile. "Talking with him brought me great comfort."

"Yeah, well, OK." The young man stood, straightened his shoulders, rubbed his hands across his face. "OK, let's do this, Kyle."

"Take your time. We're not going to rush," Kristen said. "We'll deal with Dr. Stauss when he arrives."

Aisha met Matt at the bedside chair and arranged the headset over his forehead as Kristen and Owen stepped toward the door to get out of the way.

"I'm sorry, Owen. I know how much you wanted him to live," Kristen whispered to him, so as not to disturb the young men.

"I did all this to give Kyle his choice . . . ," Owen answered in a shaky voice. "I didn't realize how much I counted on him deciding to live. But I'll be OK . . . I will . . . once I get over the . . . shock. I'll never forget the absolute relief Kyle shared during our time together, touching Oneness. I felt his joy at the freedom, as though it was my own." His heart swelled as he recalled those moments. "So, while I'm . . . disappointed, I still support him. Fully."

"I'm so grateful you pushed me to try the Witness," Kristen said, touching his arm as fresh tears rolled down her cheeks. "Now I know for certain what he wants. I get great comfort from knowing what a peaceful existence he'll experience." Her eyes shone. "I had a chance to connect with him one last time, to share my love with him directly." She reached out and embraced Owen in a big hug. "You made all that possible. Thank you. For everything."

Owen held his little sister tight, letting go of the consuming fear that he'd permanently broken her trust. It had been a very close call.

CHAPTER 45

"I just need a couple more minutes of your time," Rene said. She had no idea what was happening upstairs and needed to keep Stauss down in the cafeteria as long as possible. But she also had something to say to him.

Stauss gave Rene a withering look as he stared down at her. "What now?"

"CRINR is going to nominate you for the Kavli Prize," she said quietly. "It's an honor you rightfully deserve. You devoted your entire career to neuroscience, and you made truly valuable contributions to the field. I'll be cheering for you to win."

Stauss looked surprised. "Don't try to bullshit me, Elder."

"I've come to realize some things, Doctor," she continued, ignoring his tone. "There are hundreds, maybe thousands of us at institutions around the world who are trying to unravel the mysteries of the brain and consciousness. We'll only succeed in answering these hard questions when we freely explore all the different theories and together build our knowledge base. In truth, we scientists are all connected: we're all dependent on each other."

"Those are nice sentiments, Rene, but a little hypocritical, don't you think? After all, you're the one who triggered that investigation of me."

"The investigation was justified," she said. "But I let my disgust over that incident warp my opinion of you and damage our relationship. For that I'm truly regretful. You saved Kyle Nichols's life, and that of many others before him. When I look at the big picture, I have no choice but to give you my deepest respect."

For an instant, Stauss looked taken aback by her compliment. "I'm not dependent on your approval, Elder," he said with less conviction.

"Nor am I dependent on yours, Dr. Stauss. But whether or not we like each other, whether or not our theories are compatible, we are both on the same side: the side of the patients stricken with these devastating disabilities."

Stauss held her gaze for a long moment.

"Speaking of patients, there is one waiting for me upstairs," he said quietly, the edge gone from his voice. "Good day, Doctor," he said with the slightest of nods.

"Good day, Dr. Stauss." Rene watched him leave the room, then pulled out her phone and urgently texted Aisha, *Stauss is on his way up. I'll be in the west courtyard.*

Aisha spoke up quietly from the corner. "Dr. Elder just texted. Dr. Stauss is on his way up," she said, sounding apologetic.

Owen hadn't planned how to handle this moment. There

was no time to hide all that had been going on. He had to improvise.

Matt's connection with Kyle would have to be postponed. "Quick, Matt, take Aisha's place at the controller," Owen said. "Pretend you've been running it all along, OK?"

Aisha stood and gave her seat to Matt, who slipped into the chair just a few moments before Dr. Stauss strode in.

The physician stopped in his tracks, surveying the scene. "What the hell is going on here?" he said, planting his hands on his hips, an angry frown on his face.

Stauss held himself with a military bearing as he glared at Owen. He surveyed the room, taking in the rest of the scene. Yoshi and Aisha stood near the window; Stauss glanced right past them. Owen shot a look at Matt. The young man's head was averted from Stauss as he pretended to study the controller in front of him, but Owen could see his dejected expression. Stauss didn't seem to notice; the ultrasound headset that still rested across Kyle's forehead had caught his attention.

Stauss returned his focus to Kristen and Owen, the two boldly standing on the same side for the first time in many weeks. "Let's take this out in the hall, Doctor," Kristen said in a commanding voice as Owen herded the physician back out the door.

"Doctor, you have no idea!" Kristen said as the door to Kyle's room closed behind them. "This is the most amazing . . . I don't have words for it, even." She was so emphatic, her eyes once again filled with tears. "The Witness works! And now I know for sure what Kyle wants."

"I knew it—all that equipment. It's all Dr. Elder's, right?"

Stauss demanded. "I suspected something was up when I ran into her downstairs, damn it."

Owen couldn't let Dr. Elder take the fall. "You're wrong once again, Dr. Stauss," he announced as Stauss's face turned red. "I'm responsible for this. Dr. Elder wasn't involved in Kristen's connection with her son." Technically, that was true. Dr. Elder left the room before Kristen started witnessing with Kyle.

"That isn't your ultrasound equipment, Mr. Nichols," the physician responded accusingly, his disdain on full display. "It's obvious it all belongs to Elder."

"Yes, it belongs to her—but I stole it from her facility early this morning so I could use it with Kyle myself," Owen countered, defiant. Again, true.

"Yeah, right." Stauss's eyes narrowed.

"The janitors were going to call 911 after they walked in on me." Owen continued, "I bluffed my way out of it and came here to set up the equipment. The janitors can verify what happened." His earlier misadventure in Rene's facility was suddenly working in his favor. "Besides, I took a selfie when I was packing up the equipment; here, let me show you." Owen reached into his pocket and pulled out his phone, proud of himself for piecing together an entirely true yet sufficiently misleading account of events to throw Stauss off-balance.

The doctor glanced at the proffered phone, shuffled his stance, then tried another tack. He turned to Kristen. "Surely, Ms. Nichols, you're too smart to be taken in by all of this nonsense." His voice dripped with condescension. "I'm still convinced Elder is at the bottom of this."

Kristen responded firmly, ignoring the implied insult. "Dr.

Elder was nowhere around when I was witnessing with Kyle. But that's not relevant anyway," she said. "The important thing is that my son told me exactly what he wants. And I will fulfill his requests."

Stauss's face was crimson, his eyes fierce. "Get that damned equipment out of here immediately."

Kristen stepped toward the surgeon, her hand outstretched. "You really need to look into this Witness technique, it's—"

"It's complete and utter hogwash, Ms. Nichols," he retorted, moving away from her. "And I'll have absolutely nothing to do with it."

Kristen's face turned stern. "That's it, then. I refuse to have you present for the end of Kyle's life."

Owen started. He'd never thought Kristen's opinion could shift so dramatically.

"That's just fine with me," Stauss said, his tone infused with bitterness. "The orders for Kyle's transition are already in place. But I'll have nothing more to do with you or any of Elder's nonsense."

Stauss started down the hall, then turned and launched a final salvo, his face contorted. "Your friend Elder is a quack, and I'm going to prove it."

Owen and Kristen breathed a collective sigh of relief as Stauss finally stalked away. "Whoa, that was something. I've never seen that side of him before," Kristen said.

Yoshi came out of Kyle's room to join them. "Things were getting loud out here, so I thought I'd better check on you," he said. He turned, looking down the hall. "Is that Dr. Stauss walking away?"

Owen nodded. "I'm so proud of you, Sis. You really stood up to him."

"I've learned to stand up to bullies in court," she said brusquely. "Now, do either of you know where I can find Dr. Elder?"

"Aisha told me she's down in the courtyard," Yoshi said. "I'm going down to fill her in while Matt is having his conversation with Kyle."

"I have a favor to ask of her," Kristen said. "I'll come down in a few minutes. Matt should be finished by the time you come back up; you can have your connection with Kyle then."

"That works," he said.

CHAPTER 46

Rene sat at a small table in a shady section of the courtyard. A cool breeze rustled the leaves of the branches above her. She inhaled the fresh air, held it, and then exhaled completely. She would find out Kyle's choice soon enough.

She caught sight of Yoshi entering the courtyard and waved him over. He looked serene. She exhaled slowly. "You have news?"

Yoshi came up to her with a gentle smile and sat down next to her. "Yes. Kristen was able to connect with Kyle."

"And?"

"He's ready to move on," he said, his voice shaking a little. "Kristen said he knows he'll soon be free and is at peace."

"Were you hoping that he'd decide to live?" she asked.

"Yes, I guess I was," he said quietly. "But I totally understand his decision. I'm just going to miss him is all." He sighed. "My wife, Kimi, made the same decision."

She reached out and squeezed his hand. His warm fingers

squeezed back and held as he shared the details of Stauss's arrival at Kyle's room and Kristen's response. Their continued
touch seemed perfectly natural in her fresh new world.

Yoshi had just finished his update when Rene looked over
Yoshi's shoulder and saw Kristen approaching. With a quick
squeeze, she let go of his hand.

"Sorry to interrupt," Kristen said as she came up to the
table. "May I join you?"

They both nodded. As Kristen pulled up a nearby chair,
Rene and Yoshi scooted their chairs closer together to make
room. The rearrangement left their knees comfortably touching
under the table.

"Yoshi tells me Kyle is prepared to go," Rene said softly.

"Yes," Kristen replied with a slight catch in her voice. "We
had the most wonderful experience in the Witness together. Your
discovery is absolutely amazing." She met Rene's eyes. "I apologize for dismissing your work when we first met; someday I want
to talk with you about it in depth. But in this moment, I need to
ask you a favor. Actually, I'm passing along a request from Kyle."

Rene couldn't imagine what was coming.

"Kyle would like you to join us as he transitions to the end
of his life."

The appeal startled her. "Me? I barely know him."

"He told me that although Dr. Stauss saved his body, you
honored his autonomy, his right to choose, his very spirit."
Kristen paused.

Rene wasn't sure how to answer. Being there when Kyle's life
support ended was never part of her plan for this escapade.

"You gave him the most precious gift of all," Kristen said.
"Your presence will help ease him into this transition gently."

Rene thought of Marcella, whose death had occurred before her eyes as she stood helpless: she once again heard the keening of the child's mother as Rene delivered the news. What a contrast between the two experiences.

Rene gulped past the lump that had risen in her throat, for some reason thinking not of Kyle, but Gramps.

"In that case, it would be my honor," she said.

Rene accompanied Kristen and Yoshi back to Kyle's room. It was time for Yoshi's turn with Kyle. Rene confirmed that Aisha was willing to continue at the Witness controls and would stay through Kyle's transition. Kristen took a seat next to Matt, who looked composed and resolved.

Leaving Yoshi and Kyle to their conversation, Rene went to the nurses' station and updated Lorena, who'd come on duty with the rest of the day shift. Rene was grateful to learn that Lorena would be present to fulfill Stauss's orders and end Kyle's life support.

Seeing Rene's disheveled appearance, Lorena led her into the nurses' locker room, where Rene washed her face and brushed her hair. Joining with Kyle's loved ones for his transition was nothing like the desperate feeling of her childhood self, searching for a divine intervention to save her grandfather's life; rather, she felt uplifted by the honor of being present as Kyle exercised his choice.

Refreshed, she took up Lorena's offer of a clean white coat so she could be present with appropriate formality.

Out in the hall, Rene found Owen waiting as Yoshi left

Kyle's room. His eyes were red, but he looked relaxed. Yoshi smiled at Owen. "Your turn with Kyle, my friend."

Owen nodded and stood. "I'll let you know when I'm done," he said to Rene.

"Take your time," she said, as she and Yoshi walked down to the waiting room.

CHAPTER 47

As the two connected, Owen found Kyle's confidence surprising. *I'm practically an old hand at this Witness stuff now,* the young man thought. *Thanks to you and Dr. Elder. I'll be forever grateful. Literally.*

Owen smiled his understanding. *I will carry my love for you always.*

Kyle led him into a memory of the two of them playing a gentle game of catch. It was late in the evening, just a few hours after the awards dinner, the one where Kyle had been honored with the regional sportsmanship trophy.

Owen recalled his own memories of that same evening. As with his beach experience with Yoshi, the two were able to share their common memories from each of their unique perspectives.

It was dusk, and they were throwing the ball around under the dim outdoor lighting on the perimeter of the backyard of the house Kristen and Kyle shared. The air was cooling rapidly. Both knew it would soon be dark, so they limited their throws to soft arcing lobs that were easy to catch. The muted thwack of the ball hitting their mitts was the only sound.

It was a companionable moment as they reveled in the young man's accomplishment: Owen, quietly proud; Kyle, humble. As they revisited the moment, they silently acknowledged that the night's accolades weren't just the hard-earned result of the hundreds of hours of practice they'd put in together, but also the reward for Kyle's innate positive attitude and unselfish play.

Joined by the Witness, they shared a highlight reel of memories from different ages and seasons: Kyle as a toddler, throwing a Wiffle ball; Kristen playing catcher as Owen pitched to a little boy learning how to bat; Kyle singing "Take Me out to the Ballgame" at a Mariners game; Owen, drenched, as eight-year-old Kyle insisted on playing catch in the rain; Kyle beating Owen in a strategically challenging game of Strat-O-Matic Baseball played under Nana's tapestry in Owen's dining room. Dozens more memories flashed through their joined minds as they celebrated treasured moments together.

Eventually, they returned their focus to the game of catch they'd played on the memorable evening after the awards ceremony. Owen remembered the biting cold as the darkness finally made it impossible to continue.

It's time, Kyle said.

They met in the middle of the yard.

Do you want me to be with you? Owen sent his love to the young man. *I can join you through the Witness while you . . . transition.*

Kyle projected surprise, then gratitude for his uncle's kindness. *I'm not afraid,* Kyle sent back. *In fact, I'm looking forward to it. So you stay with the others and support Mom. I want to do this by myself.*

Owen felt the boy's inner strength. *As you wish,* he responded. He put his arm around the boy, and they walked side by side toward the back door of the house. When they reached the step, Kyle turned to face Owen as they shared all they meant to each other.

I know that you're my uncle, Kyle thought, *but in my heart, you'll always be my father.*

A tight knot deep inside Owen finally unraveled.

CHAPTER 48

Rene and Yoshi had been talking in the waiting room while Owen had his private session with Kyle. Now they walked back toward Kyle's room.

Yoshi opened the door to Kyle's room to let Rene go in first.

She scanned the members of Team Kyle, all of whom turned to look at her. Kristen sat on the near side of Kyle's bed, her face calm. Owen stood nearby, nodding gently at Rene. Matt, near the window, looked serene. Aisha looked solemn, still sitting at her station by the TCU controller.

Lorena stood out of the way, alert and prepared.

One by one, they joined in a soft round of applause as Rene entered. Words failed her. Her eyes teared as she went over to Kyle and smiled down at the soon-to-be-liberated young man. "I'm honored to be with you and witness your transition, Kyle," she said. "Safe travels."

This is for you, Gramps.

CHAPTER 49

Lorena recorded the moment when Kyle's heart stopped, information she'd pass on to the resident who would sign the death certificate.

Team Kyle continued their vigil in Kyle's room until everyone felt ready to move on.

Now Rene was part of a solemn group standing in a loose circle outside Kyle's room.

"Thank you all so much," Kristen said as they prepared to disperse. "Especially Owen and Rene, for being here for Kyle and for me. Like Kyle, I've been forever transformed by your efforts. I know a peace I never thought possible."

Rene nodded. She, too, was filled with newfound serenity. "I'd like to acknowledge Aisha. She stepped up big-time in response to my middle-of-the-night request for help."

Aisha turned to Kristen. "It was a very powerful experience, Ms. Nichols. Thank you for letting me share such an intimate time with your family."

"I'm deeply grateful for your help," Kristen said.

"Shall I take the equipment back to the lab?" Aisha said to Rene. "I can recalibrate it and have it ready for the next experiments."

"That would be great." Rene gave her a quick hug. "We'll talk soon."

Aisha nodded to everyone and carried Rene's satchel and Owen's gym bag toward the elevator.

Kristen addressed her brother directly. "Owen, would you mind staying at my place tonight? I don't feel like being alone."

"Of course," Owen answered, then walked over and offered Rene a hug. "Thanks for everything," he said to her before turning to leave with Kristen.

"I'm going home to get some rest." Matt waved and headed down the hall.

As the group moved apart, Rene and Yoshi were left standing together.

"I need some coffee," Yoshi said to her. "Mind keeping me company?"

"I'd love to," she said.

They walked down the hall hand in hand.

CHAPTER 50

It was Saturday afternoon, ten days after Kyle's passing. Rene and Owen sat in lounge chairs on Kristen's patio, relaxing before the dinner and short ceremony Kristen had planned in Kyle's honor.

That morning, Yoshi had helped Rene dig up a rosebush from her garden and transport it to Kristen's backyard to be planted in Kyle's memory. Rene helped Kristen pick a sunny spot where the bush should thrive.

As Yoshi and Owen dug the hole for the bush, Rene looked around the perimeter of the large space. "Is that old oak tree where you and Kyle buried the tanager?" Rene asked, pointing across the yard.

Kristen nodded. "I never would have guessed that the unfortunate death of that lovely bird years ago would change the course of our lives."

Yoshi looked up from his work and smiled. "Kyle's idea to share that memory with Owen was brilliant."

"He was a smart kid," she said softly.

After the bush was planted and watered, Kristen went upstairs for a shower while Yoshi got his bearings in her kitchen. Rene would soon join him and help prepare the ingredients for the sukiyaki; meanwhile, she relaxed, soaking in the sun on the patio.

Rene could tell by the way Owen was fidgeting that something was on his mind.

"I don't know if you can ever forgive me for all the ways I screwed up," Owen began, "but I need to clear my conscience."

She nodded. "I'm glad you understand the need for a reckoning," she said. "But now I see everything from a new perspective. It seems like those events happened in a different lifetime. In fact, I feel a . . . new bond with you, like comrades who've been through battle together."

"Yeah, me too," he said, offering a contrite grin.

"It's remarkable, isn't it?" she said. "Just a few days ago, we said goodbye. I assumed our work together had ended. Perhaps we'd never even see each other again. And yet we came back together in a common cause—to preserve Kyle's autonomy." She smiled back at him.

"Experiencing the Witness with him was such a profound experience," he said. "Imagine if everyone understood the implications—that we're all deeply connected at the most fundamental level."

"I couldn't agree more," Rene said, holding his eyes. "Now I know that we're never alone. We're no longer limited by the processes within our skulls. We can communicate with each other, with the universe, in ways never before imagined."

"This discovery could be as revolutionary as when Copernicus proposed that the earth traveled around the sun."

"Slow down," Rene said, frowning. "Remember that Galileo, one of the proponents of Copernicus's new worldview, spent years under house arrest, punished by the church for his support of what we know now is the absolute truth."

"Are you expecting a culture war?"

She nodded, her voice somber as she said, "I don't think opponents like Stauss and Ainsworth will stop their resistance anytime soon; their scientific legacy is under attack." She looked up at the sky. "But beyond that, there are major philosophical and religious implications of the Witness that will be deeply controversial, especially when word eventually gets out to the public."

"Well, at least there aren't any crowds picketing in front of the foundation office," he said.

"No. Not yet."

Later, Rene followed Yoshi out of Kristen's kitchen, carrying a bowl of rice into the dining room where everyone awaited Yoshi's signature dish. The sight of Yoshi and Rene cooking together made Owen smile.

The previous evening, Yoshi had invited his friends to the symphony performance in which he was playing. Rene had quietly admitted to Owen that she didn't remember him telling her that Yoshi was a professional clarinetist.

Sitting in the front row next to Kristen, Owen and Rene had exchanged glances after Yoshi's solo in Gershwin's "Rhapsody in Blue." Her eyes were wide, and she put her hand over her heart. "Oh my," she'd whispered. After the piece, when the conductor pointed to Yoshi to be acknowledged, Rene had stood and clapped vigorously as the audience gave him a standing ovation.

"You have an amazing talent," she said to Yoshi when the group gathered for dessert at a coffeehouse afterward.

Yoshi had blushed, and it soon became clear that he and Rene were hitting it off. In fact, although Rene had carpooled to the event with Owen and Kristen, Yoshi drove her home. Nothing pleased Owen more than seeing them becoming a couple.

Yoshi set the large pot of sukiyaki on the warming flame in the center of the table. He and Rene took their seats, and she passed the rice. The ceremony honoring Kyle would follow their meal, but for the moment, the group was quiet as everyone filled their bowls and began eating.

"I've never had homemade sukiyaki before," Aisha said. "This is fabulous, Yoshi."

"It's a family tradition that started before Matt was born," Yoshi replied. "I'm glad you could join us."

"Have you any updates about your research, Rene?" Kristen asked.

"I do," she said, laying her chopsticks across her bowl. "I've located a contractor who can produce the software I need, and my board has authorized the necessary funds. I'm very relieved about that."

Kristen nodded politely, but Owen knew enough about Rene's history with CRINR to understand the significance. "That's great," he said.

"What about Dr. Stauss? Is he coming after you?" Kristen asked.

"Stauss is being nominated for a prestigious international award in neurological research," Rene said. "Fortunately, he's going to be far too busy dealing with media interviews and guest lectures to bother with me for a while." She paused. "And I have some more good news to share," she said, smiling.

Everyone looked at her.

"I'm very excited to announce that Aisha has accepted my offer of full-time permanent employment. She'll continue part-time until she finishes her studies."

That brought a round of cheers. Kristen raised her glass of sake in a toast. "To Aisha," she said. "I'm deeply grateful to you for helping me connect with Kyle. Here's to a long and successful career."

"To Aisha," everyone repeated.

Aisha looked embarrassed, but then warmed to the attention. "Thanks, everyone. Dr. Elder's work uncovering the Witness has turned into the most challenging and rewarding research I could imagine. And I'm honored to be included today."

When everyone had finished eating, the talk naturally turned to Kyle. Kristen passed around photos from his life, sparking numerous anecdotes. Rene and Aisha sat quietly as those who knew him best laughed and cried, bringing his spirit to life with their memories.

As the storytelling began to wane, the energy shifted. Kristen led the group out to the backyard.

Owen carried out the specially designed urn holding Kyle's ashes to the designated space just in front of the newly planted rosebush. A friend of Yoshi's, an instructor of metalwork in the university's art department, had been commissioned to melt down Kyle's favorite aluminum bat and recast it. Other than being three inches deep, it was the exact shape and dimensions of a regulation home plate, including the beveled edges. The engraving on the brushed metal top read:

Kyle Nichols
Safe at Home

Owen scooped the dirt at the designated spot. Kristen carefully maneuvered the urn base until it rested level with the surface. Owen filled in the dirt around it.

The group gathered in a circle around the urn and rosebush. Their remembrances had been shared earlier, and a quiet fell over them.

After a nod from Kristen, Yoshi began a slow, melancholy version of "Take Me out to the Ballgame" on his clarinet. His heartfelt rendition gave Rene goose bumps as she closed her eyes and let the mournful sounds flow through her. The group held their silence as the last strains of the melody drifted into the breeze.

Then Yoshi began riffing a quiet transition, gradually increasing the volume and tempo until he unleashed a rousing version of the traditional song. Kristen began the singing, and Rene joined in as the group belted out the words in Kyle's boisterous style.

After the song, Kristen spoke. "Thank you all for being here to honor Kyle," she said, looking into each person's eyes. Then she smiled. "And now, as Kyle himself would say, it's time for the chocolate cake."

"And mochi," Matt added as Kristen led the way back into the house.

Rene gave Yoshi a hug. "I just need a minute alone," she said. "I'll join you soon."

He gave her a quick kiss and headed into the kitchen with the others.

Rene smiled. One of the most rewarding surprises of the last several weeks was meeting this warm and interesting man. The night they'd spent together after the concert had revealed a unique and important bond: they both cherished their profoundly personal experience of the conscious nature of the universe.

Rene bent and inhaled the fragrance of the roses. She relished a deep satisfaction in having honored Kyle's agency to make his own decision. She'd gained a sense of redemption for Marcella's tragedy and taken a leap forward in fulfilling her promise to Gramps. She could easily envision a future in which the Witness would assist countless people with brain disease or damage.

Beyond that, and much to her surprise, her research had revealed a presence in the universe far beyond her understanding, an energy previously unknown to science. It wasn't in the form of a personal god as Gramps or Rob envisioned, but nonetheless, it was a force of great significance that had changed her view of—everything.

Her eyes were drawn to a ladybug sunning itself on a rose petal. Delighted, she slowly extended her finger, hoping that the tiny being would deign to cross over to her. The little one paused at the edge of her fingernail, as if weighing the risks she was about to take. How could such a tiny being, lacking any kind of sophisticated nervous system, instinctively know that it was about to step onto something totally foreign? How could it possibly make such an important, perhaps life-or-death, determination?

As she awaited the creature's decision, Rene saluted all that went into her perception of this bright red insect sitting on the bold yellow petal among the dark green leaves. She paid silent tribute to the continuous flow of photons originating in the sun and finding their way through the earth's atmosphere, bouncing off all that lay before her, then entering her eyes, the rods and cones converting the sun's energy into impulses traveling through her optic nerves, where they were interpreted by her brain, creating this view and filling her with awe.

These and so many more interconnections resonated within Rene, binding her with this little being, grounding her in the universe, defining her purpose. So many questions had been explained by the Witness, and yet so many new ones had been raised.

She held her breath, waiting. Then her heart swelled as her brightly colored friend stepped bravely onto her finger.

ACKNOWLEDGMENTS

I'm grateful for all the varied circumstances that came together to allow me to discover and pursue my passion for writing. This manuscript would never have come into being without the encouragement of my family, friends, and fellow writers.

I'm very fortunate to be part of a critique group whose thoughtful insights and constant support improved every scene and helped me grow as a writer. Thanks to Douglas Carlsen, Sandra Fan, and Daniel Kamin. Mary Catlin also added thoughtful editing and offered valuable medical expertise.

Beta readers Kel Munger, Cathi Davis, Cat Johnston, and Karen Andrus provided meaningful comments on drafts along the way. I'm deeply appreciative for the time each invested and for their detailed feedback.

I've been fortunate to have worked with professional editors Tiffany Yates Martin of FoxPrint Editorial, Jennifer Udden, Kenneth Zink, and Amaryah Orenstein. Each of them challenged and guided me toward a better final manuscript.

The staff at Girl Friday Productions have been outstanding as they gently dragged me, kicking and screaming, into the real world of book production and marketing.

Family and friends are a constant source of encouragement and occasional teasing. I've been sustained by their belief in me more than they may know.

Every week, my friends in the River Rock Writers group give me the inspiration to complete this long-term project.

I thank the furry beings with whom I shared thousands of hours in silent communion with my laptop: Cinnabun (RIP), Zia, and Dax, who filled my heart with love and laughter as they slept at my feet, walked on my keyboard, and provided essential distractions.

Above all, I'm forever grateful for Ann. You bring out the best in me.

BOOK CLUB QUESTIONS

1. Rene rejected Rob's demand that an active church life be a priority when raising their children. How did you feel when she made that choice? Have differing views of religion and spirituality affected any of your relationships?

2. Rene had a difficult experience when she and Aisha tried the Witness. What would it be like to know exactly what someone else is experiencing? What would be the pros and cons of allowing someone else to know what you were thinking and feeling?

3. How did Kristen's experiences with the deaths of her grandmother and best friend shape her view of end-of-life issues? What experiences have you had that shape your perspective on death?

4. What did you think about Kristen's rejection of the Witness experience for Kyle? Was she making a reasonable choice, or was she letting her fears get the best of her?

5. Dr. Stauss was a talented neurosurgeon who saved Kyle's life after a horrific accident. He was also a highly ambitious and arrogant researcher. How would you react if he were caring for someone you love?

6. Owen was Kyle's surrogate father, at Kristen's request. Was he overinvested in Kristen's decisions? Did he have the right to override Kristen's opposition to using the Witness with Kyle?

7. Rene and Owen each chose to take significant risks to honor Kyle's autonomy and give him the opportunity to make his own life-or-death choice. How did their experiences with the Witness lead them to take those risks? Have you ever been faced with taking a big risk for someone else's well-being?

8. Many people with disabilities report feeling discounted or undervalued. Have you or someone you know ever had that experience?

9. Kyle chose to die. Were you surprised? How did you feel about his decision? What might you have decided if you were in his position?

10. Rene predicted that she would face a culture war in the future as word of her discovery became public. Why did she think that? Do you agree?

11. What would be the implications for our society if the Witness technology were real? In what ways might the Witness be used in education, therapy, law enforcement, or other arenas? What would change, and would those changes be for the better?

12. Compare the concept of a universal consciousness as an inherent part of reality with the concept of a personal god. What thoughts and feelings come up for you?

JB Maerten is available to attend book club discussions in person and virtually. Contact the author at jbmaerten@gmail.com.

ABOUT THE AUTHOR

JB Maerten has long been committed to aligning her work with her personal values. Before turning to her passion for writing, she served people living with HIV/AIDS, and, later, people experiencing homelessness. A lover of nature and the proud owner of a vivid imagination, JB explores dramas at the intersection of science and philosophy. *Of One Mind* is her first novel.

JB lives in Northern California with her wife and their two four-legged roommates. They enjoy taking long walks, birdwatching, and cheering for their favorite women's basketball teams.

9 798989 841400